LOVE PRESUMED

Cover designed by Kristallynn Designs

Used image credit in Design
Business Woman image by 4X6 on iStock
Working Man image by Italo on Shutterstock

Elsa Bayly
Visit my website at www.Elsawritesromance.com

Printed in the United States of America

First Printing: March 2019
Elsa Bayly

ISBN-978-0-9892958-5-7

This book as always, is dedicated to my husband, James, who never fails to be supportive. To my children and grandchildren and the many friends who have cheered me on over an oft interrupted path to its publishing. Enough thanks cannot be given to Hannah Neeley, my editor. A special thank you to April for her local insight. Deep appreciation goes to my beta readers, Barbara, Grace, Peggy, Abby, and Jan, for giving of their time and insight.

CONTENTS

LOVE PRESUMED

by

Elsa Bayly

CHAPTER ONE

L inda held six year old Renee's hand and guided nine year old Art with occasional light touches on the shoulder, maneuvering them ahead of her in the crush of passengers exiting the plane. She'd arrived in Alaska, a new home, possibly a new life. She smiled. It was time to do something positive about her situation. She would be working closely with Joe to make this new office successful. He should be putting a ring on her finger soon.

* * *

Joe was oblivious to more than a few women coming and going at the Anchorage airport taking an extra second to admire the six foot one inch, broad shouldered man with the black hair and the commanding presence. He stood motionless, watching passengers deplane. It had been two weeks since he'd come ahead, leaving his kids in Linda's care. He'd missed the kids and he'd missed Linda. She was the rock he'd leaned on both at work and at home, ever since his divorce from Marilyn.

There they were. Joe grinned and his heart took a couple of extra beats as he watched Art on one side of Linda, trying to look grown up but staying close enough for body contact and Renee on the other side hanging onto Linda's hand. The crowd flowed around her as if knowing better than to jostle this tall regal creature. Her eyes located him and she smiled, pointing him out to the children. Then she released them so they could race ahead and launch themselves at their father.

Joe glanced at her while he laughed and rough-housed with the kids. When the jumbled stories began to slow and they settled down, he turned to drink in the sight of her, standing there smiling, waiting for his attention. In a tailored cream colored pantsuit with her honey blond hair pulled up neatly in a sophisticated twist on top of her head, she appeared taller than her five foot eight inches.

Joe wrapped his arms around her in a tight hug. Her warmth, the fresh lavender scent of her perfume, the way she leaned into him betraying her weariness, all put his protective instincts into overdrive. He nestled her closer as the desire to hold her, protect her, make her happy and make love to her, brought on a tug of almost painful physical desire. "How was the flight?"

"Fine. The kids were restless. They're excited."

"And you? Are you excited?" He still held her, reluctant to let go.

"Yes, apprehensive too. Alaska is a big change."

"It's beautiful. You're going to love it. Now, let's go home." It occurred to him that this was the first time he had thought of his apartment as home.

He herded them toward baggage claim where each had a small bag—no big tussle with last minute items. Personal belongings had arrived two days earlier. Linda's efficiency had been applied again. His mouth turned up in a slight smile. She had been his right hand assistant at Black Capital Development Company and he liked having that efficiency applied to his personal life as well as to his business.

The job ahead of him now was to take the small, three person office the company had maintained here for the last couple of years and expand it. He intended to take advantage of the development opportunities in Alaska. Being the only son and heir apparent of his father's privately owned company, Joe was aware of the work ahead of him. His Dad, William G. Black, Billy to family and a few close friends, had been grooming him for years to take over. Expanding this office and opening up new territory for Black Capital was his first big challenge without Billy to turn to for advice. Of course, Billy was there at the end of the phone if Joe needed him, but Joe felt he should be able to handle this himself.

Linda had been Billy and Joe's personal secretary, assistant, and general get-things-done person for several years. With her managing the office end of the business he could concentrate on the projects and new customers. She had cheerfully helped with the kids after the divorce when he would bring them to the office after school. They adored her. She had taken care of social chores for him, stepping in as hostess in business occasions, and made sure he didn't let the divorce defeat him as it threatened to do. Time passed and he healed from the ordeal of the divorce. He began to look at Linda differently. She was a sexy woman as well as a beautiful person, and he had fallen in love. It was unspoken, but understood by them both, he was sure, that they were moving toward marriage. His bringing her to Alaska with him was a commitment of sorts.

He directed them to the 4-wheel drive SUV he was using. Linda would have one delivered tomorrow—company vehicles that befitted their positions.

Joe watched Linda's well rounded bottom move with each step of her long slim legs as he followed her and the children out. *Damn, she was sexy without even trying.* He wanted her in his bed, as his wife, as well as in his office, and he knew she wanted that too. He also wanted it to be perfect when it happened, to be sure it was going to work this second time around. That meant waiting until he solved the problems plaguing the new branch. This move was more than a new branch for the company. It meant a new life for him for the next few years, in Alaska until this branch was well established. It would be a big adjustment for the kids who had never changed schools. But before he could concentrate on his personal life, he had to find out why Black Capital was being targeted with dangerous accidents and threats.

* * *

Linda watched the traffic rushing by the window. Her calm expression hid the excitement caused by Joe's open affection. Watching him with the children, his solid build and the aura of strength and control he gave off, had caused her heart to miss a few beats and the muscles of her belly to draw up with a slight vibration as if a bolt of electricity had hit her. She had longed for physical contact.

She hoped the uncharacteristic public hug meant their relationship was moving forward. She'd been patient since his divorce from Marilyn and had been, as always, his dependable right hand at work. She'd taken the children under her wing and become almost a nanny to them while Joe worked harder than ever trying to get his life back on track. She'd never thrown herself at him. She didn't want him on the rebound. Finally, he'd noticed her as a woman, not just a dependable employee. Several times she thought it was leading somewhere. Then Joe would pull back into his own world, and she would be left waiting again. But he'd moved her here with them and that had to mean something.

She listened to Art and Renee peppering Joe with questions, both worried about school. Hopefully, it would go well. It was daunting for them, especially Art. He was in fifth grade and understood about things like not fitting in. Several times in the last couple of days he'd said, "Maybe they won't like me." Linda had tried to address his worries with little result. A few words from Joe would go a long way toward easing his anxiety. If Joe didn't catch on soon, she'd speak to him about it. Joe could sometimes be obtuse about the small things when he had a lot on his mind, as he inevitably did.

"I managed to get an apartment for you right across the hall from ours." Joe pulled into the lower level parking of what was obviously an expensive, high end apartment building. "I wasn't here when the moving company delivered the boxed items. Gwen came over but it's still boxed up."

"We'll sort it out. Most important is to have the kids ready for school tomorrow. Have you advertised for a nanny?"

"Not yet. Gwen said she knew someone so I held off."

An elevator took them to the fourth floor and a hallway where Linda observed thick carpeting and ornate carved woodwork surrounding the door they stopped at. Joe being second in control of one of the biggest development companies in the country and wealthy in his own right meant anything he did or had was always first class. His expression was puzzled when he inserted his key and found the door already unlocked. He ushered them in.

"Ohhhh, Goody!" A piercing squeal and clapping followed.

Linda stopped frozen. The kids cringed and moved back as a young woman in black tights, a long red sweater and a swinging chestnut ponytail raced across the room and attempted to scoop them up. Renee wrapped her arms around Linda's leg as if her life depended on hanging on. Joe stood looking surprised as Art was left attempting to fend off the woman's attempt to kiss him.

* * *

CHAPTER TWO

I just *couldn't* let your kids spend the first night here without welcoming them to their new home. I brought pizza. All kids like pizza." The whirlwind apparition stood back and looked the children over. "Oh, you're so precious. We're going to have so much *fun!*"

"Gwen? How did you get in?" Joe closed the door behind them and nudged the kids ahead of him.

"Oh, I had the manager let me in. He knows me from when the movers came. No problem."

"This is very nice of you, Gwen, but isn't necessary. Ah, Linda, this is Gwen Smith our marketing representative. Gwen, this is Linda Sloan, our office manager and my right hand."

"Nice to meet you, Miss Smith. I look forward to working with you." Linda fought to hold back amusement that threatened to become laughter while she watched the antics of her new co-worker.

"Ohoooo, it's going to be so nice to finally have an office girl. I am sooo sick of paperwork. Now, how about some pizza and maybe you kids would like to watch some TV. I hooked it up." She turned to Linda. "Joe was so sweet to get you an apartment right across the hall. I know you must be tired, so any time you want to go rest it's perfectly all right."

Office girl? Did she really say that! And she told me I can leave! Silence hung heavy as Linda waited for Joe to say something. A heavy brick was beginning to form in her stomach. *What's happening here?* A flash of doubt wedged itself into her heart. She had apparently not interpreted the hug at the airport correctly. This woman had just thrown down a challenge. Was Joe so dense he couldn't see it? Or was he attracted to her? Linda couldn't remember anyone in the company ever taking such liberties with one of the Blacks without being put in their place immediately. Okay, Miss Smith wanted to stake her claim, but she was still just an employee unless Joe told Linda differently.

"Thank you, Miss Smith, but *Mr. Black* and I have things to discuss and work yet to be done tonight. Your good intentions are appreciated, if ill timed. So we will let you be on your way and see you tomorrow at the office."

Delivered with an icy tone and an arched brow that had made many a clerk quake, Linda noted with pleasure that it was also effective with this forward little twit. She watched Gwen's eyes widen and her mouth drop open.

"Well!" Gwen turned to Joe. "I am sooo sorry, Joe. I only meant to help. People here are just friendly, not like those from -- below." She frowned at Linda.

"Gwen, it's not that we don't appreciate this, it's just that --." Joe spread his hands, apparently at a loss for words.

"It's just that we have only arrived and this is a private home." Linda picked up where Joe had faltered. "We won't keep you any longer Miss Smith. As you let yourself in, I'm sure you can let yourself out." Linda moved one hand in the direction of the door.

Snatching a shoulder bag from the kitchen bar, Gwen flounced out giving the door a healthy slam on the way.

Linda turned back to Joe who begin launching into an explanation. She had no intention of discussing this in front of the children. She was mad and she was hurt. She couldn't remember ever having been mad at Joe before. She loved him and had looked forward to getting here to be with him. *Is this the reception I get? After two weeks getting Art and Renee and their belongings ready to come, as well as my own, not to mention a day's plane ride with two overly stimulated children. And I'm met by—that woman— happily taking possession of Joe's apartment and using his first name with familiarity—and he didn't say a word when she called me an "office girl."*

"We'll discuss it tomorrow, Joe. Right now your children are apprehensive about starting a new school. If you can put Miss Smith out of mind," she took a jab at Joe, "I'll get their clothes ready for morning." Obviously a few minutes after the kids were in bed to cuddle and talk wasn't going to happen.

* * *

Joe jumped into the driver's seat of the suburban. He tried not to but couldn't help looking back at the school. "Mission accomplished."

"They'll be all right." Linda glanced back also.

"Am I that easy to read?" Joe guided the suburban out of the school parking area.

"Where the kids are concerned, yeah," Linda chuckled. Her smile faded, leaving a small crease between her eyes. "I hope their first day goes well. I'm more concerned about Art than I am Renee. He tries hard to live up to everyone's expectations, and I think he's terrified he won't be liked."

Joe reached over and patted her hand.

"He'll be fine. I'll try to spend more time with him now that we're all here.

You're wonderful with the kids, Linda. I don't tell you like I should but I do notice."

"Thank you, Joe."

She looked touched by the praise. She was always so self-contained that he tended to take her feelings for granted. He needed to change that.

"So, where do things stand now?" He reverted to business.

"On the personal side, we're here and we have apartments. We just enrolled the kids in school and the bulk of our furniture and belongings should arrive in a few days. You'll need a housekeeper and cook as soon as I can find one for you. All in all we have a good start on a new routine."

Joe shook his head. "You have no idea how good that sounds." He glanced over and found Linda's eyes focused on him with that knowing look she had when she was reading below the surface. He liked that—when they almost worked as one unit. It was intimate, almost sexy that she knew him so well.

"Tell me what I'll find at the office."

"Doing business in Alaska has special problems we don't have elsewhere. There's the remoteness of some locations, transportation headaches, supply headaches. Not knowing the players on a personal basis is a handicap. I'll remedy that. We're the new guy on the block. Donald did his best but it was a lot to get a handle on, and he was already facing retirement when we sent him up here to open a new office."

Linda nodded slowly as Joe explained about the old building they were leasing in an industrial area. He would look for a suitable location to buy and build a new facility when they had things running smoothly.

"It will be at least a year or more before we'll be moving into a new place, depending on what I find available," he explained. "So look this place over and tell me what you need. I'll get a crew in to remodel whatever you want."

"All right. It shouldn't take long to figure out what we'll need. That may change as business grows but we won't want to remodel more than once before we get a permanent place. We have two people in the office, Miss Smith and a Seth Chambers right?"

"Right, although Gwen spends very little time in the office. She was sort of both office manager and marketing rep for Donald. She knows people all over the state, brought in several deals for Donald. She's invaluable at getting a toe in the door with a lot of people."

"Is she an engineer?" Linda inquired.

"No, but she has a lot of experience with drawings and can read plans as much as she needs to."

Linda remained quiet.

"What?"

"Joe, are you interested in this woman personally?"

His mouth dropped open and he gripped the wheel hard. His lips tightened as the warmth he felt flooding through him made him feel angry and sick.

"How can you even ask me that? I know you didn't get off on a good foot with her but for God's sake, Linda!"

Linda's chin rose combatively. "I've never seen anyone allowed to take such liberties with Black Capital management as she did last night. I have to wonder why she feels she can do that—and why you didn't correct her. I need to know—so I had to ask."

"You of all people should know that I have no personal interest in Gwen Smith."

"I hope she knows that. I have yet to work with the woman but I'm willing to bet she is way out of line in what she thinks her position is with Black Capital. I suspect Donald let it slide rather than challenge her, especially if she was bringing in business. You need to decide just what her position is and explain it to her. AND you need to stop this business of her calling you by your first name. It is not respectful to a superior, much less owner of the company, and it doesn't give the impression of Black Capital you want to establish here."

Joe parked next to the building and shut off the motor. For the first time he could think of he was angry with Linda, and he was hurt. He loved her, wanted to marry her, and had spent sleepless nights thinking of what her body would feel like laying against him, those long legs wrapped around him. Now he couldn't remember there ever being a time she had criticized him. Didn't she have any more respect for his management ability than this? She didn't like Gwen. Well, Gwen was different, but Linda would see how important Gwen was right now, if a little over the top at times. He didn't need to ruffle anyone's feathers over company protocol until he figured out the answers to some problems.

"Okay, Linda. I'll be mindful of our impression." He forced a smile but her lack of trust in him had just come between them. The smile was brief.

* * *

Linda took in the fading paint and rough wood of the old building. "Sort of like the shoemakers kids, isn't it?"

Joe was already getting out of the SUV. "Not for long."

Linda followed quickly. His impatience was palpable. She knew the only thing that was going to relieve his stress was getting to work.

Joe held the door and she walked past him into the building that was to be where she would spend most of her time. Her anticipatory smile faded. The walls assaulted her with a nauseous shade of yellow. Two old chairs and a small couch available for clients were covered in a dirty worn brown velvet.

"Oh, my God!" It came out a breathless whisper.

"I know it's bad but you'll get it fixed up."

Joe's hand on her waist turned her toward the back of the large room where a pleasant looking young man sat at a drafting desk. Linda put his age in his late twenties, of medium height with light brown hair. In a crowd he would blend in as average. He was surrounded on two sides by a long counter that apparently did double duty as a reception desk. He stood as they approached and came around the counter, his hand held out.

"Linda, this is Seth Chambers, our local technical man. He takes the plans the architects send and orders supplies, double checks for problems peculiar to this area and tweaks things if needed. He's also our go-to man for information on local codes and requirements."

"Seth, this is Linda Sloan. She will be running the office and be in charge when I'm not here."

"Happy to meet you Mr. Chambers." Linda accepted his hand with a smile. "I look forward to working with you."

"A pleasure, Ms. Sloan. Happy to have you here. Call me Seth."

A door opened noisily in the back of the room where a hallway split the rest of the building in half. Gwen emerged in khaki colored slacks and a print blouse that fit closely to well-formed breasts. Her chestnut hair floated loose around her face. She looked miffed.

"Good morning, Joe. I expected you earlier. I told you I could help expedite things at the school. I know people there. It wouldn't have taken but a few minutes." She turned stiffly toward Linda. "Good morning."

Linda nodded her acknowledgement.

Gwen turned back to Joe with a bombardment of problems and decisions that Joe just *had* to look at and take care of right now. He glanced at Linda.

"Have Seth show you around while I look at these. I'll catch up with you."

Linda watched them walking down the hallway. *Gwen is definitely going to be a problem.*

"Where would you like to start Ms. Sloan?"

Refocusing on Seth, Linda found it obvious he was nervous, perhaps unsure of her. She smiled, hoping it would help to put him at ease.

"I would like to see the entire building and the area around it. We'll go from there.

* * *

Joe followed Gwen to his office. Positioning a chair as close to his as possible, she leaned forward, pressing her breasts against his arm as she spread out various folders and papers. She chattered on, relating what needed his attention and what should be done about various problems.

As Gwen jumped from one subject to another, Joe separated the folders into various projects and scanned them. Gwen was assuming he would rush right out to the sites to handle relatively small and routine problems that should have been taken care of by the site foreman.

Why aren't they taking care of things like this as they come up? Were the people on his sites incompetent? He'd only been here two weeks and Donald had been eager to leave. He possibly hadn't gotten all the briefing he should have. Donald had assured him that Gwen could tell him anything he needed to know. With the logistics of getting settled in at work and finding suitable apartments, he hadn't yet visited the sites. Every site had something holding up the project. Most were easily solved—or should have been.

"Tell Ted to have the chopper ready in the morning. I'll start with the White Mountain site."

"Wonderful. I'll call him right away." Gwen hustled out of the room, closing Joe's office door behind her. After glancing up and down the hall and seeing no one she grinned and ran her tongue over her upper lip like a cat with cream on her mustache.

* * *

CHAPTER THREE

Joe stopped the Suburban in the school drop off area.

"Bye Daddy." Renee kissed his cheek, received a hug and bounced away smiling.

Renee had chattered happily last night about her first day at school. She met a girl named Sarah and another called Misha. She played with them at recess and the teacher did a lot of fun things during the lessons.

Art hadn't been happy at all. He had been met with indifference. The boys didn't ask him to join their games. He was a new kid from out of state, the odd one out, and they had ignored him. His worst fears, it had seemed to him, had come true; he didn't fit in. Joe remembered what it was like to be the outsider at school. He struggled to find the words to tell Art how to deal with it—something besides, "Suck it up and live with it." Joe had talked to him for a long time.

"They don't know you yet. Be patient. Don't let it get to you. They'll come around."

Art seemed to be encouraged when he went to bed. Today he would go to soccer practice after school and get a uniform. He was small for his age, but fast and an excellent soccer player. Joe didn't want him to be discouraged again before he even got to school this morning, so he had decided to drop them off himself. From the glum look on Art's face he didn't think he had been successful. So here he was, VP of Black Capital and head of its new Alaska branch, late getting to the airport so he could take his kids to school. The kids were the most important of course. But somewhere in the back of his mind was a little voice telling him if he were a good manager he could do both.

"Go get'em tiger." Art considered himself too old to hug so Joe contented himself with a fist bump. Art gave him a weak smile and followed his sister, planting his feet deliberately ahead one at a time.

Joe resolved to call Linda this afternoon after she picked the kids up and see how their day had gone. She was often more in touch with what the kids were thinking than he was.

He felt a bit like *he* might be back at school too, sent to the principal's office, when he arrived at the heliport and Gwen answered his cheerful, "Good morning," with a childish sulk. He wasn't sure what to think about her. She seemed to swing from spoiled child to sultry siren to responsible businesswoman. She had made advances in the two weeks he'd been here. *Was that why he'd felt defensive when Linda questioned him about her? Linda seemed to have a sixth sense sometimes.* It wasn't unusual for a female employee to make advances toward the good looking heir to Black Capital, but they were always rebuffed immediately. He'd done his best to sidestep Gwen's forwardness without offending her. He needed her knowledge about what was going on right now and how things might work differently here, and he'd already found out he had to keep her happy to get information, otherwise she clammed up.

He glanced sideways at her as they boarded the company helicopter. He'd like to query her about things that had happened at the White Mountain site, but when he put on his headphones the intercom crackled in his ears. He'd talk to her later. The sites had been plagued with late deliveries, deliveries of the wrong supplies, damaged or substandard materials, and the list went on. These things happened, but not often on Black Capital projects. Their brand stood for quality work, and they demanded quality materials and service from those they did business with. What had been happening here was unusual in the extreme, in some cases bringing the entire project to a stop until a mistake could be corrected.

Joe watched the forested mountains moving past below them. He understood why their customer was building an upscale resort in this remote area. They were going for wealthy sportsmen who could easily pay the high price for a unique wilderness experience. That same location made it a major challenge for Black Capital. Supplies and equipment had to be ferried in by the big company helicopters. The one they were riding in carried a full load as well as Gwen and himself.

The supply problems, Joe felt could be corrected, but lately there had been accidents and even threats. Donald had gone to the law but there wasn't much they could do without more to go on. Joe had inherited a mess of headaches. Now that Linda was here and he could depend on the office running smoothly, he'd get to the bottom of it all. He planned to start with the sites and work backward. He preferred quietly getting his facts together before he started making sweeping changes. In the meantime the projects needed to continue on time.

Their landing site came into view, and Joe surveyed from the air the magnitude of this undertaking. He waited impatiently while the pilot set the chopper down.

* * *

From their position on a rise, Joe, John Everett, and Gwen surveyed the project.

John had come up from Colorado to head it. He had been with the company for many years, and Joe could almost see pride in the work they had done here oozing from his pores. It was comforting to have him here in charge of this major job, a person Joe knew he could rely on.

"This is impressive, John." Joe swept his hand from left to right, encompassing the entire horizon. "It's looking good but we're way behind. What do you need to change that?"

"Same thing I've been telling Donald and Gwen. I need the supplies I order, good supplies we can use, and I need some good men. I hear word is out that it's dangerous to work for us and men are being warned off from hiring on."

Joe whipped his eyes to John. "Why haven't I heard of this?"

John pursed his lips and glared at Gwen. "She knew. I've been telling her for weeks now."

"Oh, for goodness sakes, John." Gwen tossed her hair, giving John a contemptuous look. "That is just a rumor and you know it. I checked it all out and found nothing to prove anything has been said against us. You'll be starting rumors yourself talking that way."

Joe let Gwen's remark slide but his tone turned serious. "Let me know immediately if you hear anything else. Same with any threats or accidents, day or night, okay John?"

"You got it."

Joe started back down the hill. Gwen moved up and took Joe's arm as if she needed support and John followed behind. At the small temporary office that had been constructed for John, Joe stopped and looked around him. Men were gathering in the large tent that served as dining area.

"It will be dark soon. I've cut back working in the dark, even with good lighting. We've had three accidents. We're getting more daylight every day now this time of year. That's the best I can say. I know we're behind and need to work them overtime—they want overtime—but I won't risk someone getting hurt or worse."

"You might try telling them not to be so careless." Gwen threw her hands out in an impatient gesture.

"That's fine. I agree." Joe nodded to John, ignoring Gwen.

"Shall we go over and get you two some chow before you fly back?" John asked.

"No. Linda and the kids flew in a couple of days ago, and I want to be back tonight and see how school is going for the kids and how Linda is doing shaping up the office. I'll take a rain check."

"Hey!" John grinned widely. "Linda and the kids are here? She running things? Now at least I won't have any more problems coming from the office."

Joe turned to Gwen who was looking at John like she could spit nails.

"Why don't you go tell Ted to fire up the chopper and we'll get started home."

Gwen hesitated, opened her mouth and then closed it, obviously not wanting to leave the conversation, then whirled around and left to find the pilot. Joe followed John into the small office. Leaning against the desk Joe folded his arms.

"You've had problems with the office?"

"Oh, yeah. Lost paperwork and a lot of payroll mistakes. That doesn't make for happy workers. Especially when they're working long hard hours out here in the middle of nowhere. I expect that has accounted for a few of those that quit."

"You have paperwork on all that?"

"Nope. We don't keep much out here that we don't need. Bundle it up and send it to the office. It should all be there."

Joe nodded and retrieved his briefcase. "I'd like you to copy any paperwork you have on problem supply deliveries. Send it to the office marked personal to me in care of Linda."

John rubbed his hands together and smiled broadly. "Hot dog! I can feel things getting better already."

Joe smiled at John's optimism but his gut clenched as he wondered if some of his problems might be coming from his own office. His smile faded as he thought about the possibility of Linda accidently becoming more involved in the more serious problems that had included accidents and threats. He wanted her completely isolated from those. With a final handshake he headed for the chopper.

* * *

Joe taking the kids to school gave Linda an earlier start than she would normally have until she hired a nanny. She'd get started on that this morning.

Letting herself in, she locked the door behind her. It was 7:30 A.M. and the office would open at 8:00 A.M. Most business offices opened at 9:00 A.M. but construction workers started early and it had been the policy ever since she went to work for Black Capital that if the men who did the back breaking labor could start early the offices could open and be available also.

By the time she unlocked the front door at 8:00 A.M. she had delved into the files and found a disorganized mess stuffed into three old beat up metal file cabinets. One had drawers that were sprung and didn't close completely. She would never have believed Donald would have run an office that way.

Making a mental note that Seth was late she retraced her steps to the office. She was itching to get into the daily office routine but first she needed to get moving on remodeling the place so they could operate in some semblance of an organized business. Ten minutes later she heard the front door shut and soon Seth stuck his head into her office.

"Morning. You're here early."

"Good morning. A bit early, yes. What time have you been opening the office, Seth?"

"About 8:00, sometimes later." His attitude had gone wary. "Why? Is there a problem?"

"Did Donald set any office hours?"

"I don't remember it ever being mentioned. Are you leading up to my being here ten minutes late?"

"I'm just trying to find out what has been the norm here and what we need to clarify. Are you the one that opens and closes?"

Seth shrugged. "Me, Gwen, Donald, whoever was here first or last out."

"Okay. Company policy is the office opens at 8:00 A.M. It may not seem we need to now but we need to establish a routine. From now on I'll expect that."

"Yes, Ma'am." His face was expressionless.

"Do we have a crew available to remodel this place?" Linda consulted the list on her clipboard.

"We've been working short-handed everywhere but the shopping center job in Fairbanks is on hold for a few days while the city runs utilities in and puts down paving. Some of those men might be willing to come down and work on this for a few days."

"Good. Get me six framers and dry wall men, an electrician, four painters and a roofer. I want them here at 9:00 tomorrow morning. I'll probably be taking the children to school and won't be in as early as this morning."

"I'll get right on it."

"Good. Thank you, Seth." Linda favored him with a warm smile that took the sting out of her pointing out he was late. "Oh, and Seth," he stopped in the doorway, "you seem to be working in a pretty basic situation up there. You will have an office now. I want a list of what you need to run a first class planning room, tables, computers, lights, electrical outlets, etc., anything that will need to be considered in the remodeling. On my desk before you leave."

A wide smile broke out on Seth's face. "Yes, Ma'am."

Linda's mouth ticked up at the corner. *Seth will be fine. He just needs polishing into a more professional employee.*

On her tour the day before, Linda had noticed two rooms full of stored office furniture. She entered one of them now. *Is nothing ever locked around here?* Most of the discards were junk, broken and beat up folding and work tables, battered and rickety book shelves, some old work desks and a few discarded typewriters from days gone by. Then, shoved in the back under years of dust and dirt she spotted an elegant old roll top desk. It had seen a lot of use and abuse but under the scratches and gouges, the old varnish and the dirt, was solid oak. It stood there with a sort of majestic dignity, enduring its fall from grace and the humiliation heaped upon it.

"Don't you worry," she spoke to it. "You're coming back to the front office." She ran a finger over its dust covered top. The second room, with more of the same, offered up an over-sized legal bookcase and a huge and much abused oak table. She roamed the remaining rooms until she reached the end of the hallway where a door opened into the warehouse area at the back. Returning to the main office, she logged onto the only computer there and was soon making calls.

Two hours later she finished the calls and sat back to study the three sheets of notes on her clipboard. Linda put a call though to Seth's desk. "Do we have a janitor?"

"We get someone in from the temp agency when we need them. Never had a regular janitor."

"Okay." Linda hung up. At least one item that wasn't a problem or needed attention.

At noon Seth poked his head in again. "Time for lunch. You want to go first?"

"No thank you, Seth. You go on. I'll listen for the door and answer the phone."

He nodded and left. Linda stood up and stretched her shoulders. She had an appointment in ten minutes to interview a prospective nanny and two more after that before she had to leave to pick the kids up. This afternoon and evening would be spent with Art and Renee. She fervently hoped that Art had a good day and crossed her fingers that Joe would be home in time for dinner. When the kids went to bed, she wanted to settle down with Joe and a glass of wine and hear what he had learned at the site, tell him about the office and what her plans were. She wanted them to have some private time to hold each other, maybe make love if the kids were asleep. It had been a long time. Joe always felt guilty, she was, after all, his employee. Maybe, just maybe, they could discuss the future--their future.

The usual squeak of the front door told her the first appointment had arrived. Linda greeted a young woman, probably in her early twenties, with blond hair hanging loose around her shoulders. Her outfit was new but would have looked more at home on a trendy teenager. Linda smiled and held out her hand.

* * *

"Joe, we need to talk about this White Mountain project." Gwen's voice sounded tinny coming through the headset on the chopper. He nodded in reply. "I would suggest we talk over dinner, but I know you want to have dinner with those precious kids of yours. I could order something brought in and join you and we could talk after dinner. You really do need to understand about this project as soon as possible. It's important you know the facts."

Joe was going to be later than he had hoped. No doubt he'd miss a lot of meals and even be gone for days at a time in the near future, but for these first few days he had hoped to be there for them, talk to them, and be sure they could navigate the new waters of their life. He hadn't had a chance, actually had been immersed in business, and forgot to call Linda as he'd planned. But... he also needed to know what Gwen knew about all the projects and especially this one. She was currently his only link to information until he could make his own contacts. She was an invaluable source and, while she needed training that Donald had neglected to give her on company policy and behavior, it was looking like she was destined to become his mainstay in getting this branch off the ground. He would just have to spend the time needed to shape her into a stellar employee.

"All right, Gwen. Come on by and join us for dinner. I want to know everything you have on this project. Then I need to make arrangements to visit the Fairbanks project as soon as possible."

"We could have Ted fly us up tomorrow. You can let Linda start taking the kids to school and we could get on with business, have more time than we had today with such a late start."

Joe nodded. "Make the arrangements."

* * *

Linda carried the hot lasagna pan to the bar and set it next to the garlic bread. She had stopped at the market on the way home from school and let Art and Renee pick what they wanted for dinner that would be easy to make under the circumstances. They opted for the pre-made lasagna. She had added the garlic bread and a bag of ready-mixed salad. The kids were perched on top of unpacked boxes in place of bar stools.

It was 6:00 P.M. and she hadn't heard from Joe. She had no idea what time he would get back but had expected him in time for dinner. The kids had done their homework. Renee was happy and a chatterbox and Linda felt that she was going to be fine with the change in her life. Art was harder to read. He didn't seem happy, but if he was unhappy he hid it well. He was more reticent than anything. *Much like his father, God help us.*

Her inquiries about the soccer team were met with short answers.

"Did you get your uniform?"

"Yes."

"Were the boys on the team nice?"

"I guess."

"Did you talk to any of them?"

"Not really."

"Do you like the coach?"

"He's okay."

She detected no enthusiasm. Well, she was sure he would share more with Joe when he got here.

"Looks like your daddy is going to be a little late. Let's go ahead and eat while it's hot and we'll save some for him."

The chirp of her cell phone alerted Linda to an incoming text. It was from Joe and a big smile spread across her face as she opened it. The smile faded.

"Home in 10 min. Gwen joining us for dinner. J"

* * *

CHAPTER FOUR

Linda's breath froze in her throat and there was pain around her heart, her hands balled into fists. Disappointment, anger, dismay, all fought for dominance, but anger won out. A picture came to her, Joe in the car, claiming to have no interest in Gwen. *Why is Joe bringing that woman home—tonight of all nights?* The kids need his attention, especially Art. Was a couple of hours over dinner and bedtime too much to ask? Art would clam up in front of Gwen and in any case Gwen shouldn't be privy to Art's life. *But he's bringing her here anyway.*

Linda had planned to talk to Joe tonight, over a glass of wine, after the kids went to bed. It was important that they work together now. They needed some private time to just be together, to share their lives as well as their work. *But tonight he would be sharing his time with Gwen.*

She took a deep breath and managed to get her shaking hands under control enough to fill the kid's plates. They dove into the lasagna, not noticing her grim expression, and were happily taking second helpings when the door opened and Joe ushered Gwen in. Linda grit her teeth and smiled. The children were less circumspect. Loud exclamations of "Daddy!" died in their throats as Gwen proceeded Joe into the apartment. Renee hopped off her improvised seat and ran to Joe who grabbed her up in a bear hug.

"How's my beautiful girl?"

Renee giggled and hugged his neck. Art remained where he was, seeming to draw even more into himself than he had been earlier. Joe put an arm around his shoulders and hugged him.

"Hi, Tiger. How'd it go today?"

"Okay."

"Really? Great." Joe paused, catching on that he wasn't getting the full story. He moved over and put an arm around Linda's shoulder.

"Sorry I'm late. How is everybody?" He shifted his eyes to Art in a question.

Linda shrugged. "More communication would probably improve things for everybody."

Joe blinked, hesitated, and nodded.

"I see. Everyone—Gwen is going to have a bite to eat with us and then we have some business to talk about." He turned to Gwen. "Looks like the grown-ups eat standing up due to a shortage of suitable boxes." Joe laughed heartily.

"You should have told me about this. *I* would have seen to it you had a proper place to eat."

"Not necessary, Gwen. Everything will be here in a day or two" Joe helped himself to a paper plate and handed one to Gwen.

"Hello, Linda." Gwen finally acknowledged Linda with a bright brittle smile.

"Hello, *Miss Smith*." Linda replied pointedly, struggling to be polite and relaxed, if not warm at least neutral.

Gwen chattered brightly as they ate. She was full of "fun" suggestions for Renee and Art on everything from going out for dinner to a pizza place to movies and parks and sports games, even fishing and canoeing.

The kids finished their dinners quietly. Renee listened to Gwen in awe.

"May I be excused?" Art directed the question to Linda.

"Of course. Why don't you check your clothes for tomorrow and let me know if you need anything." Linda took his plate.

"Can I watch TV?" Renee asked hopefully.

"Thirty minutes, then you check your clothes too. Okay?"

"Okay." Renee laughed happily and raced off to the living room where the TV was sitting on the floor awaiting the furniture's arrival.

Linda cleaned the kitchen, more than it needed, as Joe and Gwen discussed the White Mountain project. She listened incredulously as Gwen explained to Joe that the men on the project were always careless and how a certain amount of accidents were to be expected.

Taking a deep breath she counted to three, then went to pull Renee from the television. By the time Renee had picked clothes for school the next day and Linda had pointed both her and Art to a bath she expected Gwen to be leaving. She tucked the kids into the temporary cots they were using until the furniture arrived, promising to send Joe in to tell them goodnight.

Renee couldn't wait for him to come. Art said he didn't need to come, he knew Dad was busy.

Returning to the kitchen Linda found Joe and Gwen still perched on the boxes vacated by the children. Gwen was telling Joe that the problem with a lumber supplier was because of John Everett. The fact that Joe sat there listening attentively to every word Gwen uttered about John Everett, a man Linda had often dealt with and who was one of Black Capital's best employees, left her more speechless than she already was.

Finally, Gwen paused, looking pointedly across the counter at Linda. Joe looked up and smiled.

"The kids are in bed. Renee wants you to come and say goodnight. Art said he knew you were busy."

"I'll go right in." Joe rose and circled the counter. Linda raised a hand to get his attention and he stopped.

"Are you going to be long here? We need to talk about some things."

"Oh, Linda, we have at least another hour of going over things on this project. I'm sure you can discuss household things with Joe later?" Gwen smiled but there was steel in her eyes.

Linda shifted her gaze back to Joe. He looked uncomfortable. "Well, ah... Gwen we can cover it all later."

"Joe! You need to know all this before we go to the site tomorrow."

Joe studied his boots. Finally he raised his head, looking at Linda.

"Gwen and I will finish this tonight and I'll get with you tomorrow when I get home."

Linda felt like she had when she was twelve and her favorite pony kicked her in the gut. Her mouth opened and she had trouble breathing.

"I'll see you in the morning. I need you to take the kids to school. Gwen and I are flying out early to Fairbanks."

"Yes, Sir. I'll be here early, Sir."

Joe started at Linda's "Yes, Sir," then opened his mouth to say something, but before he got it out Linda had turned and without a look backward let herself out of the apartment. She crossed the hall to her own apartment, kicked off her shoes and let the tears come.

Lowering herself into a tub of hot water she tried to make sense of it. *What had just happened?* Joe had been here two weeks and this woman seemed to have taken control of him. Linda had been his dependable right arm at work ever since Black Capital opened the office in California and she had been selected to be the assistant to him and his dad, Billy. Joe had begun to show feelings for her. They had fallen in love, at least she thought they both had—she had for sure—and she had been certain the move to Alaska would lead to marriage. Her relationship with Joe had been so sure. If there was any uncertainty in their personal relationship there was none in their business relationship. When Linda issued an order it carried the weight of management authority and now she was being over-ruled by this woman he had known for two weeks. What was she supposed to make of that? She was oblivious to it when the water grew as cold as her tears.

* * *

21

Stopping in a drop-off space, Linda hugged the kids as they gathered their backpacks and moved off, merging with the noisy crowd of chattering youngsters. When she had crossed the hall to Joe's apartment earlier in the morning it had been chaotic. Joe was rushing around getting ready to leave with the kids attempting to get themselves ready for school. She had taken charge and soon all three were on the way to being ready. She'd hoped to speak to Joe about Art, but when she tried, his cell phone rang. Gwen was already at the heliport and they were waiting for him. He had rushed out.

Seth greeted her at the office with a cheery, "Good morning, Ms. Sloan."

"Good morning, Seth. Did you get my men for me?"

"Sure did. They'll be here in about thirty minutes. Anything else you want me to do before they get here?"

"As a matter of fact," Linda displayed a broad smile, "there is. You can start moving everything back to the warehouse. The men can help you with tables and such. The main office, the other rooms, everything goes. We'll need long cords we can run back for the phones and computers."

"We're moving to the warehouse?"

Linda laughed out loud at Seth's expression of disbelief. "We need to be out of the way so the men can remodel this. If they have to work around us it will take twice as long. We won't be there long."

Twelve men arrived just before nine, and Seth promptly showed them to Linda's door. On a quick tour of the building she explained what she wanted done, and they all returned to her office.

"I have more detailed information." She picked up several sheets of paper. "I'd like to see this done in a week. Anyone see why we can't do that?"

A large man with a weathered look shrugged. Linda judged him to be somewhere in his thirties. "Can't tell till we get into it. Might take a month."

Linda stared at him, a bit taken aback. He wore an expression somewhere between threatening and a kid that had smarted off.

"Your name is Ralph, right?"

"That's me."

"Well, Ralph, if it takes a month there better be a *very* good reason or I'll have another crew in here." She looked the other nine men over. "Who's the senior man here?"

A balding, older, overweight man spoke up, nodding diffidently. "Reckon that's me ma'am. Name's Louie."

Linda handed him the papers she was holding. "Good. You're in charge, Louie."

She turned her attention back to the group. "Let me be clear, Gentleman. You work for Black Capital and I expect your work to reflect that. I'd like this done as quickly as possible but we don't cut corners to accomplish it. We want an end product to be proud of. Louie, anything you need, let Seth or I know. We're moving everything to the warehouse so you have nothing to hold you back. Seth and I will need a couple of you to help with that so let's get started."

Everyone smiled but Ralph, who looked like he had a lemon in his mouth as he filed out with the others.

Before the morning was out two trucks arrived. One hauled off the old furniture from the back rooms and the other took the roll top desk and other items Linda had decided to have repaired and refinished. The building hummed with noise and activity.

Linda and Seth sat in the warehouse near the hallway. The door had been removed. They had one phone line that she had hooked up to her phone. Seth had not been able to come up with enough phone cords for more but promised to pick up what they needed by the next day. A small portable heater sat between their desks. Neither were going to be able to get much done under these conditions. Daily work would pile up but in a week they should begin to operate smoothly.

A call came in informing her that the truck with their belongings would be arriving the next day between 10:00 A.M. and 4:00 P.M. Linda groaned, *Could it be more difficult? I should have been born a twin so I could be in both places at once.* She desperately needed a nanny but the three she had interviewed didn't even come close to being suitable. Now it would be Friday before she would be able to schedule more interviews. She wasn't about to settle for less than the best when it came to a nanny. She had been with the kids as they watched their family fall apart, held them when they cried and reassured them when they needed it. She had come to love them dearly and was fiercely protective. When she left to pick them up from school the front of the building was empty and two men were dismantling a wall. It would be interesting to see if they really could have it all done in a week.

* * *

Joe listened to the beat of the chopper blades as they approached Fairbanks. This shopping mall was a large project. It would have high visibility and be a major representation of Black Capital. Black Capital had sent two of their architects up to work with the customer on the plans. Everyone was happy except that they were running behind because of problems and delays at this location also.

The manager in charge of this site was George McClellen, a big bear of a man, incongruously called Baby. He met them at the airport. It was Joe's first time to meet him, as it was with most of his managers and employees here. They shook hands all around and followed Baby to a company passenger van.

"Sorry there isn't anything going on now for you to see. I have a good bunch of workers. I've been trying to stay on top of the city to see they don't drag their feet getting this paving and utilities done but it doesn't seem to have done much good. They keep telling me about permits and environmental reports. All things that have to do with them and not us so there's not much I can do."

"Okay. We'll tour the site and you can fill me in on anything I need to know."

By afternoon Joe had walked the site and observed everything with the critical eye of a professional. The work was good, but in a couple of places he recognized materials that were not of the quality he wanted. He questioned Baby about it.

"It's not what our specs called for, but it's what was sent to us, and we were told to use it." He seemed reluctant to discuss it, and Joe sensed defensiveness in his answers.

"Do you have the paperwork on it?"

"No, we send it all to the main office. All we keep here is the stuff we need like permits and so on. Permits and environmental questions and other problems getting the utilities in are what has us running behind schedule. I was hoping you might be able to do something about it."

"I'll see what I can do. When do you expect to be able to resume work?"

"Hopefully, another couple of weeks. But every time I think it's about done they have some other delay. We have no control over it because it's all public utilities. I've never run into this much trouble before."

"Can we go on with anything while we wait?"

"You see how we back up to that rock cliff, so there's no way in that way. The utility companies dug up a huge trench, bigger than any I've ever seen all around the front. They won't let us put a temporary crossing over it, just roped it all off. The only entry we have is that walkway up the side of the hill that we just came down. We can't get a truck with supplies up there."

"Why aren't we using the choppers to bring supplies in here?"

Gwen spoke up. "The city won't let us set them down anywhere but the airport, and then we would have to truck the material from the plane to here. The choppers are busy taking supplies to more remote sites. Since we would have to transfer the supplies to trucks anyway we just truck it the whole way."

Joe frowned. "I'll try to speed things up. In the meantime tear out that substandard stuff and reorder what the specs call for. Anything that arrives the men will have to pull up that hill on dollies. If I can't get this access delay fixed we'll have to come up with something else."

"Take it all out!" Baby's mouth hung open. "That could set us back as much as a couple of weeks. That will mean fines if we don't finish on time."

"Quality is more important. Keep me informed every couple of days on the progress up here, and I'll see what I can do from my end."

Baby answered with a subdued, "Yes, sir." He recovered from his surprise as they walked back to the van for the ride to the airport.

"I hope those guys I sent you do a good job. I tried to pick the best of the ones that wanted to go and work a few days while we're shut down here."

Joe stopped in his tracks and turned to Baby. A few seconds ticked by. "What guys?"

Baby looked confused. "Seth Chambers called up here and asked if I had any guys that wanted to work a few days remodeling the office. I sent a dozen guys up this morning."

"A dozen guys!" Gwen blurted out at the top of her voice. "Has he lost his mind? It only takes a couple of guys to paint a few offices. Oh, Joe, this isn't because of your office girl is it?"

Joe smiled. "Yes, Gwen, I'm sure it's at Linda's direction." He resumed his walk to the van. "I'm sure they will do fine, Baby." *If they don't they'll wish they had if Linda is overseeing them.* Joe chuckled softly, suddenly impatient to get home as his thoughts went from the construction site to Linda's blond hair, unbound and waving softly down her back.

* * *

On the flight home Gwen tried insinuating herself into Joe's evening plans again with the offer to return the favor of dinner and take him out to a favorite place of hers, and the kids also if they hadn't already eaten. When that didn't work she suggested they go by the office and check on anything being done there. Joe assured her the office was in good hands and didn't need their attention. She sulked.

Joe wanted to spend the evening with Linda and the kids. Last night had been a disaster. The two women didn't like each other, but he needed everyone to work together now. Linda had always been his strong right hand, and he didn't understand why she wasn't working with him on this. He wanted her approval and it hurt that she obviously didn't think he had good judgement where Gwen was concerned.

He opened the apartment door to the aroma of take-out chicken.

"Hope you didn't eat all that chicken I smell." Joe laughed as Renee came running and launched herself at him. He even got a smile out of Art.

Linda watched him from behind the kitchen bar as he approached still carrying Renee. He felt a pang of guilt at her wary expression when she glanced behind him as if to assure herself he was alone.

"I'll fix you a plate." She gave him a weak smile and turned to fill a paper plate with chicken from a cardboard bucket.

Chatter filled the apartment as the kids rushed to tell him about school. Renee was still happy and regaled him with all things exciting about first grade. Art even managed to have some enthusiasm as he related that he had played well at practice. The coach had actually said, "Good" at a couple of his tries at scoring a goal over his teammates.

"Great." Joe laughed, happy that Art seemed happy, gave him a high-five and asked some questions about practice.

"Linda showed me how to work the washer and dryer so I can wash my uniform every night. As soon as it's dry I'll show it to you since you couldn't see it last night."

Art made his point. Joe knew that Linda wasn't the only one he was in the doghouse with. His lessening guilt came back to slam his conscience again.

He was acutely aware of Linda and the faint lavender scent she always wore as he listened to the kids. She wordlessly served the kids and himself second helpings, ate her own dinner, and cleaned up the kitchen. When she was done she poured herself some wine in a paper cup and turned to Joe.

"If you have a few minutes....... I would like to speak to you. After you have Art and Renee in bed. I'll wait in the front room."

Joe nodded at her wine. "Pour me one of those and I'll be with you in a little while." He followed Art and Renee down the hall to their bath and bed. He had to fix this tension. He had never seen Linda react to anything this way before. He wanted her to like it here in Alaska—enough to marry him and start a life together.

With the kids tucked in he returned to find Linda sitting on the floor with her wine glass, watching a local news program. Just looking at her sitting there on the floor lowered the stress level brought on by all his problems. Dropping to the floor beside her he put his arm around her shoulders and pulled her close.

"I love getting home at the end of the day."

"Even with no furniture to sit on?" Linda raised her eyebrows. "It arrives tomorrow so things should improve then." He felt her defensiveness melt a bit.

Joe leaned in and lightly kissed her temple. "Furniture is not a necessity. You and the kids are. I'm glad things are good for the kids at school." His lips moved from her temple to her ear and on down to the nape of her neck. Linda smiled and coyly bent her head forward giving him more access to her neck.

"Mmmm, you need to talk to Art every day for a while. He's still insecure. How did you find the project sites?"

Joe sighed and pulled his arm back, cradling the paper cup in both hands. "Problems on top of problems. John Everett will be sending things to me through you marked private. I also want to see all the paperwork from all the sites until I figure out where the problems are. Today is only the second one I've been to and I have three more to see. They all seem to have the same problems. I'd like you to go back to the opening of this branch if possible and verify that all the payroll was correct and if it wasn't, correct it."

"There are payroll problems?"

"So John says. Apparently it's been a big gripe with the men." He turned to face her with a big grin. "I heard you commandeered part of my work crew."

Linda burst out laughing. She snuggled into his side and he put his arm back around her. "Word gets around, doesn't it? Maybe I better tell you what the situation at the office is."

* * *

While Linda was telling Joe about the office and what she had planned, that office was a subject of ire across town where Gwen was beating on a door with both fists.

"What the hell is going on?" She screamed at Seth as he opened it wide to allow her to pass by him.

"I assume you've been to the office." He closed the door behind her.

"Baby mentioned today that you had a dozen men transferred down here. I stopped at the office. What the hell is wrong with you?"

"I got exactly what my boss, *our new manager,* told me to get. Want a drink?" Seth calmly moved to the bar in the kitchen and poured himself one and then held up a second glass, lifting his eyebrows in question. At Gwen's nod he poured the second one and walked around the bar, handing it to her.

"I think you're up against a formidable foe, sweetheart. The lady is smart and seems to carry a lot of authority. She's in charge of his kids and his private arrangements. She gives an order and expects it to be carried out. I suggest you clean up your act or you may never make it into his bed."

Gwen's face suffused in dark crimson. She tossed off her drink and viciously hurled the glass at the sink sending glass shards flying around the kitchen.

"*Formidable* is she! We'll just see who's the most *formidable* one around here you milksop." She stormed out leaving Seth cringing as his door slammed hard enough that he checked to see if anything had cracked or come lose.

* * *

CHAPTER FIVE

Linda was cheerful, humming along to a song being played by a popular radio station as she pulled into the parking area the next morning. Seth arrived just ahead of her and she parked next to him. Workmen were arriving in a couple of vans. She exchanged greetings with Seth as he unlocked the door. Stepping inside they froze. Mayhem confronted them. Ladders were tipped over, paint and a black substance that looked like tar was splashed on walls and the floor, wooden trim intended for baseboards and doors was broken into pieces, now unusable.

"Ah, shit!" Seth exploded. "What the hell happened?"

Getting past the first shock of what she was looking at, Linda moved around the wet sticky mess and proceeded down the hall, checking every office as she went, finding much the same condition in each. Panic hit the pit of her stomach, and she hurried to the warehouse where all the business records had been moved. It took all her self-control not to cry. Computers were smashed, phones destroyed, file cabinets were emptied, contents strewn over the floor. Chairs were smashed and an axe had been taken to the work tables. Workmen filed in behind her. Seth waited for her to say something. She swallowed twice to get the lump out of her throat before she could speak.

"Seth, call the police." Turning to the workmen she took a deep breath. "Nobody touch anything before they come. You'll have to make a list of what you need to clean up and what you need to replace. Let Seth know what you need and let me know of any problems you have. In the meantime one of you go for doughnuts and coffee and bring it back. I expect that's all we'll be doing for most of the morning."

The men moved off, finding various places to sit, while they waited. Most were bored but Ralph yawned and after giving Seth a big smile, pulled his cap over his eyes and settled down for a nap. Linda called Joe on her cell phone.

"What's up?" Joe sounded cheerful.

"Have you dropped the kids off yet?"

"Just did. I'm on my way to the office now. Why?"

"Come right here. You know those problems you mentioned last night? I think they just hit home." She clicked off, not wanting to discuss it on the phone in case any of the workmen might hear.

Seth looked up from his phone. "Cops are on the way. What do you want me to do?"

"Nothing we can do until they get here and do whatever they do. Frankly, I doubt they can do much about it."

"Who would do something like this?" Seth shook his head. Linda didn't answer so he tried again. "Shall I start getting these files put back together or at least picked up?"

"No. Leave it for the police to see. There's no hurry now."

Ten minutes later a police vehicle pulled up and Linda ushered in two officers.

"Wow!" One of them commented. "This goes above and beyond the usual vandalism."

"Anyone who might have a reason to do something like this?" The other cop asked her as he surveyed the damage.

Joe walked in at that moment and reacted much the same way Linda and Seth had at first sight of the destruction. Linda introduced him to the officers and they in turn began taking statements, starting with Joe. They called for a police photographer to come and record the damage on film. Joe had obviously just arrived and had nothing he could tell them. Linda and Seth came next but here again they were limited as to any information they might have. They took statements from the workmen more as a matter of procedure than any expectation of useful information.

About 10 AM, Gwen came in. She was shocked and sympathized with the work Linda would have to do to get things up and running again. She turned to Joe.

"You know I did all of Linda's work as well as marketing before she came and never had any problems. If I can help with this, I'll be glad to. Linda seems over-worked. Maybe I should take some of this back from her.

Joe assured her Linda could handle it. She whirled around and went to find a place to sit until the police were done. Passing the workmen she gave Ralph a brief amused smile. He rolled the toothpick in his mouth from one side to the other and stretched to a more comfortable position while returning Gwen's smile with a short grin.

The end result was as Linda had expected. The police would file a report but there was no evidence to follow up on. They left. Using her cell phone Linda contacted a security company and arranged to have two guards around the clock for at least the next few days. Her plan to have the office mostly remodeled in a week had just taken a huge setback.

Linda's legs began to tremble, and she sat down only to find out that her hands shook also. She hadn't realized they would have enemies here that would resort to an act like this. Joe had finally admitted there were "some problems" at the sites beyond supply troubles but had evaded her more in depth questions. He had obviously not included her in everything. Why?

Getting a grip on herself, she gave Seth the go-ahead to pick up the files and paperwork and try to sort it to some extent. She supposed they were lucky that the vandals hadn't destroyed the files. That would have been a disaster. But then, maybe they didn't think about destroying the files. She dismissed the thought.

* * *

Coming into the office, Joe smiled. A week had made a difference on both the home front and the office. It was shaping up into an impressive place for them for the next year or so. Linda had outdone herself the last week in overcoming the problems of getting them settled. While Joe spent his days visiting the remaining construction sites, she had juggled both the remodeling disaster at the office and the arrival of their furniture. No one they sent from the employment office had been suitable as a nanny for the kids. When Linda decided to look after the kids herself at the office after school and just hire a good housekeeper her luck had changed.

Mary Ramsey was a care-worn widow in her fifties, the mother of five grown children, all out on their own. Her husband had died in a fishing boat accident with the children half grown, leaving her to bring them up though the troublesome teen years by herself on a waitress wage. She had lost her job to younger and the quicker waitresses, and had reached the end of her unemployment some time ago. She was friendly, down to earth and honest in her answers to Linda's questions. They had agreed on a trial period where she would not only function as a housekeeper and cook but as a nanny before and after school. She had worked out splendidly, and life had improved immensely with no worries about transporting the kids to school and back, and she was a good cook to boot.

The office remodeling had been set back a couple of days by the vandalism, but the project was expected to be finished in a matter of days. The roofer, after some minor maintenance work, had declared the roof in good shape and departed for home. The structural work was done and most of the electrical work. The framers and drywall men had also left for home that morning. The painting crew were still busy and the electrician would remain until the last in case of unforeseen needs. Much of the flooring had been removed and replaced because of the tar and the reception area and hallways now had heavy planking that had been finished to a high gloss. Painting had been completed in the reception area and an elegant looking desk sat prominently attended by a receptionist. Comfortable chairs sat here and there by low tables with large area rugs in warm hues in front of them.

Joe strode to the desk where Linda's new receptionist, a young man named Wallace Kingfisher sat. She had hired him from a local college where he had just graduated. His dream had been to work in construction where the big paychecks were. Unfortunately, he was small in stature and a Native American, both of which worked against him in competing for the lucrative jobs. When Linda offered the receptionist job he jumped at it, grateful to have a job of any kind and thrilled to be working for Black Capital, even if as a receptionist.

"Good morning, Wallace. How's your first morning?"

"All right, sir. At least I think so."

Joe smiled at the obviously nervous young man. "After today it will all seem routine. Just go to Linda, or Seth if she isn't around, if you have a question."

"Yes, sir. I'll do that."

Joe moved on into the hallway past offices that were still being painted. He threaded his way between ladders and paint supplies on his way to the warehouse. Linda and Seth sat at folding tables, each busy with stacks of paperwork. Looking up, Linda returned his smile.

"The reception room is beautiful. Wallace is nervous." Joe grinned at her.

"Yes, I know," she chuckled. "I just gave him some basic things to do for today. I'll work more in as he gets more comfortable."

Joe pulled up a folding chair and sat down. "When you get done with him, he'll be yours forever."

"I hope so. Faithful employees are the key to everything."

"I want to go back up to the White Mountain project but I would be gone over the weekend. I hate to be gone then but it's important to get things moving as soon as possible. Has anything come from John?"

Linda nodded her head and reached for a folder on the table. "I printed an extra copy for you and I'm taking the original home in my briefcase until we get tighter security. I didn't copy you the payroll information as it's routine, but there is a progress report and information on a couple of rumors John heard. Also, he has some supply deliveries that are late. Do you want me to check on them?"

"No. You've got your hands full here. I'll do it or have Gwen do it." Joe didn't miss the muscle twitch in Linda's jaw.

"Speaking of Gwen, we haven't seen her around here in two or three days."

"She's out of town meeting with a couple of prospective customers."

"Shouldn't you be meeting them?"

"In time I will. For now she can handle it and I can try to get these other problems straightened out."

"I haven't seen any information that we usually file and study before making a bid on new projects."

"She told me about some of it. It's okay for now."

"When we get into the offices we will have to use the company system to keep track of things."

Joe nodded and stood. "Well, I'll go home and pack and catch the chopper up to White Mountain today. You sure you're all right with the kids for the weekend?"

Linda nodded and Joe bent to give her a light kiss on the forehead. He would really be happy when he got all these problems solved and could give more thought and time to Linda and the kids.

* * *

Miles away in Juneau a large overweight balding man in an expensive suit rested his feet, clad in expensive shoes, on an expensive coffee table. He was sitting in a plush chair upholstered in deep rust velvet. He reached up and accepted the drink offered by his longtime aide.

"So, Black has arrived. You say she's working on him?"

That brought a short laugh from his aide, Beacher Yates. "Oh, yes. From the minute she saw him she decided she wanted to be Mrs. Black. Unfortunately, he seems to have a secretary that's first in line for that... or so it seems."

"Don't count the little minx out if she wants him. What about what I want?"

"She's been doing well on it but now that he's here he's attempting to find out what's going wrong. Want me to tell her to step it up?"

Senator Alfred Robard toyed with his glass and contemplated the question. "Tell her to step up the pressure but for God's sake be discrete. We need something to happen to get some attention and bad publicity for this Black Capital bunch. I want them out of this state before they have a chance to get a toehold. If she goes along as his wife that's fine but they have to go."

"I'll tell her."

The Senator looked up. "You have someone keeping close tabs on her? She can be a loose cannon."

"Oh, yes. I'm watching her.

* * *

Gwen finished with the prospective new customer and took a private bush plane home. Home, which she never talked about, was an old cabin in a remote area where her father sometimes pretended to eke out a living from trapping and an old gold claim that had exhausted its meagre offerings many years before. In reality he spent most of his time in the place he had been born and raised, on the docks where he had his hand in a considerably large part of the crime and illegal dealings that plagued the state.

Gwen emerged from the plane and set off toward the cabin, passing the line of small dog kennels with a dog chained at each. Her cousins might enter the Iditarod every year but it was her father's fourth wife, a Native American that kept, trained and supplied the dogs. Her father waited on a platform that served as an excuse for a porch.

"What do I owe a visit from my devious offspring to?" He watched her shrewdly as she passed him by and slammed the door behind her.

He raised his eyebrows in a question to the man following her. The man shifted the bag of supplies Gwen had brought along from his arm to the porch. He shrugged his shoulders and shook his head in answer to the silent question. He retreated to the plane to wait. He'd been a bush pilot here for many years and didn't want to be anywhere near a family problem, especially this family.

Bull Smith joined Gwen inside, where she was sitting down to a plate of stew served by Bull's silent wife Mit. Mit rarely spoke. She'd tried to speak to her mother when she was fifteen and Bull Smith offered her father money to hand her over to be his wife. Her mother told her to be quiet or her father would beat her. On her wedding night she tried to speak to Bull and he beat her. Then he showed her what he expected of her. When he was done, he told her to clean herself up and fix food for him and his drinking buddies. She vomited when he left. Then she did as she was told. She never spoke again unless asked a question. Observing her husband and his offspring she vowed to never have a child. Remedies passed down for generations helped her keep that vow. Bull took a seat at the table and accepted the beer Mit brought him.

Gwen wanted something or she would never come here. She had grandiose ideas and (if encountering him on a city street) would pass by without blinking an eye.

"I need more help with stopping the projects."

"I pulled in favors to have a lot of workmen make problems for you but they will only do so much of that. They get caught, they're out of work, and they'll talk. This is your baby. You took it on, you deliver. Don't try to dump it in my lap."

Gwen shook her head while spooning stew into her mouth.

"Not that kind of help. Some worker sabotaging something or some clerk screwing up a supply or transportation order isn't going to be enough. I want someone that can move around quickly and do damage. I want Rodney."

Bull snorted. "Don't want much do you? He ain't been seen since he broke out of prison. Even the officials think he drowned. Trying to escape in a little boat in a major storm, he didn't have a chance. Not even anything left of the boat but a few sticks that floated up."

Gwen pushed the now empty plate away and leaned back in her chair.

"Rodney would never take a risk like that. Whoever went out on that boat, if anyone did, it sure as hell wasn't Rodney. I figure you know just where he is and how to contact him. I doubt he had much of a stash, if any, and that he needs money by now. I can make it worth his while."

"You better be able to pull this off. Your boss can be right unpleasant when he's let down."

"My only boss is Joe Black, and I plan on becoming Mrs. Black."

Bull leaned forward and frowned. "You're playing a dangerous game gal. You be very sure you know what you're doing or you may find yourself roadkill on a road of money."

Gwen pushed her chair back and stood up, glaring at her father.

"I'll expect to hear from Rodney—soon." She stomped out the door, slamming it behind her.

Mit carried the dirty plate and spoon back to the rough table she used as a kitchen. After Bull followed Gwen outside, she watched through the small window, without expression, as Gwen and the pilot entered the plane and took off back to whatever place they came from.

When Bull came back, he made up a bedroll and set the bag of supplies that had been meant for Mit beside it. Then he went out and saddled a horse. An hour later he was gone and so were her supplies. He didn't tell her where he was going or when he would be back. He had done this every so often for several months, always coming back the following day.

* * *

CHAPTER SIX

Linda took the kids to a movie, and they ate at the food court in the theatre. Pizza, popcorn, candy, and soda combined to worry Linda about the possibility of a couple of sick kids that night. But they were delighted and enjoyed the novelty of their first trip to the theatre since arriving. Both were unhappy Joe wasn't with them but understood that from time to time he had to be away. Linda was definitely not happy and had to dig deep to maintain a happy face for Art and Renee.

Saturday morning Linda loaded the kids into the suburban along with school books, homework, a soccer ball and a random game or two. They romped through the nearly completed offices commenting on this and that as only observant children can do. Linda settled in at her folding table in the warehouse and pointed out the large empty space behind her where they could play soccer to their hearts content.

She had spent the last week trying to stay on top of the daily work—difficult, under the present circumstances. Hiring Mary had freed her of having to take the children to school and back and arrange for meals. With Joe gone most days—with Gwen—Linda could work as long as she wanted. There was no reason to go home when the work day was over. Joe was spending long days out of the office—with Gwen—and when he did make it home the kids needed his attention.

Unease stalked Linda. Dreams of the office being ransacked again were frequent. She was easily distracted at work and began making all her decisions around her worries. She needed to get a routine in place and the rules laid down as soon as possible. If all went well, by Thursday she could let the IT firm come and install the new computers and other equipment she had ordered. It was the latest technology, and she ordered it all with as much security as could be had. Giving in to the bad feeling she had been plagued with ever since the vandalism, she ordered, without speaking to Joe, a large safe to put confidential information in.

She began with sorting paperwork from the files that had been scattered. After a few hours the kids were hungry and asking when they were going to eat. She took a quick break and went to the drive through at a fast food place and bought them a generous lunch to take back to the warehouse. She set them to arranging their lunch into a picnic in the cavernous warehouse and went back to her work, nibbling on chicken strips while she worked. Every so often one of the guards would come through on his rounds. One of them joined Art in a gentle game of passing the soccer ball back and forth which went a long way toward keeping Art happy.

She worked until well after the dinner hour. The kids were bored, tired, and hungry again. Rolling her chair back she looked at the files with satisfaction. She was over half done and if she repeated her efforts tomorrow she would have them in order for Monday morning. Her next job would be to go through each file separately. Before that however, she needed to go back to the beginning and scour the payroll files. By the end of the week the IT people would have her computer network set up and she could begin digging for payroll information. The computers had been destroyed in the attack on the office but the IT people were able to save the information on the hard drives. Linda had it put on external drives.

By Sunday evening she was tired and the kids were beyond bored with playing in the warehouse. At least she had the files in order and back in the old file cabinets. She was ready to get things under control. Tuesday the carpet would go down, Wednesday the new office furniture she had purchased would arrive, minus the specialized drafting tables and items for Seth that were not normally kept on hand. He didn't mind. He was delighted to just be getting them at all. Thursday was the day she looked forward to. The IT people would come and she would have all the information at her fingertips, or would when she got it input.

She was close enough now to having it all up and running smoothly that she would have to have a talk with Joe. Every time she had tried to approach the subject he got defensive and walked off. But the office was her domain and come Friday, when it was functional, there would be procedures to be followed and even Gwen would have to comply.

* * *

Joe made it back Sunday night just as Linda was putting the kids to bed. His arrival granted the already tired and cranky children a reprieve of an hour to be with their father.

Linda checked the apartment to assure herself everything was ready for Mary's arrival the next morning and the kid's departure for school. She had a momentary twinge of guilt for the poor teachers that would have to deal with the tired state the kids would be in the next day. She poured a glass of wine for herself and a whiskey for Joe and waited.

Joe came in and smiled at the drink waiting for him and sighed as he sank into a chair. Linda studied the tired lines around his eyes.

"How was it?"

"John is doing the best he can, and there have been no more accidents. A few materials have been slow arriving. I'll get on that in the morning. Then I want to go back up to the Fairbanks project and go to city hall. I made some calls about the hold ups on permits, our blocked access and the delay on the work around our project, but all I get is a run-around. I think it's time I meet some officials face to face."

"When are you going to Fairbanks?"

"I think Tuesday. I'll call tomorrow and set up some times for a meeting. I hear from the kids that you worked all weekend."

Linda nodded and sipped her wine. "The files are sorted as best I can until I go through them one by one. Tomorrow I can concentrate on just the daily items that have been backing up. Next week should see us up and running like a business."

Joe smiled. "You are a treasure. Not only are you a miracle worker at business but you're beautiful too." He studied her for a minute. "I'm sorry I wasn't at the theater with you."

Linda blinked away the dampness that started to gather in her eyes. "Me too. We all miss you when you're gone."

They talked for a while but seeing that Joe was tired she excused herself and after a tight hug and a gentle kiss she crossed the hall to her own apartment.

* * *

Sitting at a table near Linda's, Joe made calls about the slow deliveries to John. In almost all cases the shipments had gone out on time from suppliers or were ready to go out. Three transportation companies had been involved. One showed no delivery problems. By the end of the day he had determined that the others had not picked up on time, been slow delivering the goods to the airport where they had to be taken on by the big helicopters, or had problems on the road that delayed delivery anywhere from a day to a week. He talked to Ted Wane, the head chopper pilot, and was told that things often came in all at once. The ordering system was supposed to prevent that with supplies requiring chopper transport. Supplies could pile up at the airport if the choppers couldn't keep up with the sudden influx of goods. Joe recognized the irony of the theft problem he had solved a few years ago in Denver also having been centered on the transport of materials.

Shifting his position he watched Linda, her head bent over folders at the work table. Tired and pre-occupied as he had been the last few weeks she had remained a bright spot in his days. The line of her neck as she tilted her head and studied a document, the swell of her breasts against her silk blouse, the way a few strands of golden hair had escaped from the clasp holding a perfect roll at the back of her head all embedded in his brain for those times when she wasn't there to look at. He shifted his weight as her effect on him caused a reaction he couldn't do anything about.

Would it be that wrong if I took her home to bed right now? I could propose. Well, no, I can't. The time isn't right yet... But soon....

He picked up the folder she was working on, closed it and put it aside. Leaning in he brushed her forehead with a light kiss. "How about you call Mary and see if she can stay and feed the kids and you and I will go out to dinner?" A slight flush suffused Linda's cheeks and she smiled happily, something he hadn't often seen her do since she arrived.

"I'd love to."

"You call Mary and I'll get us some reservations. Then let's get out of here early and let Seth close up shop."

Twenty minutes later Joe parked at a scenic spot overlooking the water. He hadn't felt so relaxed since he got here.

"Our reservations aren't for a couple of hours yet. I thought we could drive around and see some of the town and enjoy the sights. We haven't had a chance to do that."

"No, we haven't." She sounded wistful. "I'm hoping that improves soon when you find out who is behind all these problems."

Joe settled back in his seat with a sigh and draped his arm over her shoulders. The atmosphere in the SUV was warm, relaxed, and charged with sexual attraction.

"Me too. It's becoming reminiscent of Denver in some ways; a lot of the problems are with transportation. But then delivery of supplies here in Alaska is more complicated and more work than elsewhere. I'll just have to keep digging. The accidents bother me the most. We have high company-wide safety standards and accidents are rare. It's been almost, in these instances anyway, impossible to find out what happened. Then there are the rumors about Black Capital. The accidents could be the reason for that. A rash of them with one outfit and word spreads. John tells me there were a few that were overly upset about the payroll problems, but they were supposedly corrected so they shouldn't have been bad-mouthing the company they work for."

"I haven't started working on the payroll history yet. I need the computers back up and running first, I hope by Friday. It will take me a while. I can have Wallace do some of the entry work but there's a lot of work to setting up the files for all the local activity and contracts. I'm going to set up a new file for everything to be sure no problems are imported. I'll make it a point to squeeze out some time to start on the payroll history."

"You're marvelous." Joe's arm tightened around her shoulders, pulling her against him. His lips found hers, and he kissed them lightly, his own moving gently. His tongue tasted her lips as they pressed hers, and hers parted in welcome. He moved into a world where all that mattered was the warm pocket of her mouth and the movement of her tongue in response to his.

That world shattered with an ear-splitting reverberation that caused him to jump and Linda to scream. Four teenage boys laughed and danced around them beating on the SUV while making lewd remarks and gestures. Joe swore venomously, pivoting and reaching for the door.

"No! Joe! Stop!" Linda gripped his arm, pulling back. "Just leave," she urged. "A fight with them would make a great news story about Black Capital's new boss." She pressed her lips together tight in an effort to suppress the escaping giggle.

Joe emitted something akin to a growl and started the engine. Backing away he took the SUV toward the street, leaving the laughing teens behind. Linda made it a couple of blocks before erupting in laughter. Joe glanced sideways at her and the corners of his mouth twisted up.

"Busted by a bunch of damn kids!" He couldn't help but chuckle.

Linda's laughter peeled out uncontrolled.

"Can't go home." Joe attempted to sound grieved. "Kids there too."

That sent Linda into another round of laughter, by now wiping tears away.

The next couple of hours had them seeing what there was to see and becoming more familiar with the city. Joe had seen some of it before but to Linda, who hadn't had a free minute since she arrived, it was all new. Eventually, he led her into an upscale restaurant where he had reservations. The ambiance was elegant, and Joe selected a superb wine. There was a happiness and comfort between them that had been missing since Linda arrived. She declared the entre the best fish she had ever eaten, and they finished with a dish of ice cream that they laughed over like a couple of kids.

For the first time since he had arrived here, Joe's company problems receded and he basked in the warm calm he always felt around Linda. When the time was right he would ask her to marry him. When they finished they turned toward home so Joe could spend some time with Art and Renee before they had to go to bed, and so Mary Ramsey could go home after her long day.

* * *

"Mr. Cutter." Joe clasped the new prospective customer's hand in a firm grip.

"Hey! Joe Black is it? Call me Burt. Nice to meet you. Gwen tells me you folks plan to do great things up here."

Joe responded with a polite laugh. "We'll try to live up to anything you've heard."

A quick glance at Gwen showed her wearing a vapid smile, apparently absorbed in studying Burton Cutter. Burton, a paunchy, late middle-aged man, was soaking up her attention.

"Oh, now, Burt." Gwen giggled. "You know how excited I am about Black Capital coming to Alaska and I'm so proud to be a part of it." She squeezed Burt's arm playfully. "You are going to just *love* everything we do."

Burt seated Joe in a chair facing a large coffee-table and offered Gwen a place on the couch it fronted. Joe smiled when Cutter settled his bulk on the couch next to her.

"You have a nice facility here. The addition you've planned will work nicely with it." Joe commented.

Burton Cutter beamed at the compliment. "Thank you, Joe."

Joe removed a sheaf of papers from his briefcase, extracting several sheets that were stapled together. "This is our standard preliminary contract. I took the liberty of drawing it up from what Gwen concluded you wanted after your talks. I'd like you to look it over and if you want any changes or additions we'll rewrite it."

"I'll do that, but I expect it'll be all right as it is. My gal Gwen here knows what I want." He grinned and took the opportunity to pat her leg.

"Well, in case you do find anything I'll call you next week. If it's good as is, I'll come over and we'll get everything signed and get started."

"You don't need to come. Just send Gwen here. She can take care of me. Right Gwenee?"

Obviously, the man wanted to deal only with Gwen. "Unfortunately, while Gwen is very capable, my signature is required so you'll have to put up with me. I'm sure you'll see Gwen often as we get construction started." Joe's tone was firm leaving no room for argument.

After lunch with Burt, whose attention was divided between ogling Gwen and talking construction of his industrial development, Joe and Gwen headed back. They would be late getting home, and Gwen mentioned several times how convenient it would be to spend the night somewhere and drive on home the next morning. Joe reminded her he had two kids that would more than likely be waiting up for him.

"You could call them and tell them we would take them to the movies tomorrow night. Or would they like to go fishing? I could arrange for us to do that Sunday. I'd love to spend some time with them."

"That's nice of you Gwen, but they are just getting settled into school and a routine. I don't want to overload them right now."

"Oh, of course you don't. Well, maybe soon. All right Joe?" Gwen's face had taken on a pained look at his refusal.

"Sure, one of these days, Gwen. Thank you for offering."

She retreated into silence, rare for her, and Joe's thoughts turned back to the recent meeting with Burt. It had been an eye-opener. Joe got a first-hand look at how Gwen reeled in new business. He would have to deal with her eventually. There were potential customers that wouldn't like that approach. But for now it validated his feeling that Gwen was, in these early stages of building the business, a vital part of marketing and bringing in new clients.

It wasn't long before Gwen again broke out in chatter. She had ideas about this new project and a couple of new prospects that she would want Joe to meet in a week or so. At least one of them was far enough away that they really should plan it as an overnight trip. She was so glad that the upheaval in the office was about over. It had caused so many problems and so much inconvenience for her and had slowed her being able to get new projects. Since Joe would be in the office for a couple of days, she was going to do the same and try to get her work area back to where it was before.

* * *

Linda had spent a happy weekend with Joe and the kids. Things seemed to be returning to the way they were before coming to Alaska. The remodeling was over, and her computer systems were installed. Only a few odds and ends remained to be done. She had spent several hours on Friday with Seth helping him get his systems up and running and explaining what was and what wasn't done with Black Capital procedures. He could now go ahead and create what files he needed for his technical side of things.

Linda had set the system up so that Seth, Gwen, and Wallace could access only what pertained to their own departments. Standard procedure that had never been followed in this office. She and Joe would have access to everything.

She had just finished settling Joe in his office for the first time and getting a list of things he needed before he started making calls when Gwen breezed in smiling and gooing over him. Her attitude and comments seemed to indicate a certain intimacy. Trying to tell herself she was imagining it, Linda tried to push it out of her mind. Still, it sat there unbanished in the back of her head. Her happy mood began to dim.

An hour later Gwen's scream rang through the offices. "Joe!"

Five minutes later, Joe entered Linda's office with Gwen in his wake, her lips clamped together, eyes blazing.

"Linda, Gwen is having trouble getting into and accessing her files. Is her computer up and running yet?"

Linda directed what she hoped passed for a friendly smile at Gwen.

"Not quite, Gwen. I'm downloading forms now from headquarters. As soon as that is completed, I'll go over it with you. Then you can set up your password and you'll be in business in a few hours."

"What forms? What are you talking about? I have a stack of forms. At least I did if they didn't get lost in this disastrous remodeling mess you made."

"The forms this office has been using are not standard Black Capital forms. If you noticed, the contract Joe took to Mr. Cutter was slightly different than what you have been using. There are several variations in the forms, the contract itself, workup sheets, estimates, material lists, payment agreements, environmental reports and so on. I'll go over them with you as soon as I have them all."

"You don't need to go over anything with me! If I have a question, I'll ask Joe."

"Joe will hopefully be too busy with new customers to deal with clerical questions. That's a part of my function as you will learn. Just be aware that nothing but Black Capital forms will be used. Give all the old ones you've been using to Wallace and he'll shred them."

Linda directed a calm but challenging gaze at Joe, silently daring him to contradict her.

"What about my other files? They're gone."

"I have everything backed up on a portable hard drive. If you need one just let me know and I'll get you a copy of it or arrange for you to look at it. No old files will be entered in the new system."

Joe turned to Gwen. "It's a matter of not importing problems from the old files, Gwen. We will be more efficient this way. There will just be a little difference in the way we handle things now. It will be fine, you'll see."

Gwen opened her mouth twice and closed it without saying anything. She made a visible effort to keep control before whirling around and returning to her office.

"This won't be the last time." Linda commented.

"Cut her some slack." Joe snapped at her. "She's important to me and to this office."

A flicker of surprise flashed in Linda's eyes. She directed her gaze back to her computer at the same time Joe's cell phone sounded. He listened, his posture stiffening and his jaw set.

"What's wrong?" Linda asked the minute he disconnected.

"There's been another accident. This time someone was hurt. He's being airlifted here to Anchorage. You meet the plane at the hospital and I'll take a chopper to the site. I want to know what happened this time."

Linda was already shutting down her computer as Joe strode rapidly out of the office.

LOVE PRESUMED

* * *

CHAPTER SEVEN

Joe jumped from the chopper and stomped across the tarmac, unsuccessful at suppressing his irritation at having to land at the airport instead of the construction site. The city was making it as difficult as possible to operate here. After a talk with the mayor, who had been obsequious but not very helpful, the utility installation had been moved along a bit and a narrow access had been allowed to the shopping mall site. Black Capital had resumed work, but the small access had made it slower and more difficult than normal.

He hailed a taxi, preferring to forego having someone pick him up as he would have done under other circumstances. Once on the way he called Linda for an update on his injured employee.

"He's being examined now. They know he has a concussion, a broken shoulder, neck, and leg. They flew him here because of the broken neck. There's a specialist here and while they don't think he's paralyzed, they want to be careful. They won't know more until the doctor does a complete examination. I have no idea how long it will take. I'll call you as soon as I know anything."

At the site Joe asked the taxi driver to wait, obtaining agreement only if the meter was kept running. Walking up the rutted access road he observed only two men working in the area of the utilities. *Some help the mayor had been.* A few men were visible working at the far end of the mall. At a flat-bed truck, parked about half-way along the site, he found a couple of men coming and going as they unloaded it.

"Mr. Black." One of the men touched his hard hat in greeting.

"Hello fellows. Not a good day around here is it?"

"No sir. They flew Mickey out to Anchorage we hear. He seemed hurt pretty bad."

"I just talked to Ms. Sloan. She's at the hospital waiting for the doctor to finish his examination. It's the neck they're worried about but they don't seem to think he's completely paralyzed, if at all. We just have to wait. You boys know where I might find Baby?"

"He's back up that way. I'll call him for you."

"Thanks." Joe surveyed the project while the man called Baby on a static filled mobile phone.

Baby's size and weight appeared to bear down on him as he trudged toward Joe. He stuck his hand out in a half-hearted shake as his head moved back and forth in a hopeless manner. Joe had no trouble deciding that Baby was taking this every bit as seriously as he was.

"Mr. Black. I swear to God, I never in my whole career had a bad accident like this one. The usual stuff that always happens around a worksite but nothing like this."

"So what happened? I understand a truss fell on him. How the hell does that happen?"

"Damned if I know. A load of trusses was delivered yesterday and set on top of the framework. Everything was ready to move them into place today. From what I can find out Mickey had just got to work and was climbing the ladder to the top when one came down. Slammed him into and then off the ladder and up against the framework. Rest of the crew were on their way up the road when they heard the crash and him screaming. They got the truss off him but someone thought he looked too bad to move until the ambulance got here. I swear to God that's all anybody knows."

Joe watched Baby silently and would have sworn the man wasn't holding anything back. At least he hoped so.

"Has anyone looked the site over to figure out why that truss fell?"

"Call came that you was on the way up to look at it so we didn't go up and maybe mess it up."

"I want to see that site."

Joe winced when he saw the broken ladder and the heavy truss still lying where it had fallen.

"Let me borrow your hard hat, Baby. I want to see what's up top."

Joe donned the hard hat, then climbed a ladder that had been brought in and stepped out on top of the framework. He noticed a couple of men exchange glances with raised eyebrows. It wasn't generally expected that the big boss would or could step out on a framework. Only a few older employees in the lower states who had worked with his Dad as he was building the company would know that Joe had grown up scampering around the top of building sites.

It didn't take an expert to see the scrape marks on the framework where one end of the truss had obviously been shoved forward until it tipped over and fell. Taking his time to observe everything as he went, he moved along toward the back of the structure. There he found tell-tale black smears on the light colored framing lumber along with small clumps of dirt—the kind that comes from between the treads of boots. Squatting down he crumbled one between his fingers and found it still soft with moisture. He was aware of his stomach knotting up. *It wasn't an accident. Someone came up the back side and pushed that truss over on him. I'm betting they left through those trees.* He contemplated the wall of trees and brush blanketing the bluff within a few yards of the work area.

Joe slipped out his phone and carefully snapped several pictures of everything, including the woods behind the site. Back on the ground, approaching the men that had gathered, he tried to read their faces for any unusual expression, any hint that might tell him that one of them knew something. All he saw was concern and uneasiness. Uneasiness that was taking hold of him too. That feeling among his workers could cause superstition and a massive loss of help. If word got around that this was a company cursed with accidents they wouldn't be able to get help at all.

"Any of you hear or see anything?"

A tall dark haired man spoke up. "We heard a crash and then Mickey started screaming."

"Who got here first? Did he say anything?"

"Bill and I got to him first." The speaker was young, red-headed, and freckle faced. "He was just screaming, and then he sort of passed out."

"Anybody seen anyone around the site that doesn't belong here?"

All of them, without exception, shook their head. Joe turned to Baby.

"Call the sheriff. This wasn't an accident."

Baby's eyes widened with surprise. "You serious?"

Joe nodded, following with what he had found on the top framework.

"I want you, Baby, and two of your men to go up there and take a look so it's not just my word. Be careful not to mess anything up before the sheriff sees it. My guess is they left through those trees at the back and up over that bluff. Where does that lead to?"

"About a half mile of trees and brush, and then you hit a development on the other side."

"All right. Be handy if the sheriff wants to talk to you. Work in another area until the sheriff is done looking at this."

* * *

Two hours later Joe was, if possible, angrier than he had been to start with.

"I'm not telling you again, Black." The sheriff stood toe to toe with Joe, and poked his finger at Joe's face. "You can't come in here and push us around. You run a slipshod operation and get people hurt and then you want me to run around investigating an imaginary crime."

"You can't deny the evidence. You saw it yourself." Joe's face was red and his fists clenched and unclenched as he argued with the antagonistic sheriff.

The sheriff's belly bounced over his belt as he laughed derisively. "Scrapes on lumber and some dirt from somebody's boots! This is a construction site for God's sake! Maybe you never been on one before, pretty boy. It's a dirty job! Nothing criminal about it."

"So you're refusing to do anything about it?"

"Nothin to do anything about. But I'll tell you what I am going to do. We been out here twice now today, once when that poor boy had the accident and now with you trying to make it look like something it ain't. If we get called out here again without reason I'm going to charge you with harassing law enforcement. You got that?" With a final derisive snort he turned and swaggered back down the rutted delivery road that he had declined to drive his patrol car up.

Joe was still steaming as the sheriff drove off. A truck with the markings of a city vehicle pulled into the place just vacated by the patrol car. A man got out and began putting yellow tape across the entry to the access road they were using. Joe hurried down the road to intercept him.

"I just talked to the Mayor about this last week and we worked it out." Joe told the bored looking man.

"Don't know what to tell you, man. I just got my orders to come tape it off, that it's not to be used until further notice. I just put up tape. Anything else is above my pay grade."

Joe tried calling the Mayor's office and was told he was out of town for the next week. No, he couldn't be reached.

* * *

Joe accepted defeat in Fairbanks and told Baby to do the best he could to continue working with what supplies he had, He then boarded the chopper to return to Anchorage.

This is something big. Joe watched the landscape below pass by without seeing it. *Someone has the mayor and the sheriff working against us. I'm sure the problems at the other sites have something to do with it also. But why? One thing is sure. I'm not going to find out butting heads with the locals.*

Back in his Suburban at the Anchorage airport, his first call was to Linda who was still at the hospital.

"They had a specialist examine him and all the test results and x-rays. The doctor thinks he was lucky and isn't going to have major problems like being paralyzed. They want his neck healed up completely before they release him to work and can't say if he will have any after-problems with it. It may be he can't work construction, but only time will tell."

"Can we talk to him?"

"If you're thinking about asking about the accident, I would say you can talk to him but not a chance of it being private. His wife and parents and brother are all directing their anger toward Black Capital. Gwen has been here trying to get in to see him. She presented herself to the doctor as the Black Capital official in charge. I set the doctor straight and she left in a huff."

"She's just trying to do what she thinks she's supposed to. She *is* Black Capital's representative to the customers she brings in." Joe was greeted with silence on the phone and realized he had his foot in his mouth again. He had too much on his mind now to deal with what Linda thought of Gwen's attitude. "I'll come on over and give it a try, and if nothing else, put in an appearance."

"I'll stay until you get here."

Joe had no chance to reply. He immediately got the buzz of a disconnected call. He gritted his teeth. *Damn Linda's touchy attitude toward Gwen.*

He sat thinking for several minutes, then made a call to Byron Marks. Byron ran a nationwide private detective agency out of Denver and had been used by Joe's father and Black Capital several times over the years. He was the best there was at what he did.

"Byron? It's Joe Black."

"Hey, Joe. How's Alaska? Don't tell me you called about a bear you just bagged."

Joe chuckled mirthlessly. "I wish it were as simple as that. But I do think I may have a bear by the tail. Do you have operations up here, Byron? I've got problems on all my sites. Now I have a man in the hospital and I'm getting stonewalled by a mayor and a sheriff. I'm thinking there's more here than I'm going to be able to track down myself."

"Yeah, I can operate anywhere. I need all the information you have and your observations of what's going on. I hear Linda is up there. Is she a good contact point?"

"No. I don't want her to know I have you working on it. Linda is too proactive and might put herself in a bad situation. Then there's the kids to consider. I want this to just be you and me for now."

"Okay. When can you call me with all the information?"

"I'm on my way to the hospital to check on this guy now. I'll go from there to the office and call you back. I've got some pictures I'll send you of the site too."

"Until I know more we should be extra cautious, especially if a mayor and sheriff are involved. That sounds professional. Buy a burner phone and call from someplace outside your office, like a park. Just in case you have a bug. Wouldn't hurt to check your car too. I'll get somebody to you that can check for that."

"Right. Be back to you soon."

* * *

The customary touch and hug that Linda met Joe with were more subdued than usual. Then Joe hugged her tightly and in spite of her hurt and anger over his defense of Gwen, she was overwhelmed with warmth and relief to have him there. They stood quietly, arms loosely around each other as Linda related her rather unsatisfactory encounter with the family.

Not much had changed. She pointed out the room Mickey Paxton was in. His family had stationed themselves in the hallway and occasionally passed in and out of his room.

"I'll give it a try and see what happens." Joe glanced toward them.

"Go turn on the charm. I'll go back to the office and try to get some work done before quitting time. Good luck running the gauntlet with the family."

Linda pivoted to leave just as the elevator doors down the hall opened. Gwen breezed out, gave her a smirk in place of a smile as they passed in the hallway without speaking and made a bee-line for Joe. In the elevator she waited for the doors to close as she watched Gwen launch herself at Joe, throw her arms around his neck and kiss him on the cheek. His arms circled Gwen and he patted her on the back as if comforting her. The doors closed and the elevator descended, but its drop was not the cause of the lump in Linda's throat.

At the office she cleared the daily work waiting for her and decided it was time to start checking the payroll history. She was no longer needed to rush home to the kids. Mary Ramsey was dependable and efficient, and they were her job now. There hadn't been much evening interaction with Joe. He was putting in long hours out of the office and hadn't been very communicative with her about what he was doing.

She went back to the original records from when the office opened. She had settled into comparing records when Joe came in. Trailing in his wake was Gwen, following him into his office. Joe hung his coat up and took a seat behind his desk. Gwen glanced at Linda through the large glass window between the offices and with a flounce, walked over and closed the blind.

Linda clenched her fists, her leg muscles flexed as she started to stand up. *No, if he wants me to know how it went at the hospital he'll tell me. He wants her in there. She can do no wrong. I need to get out of here.*

Logging off her payroll project, Linda shut down her computer, grabbed her handbag and locked her office on the way out.

Elsa Bayly

* * *

CHAPTER EIGHT

J oe honey, what did Mickey say to you?" Gwen settled herself on the corner of his desk. "He isn't blaming us is he? That family of his would certainly like to blame us."

"I don't think there will be a problem, Gwen."

"Well, I hope not. Did he tell you how it happened?"

"Not really."

A small frown creased Gwen's brow. "So, what did he say?'

"He said he had a headache."

"Obviously he can't work for us anymore."

"Sure he can. He's going to recover just fine."

"Joe honey, I know you want to be a good guy and all, but we need to let him go. You can't be sure he's all right, and if a person is careless and gets hurt once he'll do it again."

"We will not be letting him go, Gwen. End of subject." Joe pulled a pad toward him, seemed to change his mind and pushed it back. "Any new customers today? All the projects going well besides this one?"

"I haven't heard of any problems today besides Mickey. I was too busy trying to keep up on that. You should have taken me with you to the site," she chided. "What did you find out there?"

"That we are going to be late finishing that project." Joe tapped his pen rapidly on the desk pad and stood abruptly.

"Oh, Joe, I have tried so hard to keep things moving up there. I'm sorry it's all bogged down like this." Gwen clasped Joe's hands, moving closer until she was directly in front of him. "I did the best I could today. I tried to talk to Mickey and head off trouble, but Linda had the doctor bar me from the room. I don't understand why she dislikes me so much, but it makes it hard to do my job." A tear escaped and traced a path down Gwen's cheek. Releasing Joe's hands she wiped at it.

Joe, attempting to comfort her, patted her shoulder and suddenly she was clasping him tight, arms around his neck, face buried in his shoulder. Perplexed, he patted her back. *Damn, sometimes I think Linda is right, Gwen is way too forward. But things are different here and Gwen is well-intentioned if overly affectionate. And she's good in the sales and the customer end of things.*

"Everything is going to be fine." Joe disengaged her from around his neck and managed to step back as she continued trying to cling to him.

"Thank you for being so understanding, Joe. You are just so wonderful."

In one swift unexpected move, Gwen was kissing him, not on the cheek as she had previously been prone to do but full on the lips. She held the kiss several seconds and just as Joe was beginning to recover from surprise she moved back, smiling.

"Gwen! That sort of thing is inappropriate."

"Oh, Joe honey, you are so straight laced sometimes. All right, I'll be good. Shall we go someplace and have dinner? You know, unwind from the day?"

"Sorry Gwen, I have a lot of things to do tonight."

Grabbing his coat he held the door for her. When she had passed through he turned off the light. Intending to stop and talk to Linda, he found her office dark. Why would she have left already without discussing the problems Mickey Paxton's accident had brought about?

Hurrying out, he made a mental note to talk to her in the morning. He'd do that tonight, after all she was just across the hall, but he had to pick up a burner phone and call Byron. By the time he got home it would be late, and he would need to give his attention to the kids. It would have to be morning.

* * *

An hour later he was sitting on a bench overlooking the bay, phone pressed to his ear.

"So you only have four employees, Seth and Gwen and Donald who retired and left. The new kid, Wallace, should be okay. He hasn't been there long but we'll check him out anyway."

Joe had just given Byron a run-down of all the problems and accidents Black Capital had experienced.

"I'll need a complete list of employees at all the sites, even those who may have left for one reason or another," Byron continued in his matter of fact way. "The payroll problems are interesting. If they aren't just mistakes it would indicate it goes back a ways." He hesitated. "You understand it would also indicate that someone with access to the payroll could be involved."

"I do. I'll have to be careful until we know more. Linda is starting to check all the records and I'll send you anything she finds."

"Are you sure you don't want to let Linda in on this? I could work directly with her. Linda is sharp. She could spot something that might go right by me or even you."

"No. Not yet at least. Linda doesn't seem to be too happy up here. I'm gone a lot trying to get these problems fixed, and we haven't had much time together. Gwen is different and things operate a lot looser here. Linda has taken an exceptional dislike to her. I'm afraid she might let something slip to someone and put herself or even the kids in danger. I'll get you what you need."

"Okay, you're the boss. I'll get started in the morning. I want to dig into this mayor and sheriff. You get any information or anything else happens call me. I have a couple of men in Alaska, Jake Travers and Harry Conley. I've already contacted them, and they're just waiting for instructions. They'll only contact you personally if necessary. If you need to contact them these are the numbers to use." Byron read off a couple of numbers and after verifying them, Joe said his goodbye.

* * *

"Don't push me." Al, a corpulent man in an expensive suit spoke around a mouthful of lobster that he chewed rapidly as if he didn't hurry he wouldn't get it all.

"Listen, Al, every week that goes by she's bringing in new contracts for them. And every damn one of them is a contract we don't get. You understand that?"

"I hear you, Josh, I understand money better than you ever will. This will get done, but it has to look like it's their incompetence, not an attack on them. Gwen's working on it."

"So just what in hell is she doing besides bringing them new contracts? She needs to step it up from little shit to something that will get them out of Alaska."

"She has, Josh. She has. They had a man take a bad fall the other day, had to airlift him from Fairbanks to Anchorage. He was lucky he made it—should have died. Worked out though, seems he didn't see anything and it made the news. Bad publicity for Black Capital."

"I heard about that. How'd she pull it off?" Josh returned his attention to his meal, somewhat mollified.

Al smiled, wrapping his fat fingers around a wine glass. "She lured Rodney out of hiding."

Josh dropped his fork. His head jerked up. "Rodney! Are you kidding? He's supposed to be dead."

"You should know better. Takes a lot to kill a guy like Rodney."

Josh leaned back in his chair, a big smile on his face. "Well, I feel better now. Gwen may be queen of the connivers, but Rodney is the king of vicious and gets things done. God help that Black Capital bunch. I guess you do have things under control cousin." He laughed heartily.

* * *

Linda set a chocolate donut on a paper towel and sipped at a large plastic cup of coffee before it joined the donut at the edge of her desk. She had left early this morning, telling herself it was to have time to pick up coffee and the donut, while all the time knowing it was to avoid seeing Joe as they usually left about the same time. She was still hurt over Gwen's familiarity with him yesterday and his acceptance of it. When they closeted themselves in his office and he didn't share his visit with Mickey Paxton she started to have serious doubts about their relationship. She'd never felt that way before. They always worked like a well-oiled machine, even before they became close on a personal level and she fell desperately in love with him. She had thought he felt the same. When he had asked her to come here, she expected him to propose. Now he was shutting her out.

She heard Joe saying good morning to Wallace and wondered what greeting he would have for her. She took a large gulp of her coffee, knowing that the last thing she needed pounding through her veins was more adrenaline. Joe burst through the door with a big smile.

"Where on earth have you been? I wanted to talk to you last night and you'd left and this morning you were gone before me."

"Well, here I am. What do we talk about?"

Joe spied the donut and coffee and his smile turned to puzzlement. "Is that your breakfast?"

"Yes, I left early to have time to pick it up." She hated herself for explaining her movements to him. It wasn't as if he seemed to care.

"I wanted to compare notes with you last night on Mickey, but you were gone."

"I was here when you came in with Gwen and closeted yourself in your office. She closed the blinds, and you didn't call me in so I presumed you wanted privacy. I went home."

Joe's eyes narrowed, and she knew she'd made him angry. She waited for him to deny her implied accusation.

"Speaking of Gwen." Joe's voice was controlled but she could see the muscles in his jaw clench. "She's upset that you had her banned from Mickey's room."

Linda choked back the bile that rose in her throat.

"I shouldn't have to explain to you of all people. She is not his friend. She is not his family. She is not even his boss. She has no business being there. She is a loose cannon who has no common sense. Right now neither he nor his family blames us, but no telling what she and her big mouth would say to make things worse. If you can't see that maybe you should call the legal department and get their opinion."

Joe sighed in what appeared to be resignation. His face softened a bit. "You're right. It's just that things are difficult right now, and she does want to be a part of the company. She knows a lot of people and brings in business."

Linda's shoulders slumped imperceptibly. *The same old story, the same excuse.*

Joe came around the desk and leaned over, pressing his cheek against her hair while he whispered in her ear. "I'm going to call Mary to stay overnight, and you and I are going to dinner to spend some quality time together without a deadline to be somewhere."

He studied her face, waiting for a reply. She couldn't resist Joe for long when he was being persuasive. She smiled in spite of herself and nodded her head.

"Wonderful! Plan to leave early—we'll go for drinks before dinner."

She smiled as he sailed out the door to his own office. Maybe it was all right, maybe she was over reacting. Maybe they could be close again, like before they came here.

* * *

Joe took Linda for a walk along the waterfront. He was more relaxed than he'd been in weeks. They laughed like a couple of kids as they watched the boats coming in. They detoured around a moose doing his own sightseeing and stood several minutes drinking in the beauty of the skyline. They ate at a small bistro on the waterfront. The atmosphere was working class, the food excellent and plentiful. Occasionally a couple would venture out on a small dance floor in the corner.

Dinner conversation revolved around the kids. Art was becoming one of the better soccer players on his school team. Making friends was hard; he hadn't yet figured out how to fit into the local culture, but he was trying. Renee, on the other hand, loved school and was making friends quickly. Their grades were good but not as good as they should be. Joe and Linda both worked late and Linda was not needed to oversee them now that Joe had a reliable nanny in Mary Ramsey. They did, however, need someone to be there to help with their homework. Mary was a good nanny, but homework was not her strong point.

They'd always worked together, shared the job and work experiences. It was a logical topic of conversation. But when Linda strayed from personal to business, Joe shut her down.

"This isn't a time for business. This is a time for us." He ignored her puzzled look and ordered after dinner drinks.

"Shall we try the dance floor?" Joe stood and held out his hand. She smiled and let him lead her to the tiny floor where they joined another couple. The dance space was so small it pretty much limited dancing to 'hold and sway.' That suited Joe fine. He wanted to hold her, wanted to make love to her, and wanted her to love him. She felt so right against him. Her hair gave off a scent of lavender. Her long legs fit snuggly against his as they moved in unison. He was consumed with the feel of those legs as they moved against his with each step.

"We could go to your place." He whispered next to her ear. *What was he thinking? This was the woman he loved and wanted to do everything right for. Here he was asking her if he could come home with her.*

"Yes, we could." She whispered back.

They drove in comfortable silence, stealing glances at each other and exchanging small smiles like two co-conspirators. Joe hesitated at her door. *This wasn't the way he had wanted to do this. But, damn it, he needed her. And they would be engaged and married soon, as soon as he could be sure she and the kids were safe.* When she reached back and took his hand he was reassured and followed her in.

Linda shrugged out of her pantsuit jacket, dropping it across the back of the couch. He gathered her up, wrapping his arms around her, feeling the silkiness of her blouse, the softness of her against him. He kissed her face, her eyelids, her forehead, her cheeks, and finally her lips, exploring, seeking the warm cavern of her mouth, still tasting of the wine they had shared.

She ran her hands up his chest and under his coat, pushing it off and letting it fall to the floor. His finger explored the v shaped line between her silk blouse and her skin. She shivered under his touch, and he dipped deeper behind the silk, between her breasts. One by one he dealt with the buttons of her blouse, parting it to expose a lacy delicate bra bulging with creamy flesh. He was unwrapping an exquisite beautiful and perfect piece of art.

He kissed and nibbled at the edge of her bra, then moved to find the hard sensitive center that told him she wanted him every bit as much as he wanted her. She groaned, and he opened the front fastening of the bra, setting her breasts loose for him to feast on. Tongue pressed against her nipple, he sucked, closing his eyes and losing himself in the exquisite sensations rolling over his body. He felt her hands unbuckle his belt and open his pants. She ran her hand down his belly and delved into his open pants. His chest froze, and he ceased to breathe when her fingers closed around him and his manhood jerked.

Almost as one they moved apart by inches and never taking eyes away from the other their clothes found the floor. He heard her intake of breath when his penis, freed from restraint, arched toward her.

"Bedroom?" He managed something between a whisper and a gasp.

"Oh, yes." She nodded, her voice husky and breathless. Her hand caressed his shaft.

"Don't." He whispered, his voice hoarse. "I won't be able to wait."

"Joe." She sighed, leaning into him.

A noise from hell sounded like a fire alarm from the pocket of his jacket. His damn phone broke up the moment, and he frowned. Could he just let it go and deal with whoever it was in the morning? No, might be something important, like another accident. He sighed and moving away from Linda, retrieved his phone.

"It's Mary." He told Linda and saw the same concern come to her face that he was feeling. "The kids!" He put the phone on speaker.

"Joe, I'm sorry to interrupt you, but I got this call from Gwen Smith, and she sounded frantic. Said she'd been trying to locate you all evening. She left a message that there is an emergency and for you to come to the office. She said she'll be at the office until you get there if it takes all night. She wouldn't tell me what it was."

"All right, Mary. I'll get back to her. Thank you for calling me."

He called the number for Gwen's phone, listening to it ring while watching Linda pick up her clothes from where they'd landed on the floor. The mood wasn't broken; it was shattered in a million pieces.

"She's not answering. I'll have to go to the office." His heart bled when he saw the hurt on Linda's face. "I don't know what else to do, Linda. I don't know how serious it is."

"Go, go on, get dressed."

He dressed quickly and stepped into the bathroom and ran a comb through his hair. When he emerged he found Linda had put on a robe. He wanted to speak to her, but she disappeared into the bathroom, closing the door behind her. He pulled on his jacket and opened the bathroom door.

"I'll call and let you know what's happened as soon as I know."

"All right." The answer came from within a cloud of steam in the shower. He waited for something else, but when she said nothing more he closed the door and left the apartment.

What the hell can have gone wrong now? Other than the fact that I just had the most marvelous evening with a nightmare ending. His foot pressed harder on the gas pedal and he sped over the road toward whatever the next emergency was.

When he pulled in and parked next to Gwen's car, Joe's headlights illuminated the guard making rounds.

"Evening, Mr. Black. Been watching for you. Ms. Smith said you'd be along."

Joe returned the greeting and let himself in the front door. A faint light shown down the hallway, and he hurried toward it. Gwen rushed from her office to meet him.

"Joe! I'm so upset. I haven't been able to reach you anywhere and you're my rock when I have problems."

"What's happened, Gwen? What's the emergency?"

"Well, I tried to check on the schedule, but I can't access it and your office and

Linda's are all locked up. I swear, Joe, ever since she came everything is so secretive that you can't get anything done around here."

"Gwen! What is the emergency?"

"Well, no need to be cross, it's not my fault you know. I was having a drink with a girlfriend and I heard someone at another table talking about a cargo ship running behind schedule, and I think it might be the one our next shipment for White Mountain is on. That will slow things down, and I don't even know how late the ship is running. I can't get any information on the order because everything is either locked up or not accessible to me on the computer. I have been trying to get you ever since I heard it. Where have you been anyway?"

"Stop!" Joe held up his hand palm out in an effort to stanch the flow of words gushing forth. He rubbed the bridge of his nose between thumb and forefinger of his other hand and grit his teeth to keep from saying something he shouldn't.

"*That* is your big emergency? That's all of it?"

"Well, yes. I thought you'd be concerned too."

"A rumor about a ship is something that can wait until morning. A ship being late that is a fact, and not a rumor, can wait until morning. If our order is on a late ship it can wait until morning because there is nothing we can do about it. It is *not* an emergency. Now go home and go to bed and *don't* call me about an emergency again unless it is truly an emergency.

His rhetoric was met first with shocked silence, and then Gwen's eyes filled with tears.

"Oh, Joe, I never meant to make you mad. I was just trying to do what I thought I should. It's so hard to know what you want sometimes." The tears spilled over and down her cheeks.

"I understand, Gwen. We'll just call this a learning experience."

She began to cry softly. "I don't suppose you could go home with me for a while? I feel awful that I made you mad. We could talk it over. I'm pretty good company, you know." She smiled, blinking away the tears.

"I'm sure you are, but I need to go home now. I'll see you tomorrow. Goodnight." Joe turned on his heel and left.

* * *

Gwen watched him go and as soon as the door shut broke out into a big grin. When she found he had left early with Linda she had sent a man to find them and got a report that they were wining and dining and had gone back to Linda's apartment.

No, it wouldn't do to have him more involved with Linda. She had taken care of his little evening with the ice witch, and she would make sure there were no more. Linda was a major stumbling block in her plans to get Joe to the altar. So far Linda had proved a formidable problem. Gwen needed to get her out of the business. She should have convinced Joe that she could run the office before the bitch came. That had been a mistake but she wouldn't make another. Too bad he hadn't come home with her tonight. She'd have to work on that.

* * *

CHAPTER NINE

Joe arrived at the hospital well before they served breakfast, and not wanting to be thrown out because it was too early for visitors, made his way stealthily to Mickey's room. The hospital was coming to life. Nurses were making morning checks, administering medications, and changing shifts. Quietly slipping in the door of the private room Black Capital was paying for, he found Mickey awake and, as he had hoped, with no family member sitting watch. Mickey wore a large awkward device designed to keep his neck immobile.

"How're you doing, Mickey?"

"All right, so they tell me. They keep me pretty well doped up so I don't move around from any pain. It's getting better."

"I'm relieved to hear that. Anything I can do to help, you just call."

"I appreciate that." Mickey's Adam's apple bobbed as his eyes watered, and he swallowed. "The docs won't guarantee I'll be able to do construction again, but they think I probably can. Tell me honestly, Mr. Black. Will you give me a chance to come back when I get out of here?"

"Mickey." Joe pulled a chair to the side of the bed where Mickey could see him easily. "When you recover from this, you are going to have a job with Black Capital. If you can't do construction we'll find something else for you to do. I promise you that."

"Thank you." Mickey took a deep breath. "I'll rest easier now." He paused and studied Joe. "Mr. Black, I know this sounds crazy, but it wasn't an accident that those trusses fell on me."

Joe nodded and frowned. "I was sure of that. I found where someone had been up on top, but the sheriff won't buy it."

"I heard the trusses start to come down, and when I turned to see what was happening I saw them out of the corner of my eye. There were at least two, but I didn't see faces, just a glimpse of guys in jackets. Then the lights went out for me."

Joe followed up with a few questions, but Mickey could add nothing else.

"Listen, Mickey, I've been waiting for a chance to talk to you in private. I don't want to alarm you, but we've had problems at all our sites. This is the first time anybody got hurt. Whoever did this didn't expect you to make it. Right now the word is you think it was an accident. I would advise you to stick with that, even with your wife and family if you haven't mentioned it already."

"I'm way ahead of you. I haven't told anyone but you and I don't plan to."

"Excellent. We're working on trying to figure out who's behind this, but it may take time. If you think of anything else you saw, no matter how small, call me for something, money, help with a car, anything to give you a reason to call. I don't mean to over react but I would prefer they don't know we're working on it."

"You got it Mr. Black."

Joe smiled and gently took Mickey's hand which stuck out of a cast immobilizing his arm and shoulder.

"Call me Joe."

"All right Joe."

As he passed through the lobby on his way out, Joe passed Mickey's wife but she didn't see him. He decided not to stop her. After all, what could he say to her?

* * *

Joe's spirits lifted when he arrived at the office and found Linda smiling. Maybe they could get past the disastrous ending to the previous night. He'd felt they were connecting again, like before he'd taken over this office. Then Gwen's call had come ...

"Your day must have started off right." He wrapped her in a hug and kissed her cheek. "I'm sorry about the way last night ended."

"I'm sorry too. Was it a big problem?"

Joe dropped his arms and shook his head. "No, no, it wasn't and hopefully it will never happen again. Now, is there a particular reason for that sunny smile?"

"As a matter of fact there is. I just talked to Ashton Baxter, and you will be glad to know he's to the point where he wants the decorator to come."

Joe smiled broadly. "Damn! Some things are going right for a change." He swept Linda into his arms and whirled her around the office. They both laughed.

"So, is Josie available right away?" Joe would enjoy seeing his step-sister as much on a personal level as for her being head of Black Capital's relatively new decorating department.

"I was just about to call her. I hope Seyma won't be a problem. I'm sure Mrs. Ramsey won't mind caring for her. I know Josie will be busy. It's tough for a single mother to make arrangements for a four year old with all the traveling she has to do."

"Well, call her and find out." Joe took Linda's face in his large palms. "I know you're looking forward to seeing Josie, but she may not want to come herself. She has an assistant now, and she may send her instead."

Linda's expression sobered. "I know. I hope she comes, but if she doesn't I'll understand."

"I hope she comes too." He leaned forward and quickly kissed her forehead. "Let me know what she says."

Joe was hardly settled in his own office when Gwen entered with a bright smile. She wore a navy blue suit whose only concession to being called a business suit was its cut and color. The lapels came together well below her bust line, revealing an underlying blouse of a gauzy material that left little to the imagination. The skirt and jacket gave the impression they would have to be peeled off.

"Good morning, Joe honey." She strutted across the office to the front of his desk.

"Good morning, Gwen." Joe returned her smile. "What can I do for you this morning?"

"Oh, honey. It's not what you can do for me but what I can do for you this morning."

"And what would that be?" Joe patiently played her game, having learned she would not get to the point until he did.

"I have a new client that wants to put up a fifty unit retirement complex in Juneau. He wants to go first class. This will be for those who can afford whatever they want, so he wants this to be a showplace."

Joe leaned back in his chair and gave her his full attention. "Tell me what you know so far. Does he have plans or does he want our services on that also?"

"He hasn't decided yet. He wants to have a meeting and go over it all. I made an appointment for us to meet with him at 7:00 A.M. tomorrow morning. He wants to work a couple of hours and then go to breakfast and finish up what we need to afterwards."

Joe frowned. "Why so early. It takes time to get there."

"That was how he wanted it. If we want to be fresh and ready we should go up this evening. I've already arranged for the chopper to be ready by 4:00 P.M. and booked us at the nicest place in Juneau."

Joe frowned again. He didn't want to be gone overnight. He wanted a somewhat normal life for the kids and that included being home at night like he had been before this move. But he didn't see any way out of it this time. It sounded like Gwen had an important project on the line. He was here to build the Black Capital office and this was the way to do it.

"All right. I'll see you at the heliport at four."

Gwen was all smiles as she almost skipped out of the office.

* * *

Linda replaced the phone and heaved a happy sigh. Josie would be here the following Monday. She would bring Seyma and let Mrs. Ramsey care for her. It wouldn't be a long stay, a week, possibly a bit more.

Linda wanted someone to talk to, someone she could trust not to repeat anything, and who would understand and possibly give her another perspective on Joe's behavior.

She turned back to her computer and the slow work of checking all the old payroll records. She had, even in these early efforts, found a few mistakes. Even a few was too many. The Black Capital operation she was a part of had no tolerance for mistakes.

* * *

Joe spent the hour after Gwen left chewing over his problems. He was trying to come up with new options and finding he had few. He moved his problems around in his mind as if it was a chess game. Then, an idea popped up. He knew what he hadn't done and should have. He made a call to a company specializing in electronic security and made arrangements for an appointment in one hour. A moment later he was in Linda's office.

"I should have thought of it before. We have cameras on site but nothing real time and monitored. I'll make arrangements this afternoon to have the systems put in. It will be expensive but worth it if it prevents something else happening. Call all the project managers and explain it. Make whatever arrangements we need for around-the-clock monitors. They have to be reliable and not the type that are off pouring a cup of coffee when they should be watching the screen."

"Linda nodded, made notes, and reached for the phone. Joe was rushing out, impatient to get to his appointment, when he stopped suddenly and whirled around.

"By the way, I'll be gone overnight. Gwen and I have a 7:00 A.M. appointment in Juneau with a new client. Get me by phone if you need me." He raced off, too busy with his objective to notice the frozen look on Linda's face.

* * *

True to her word, Gwen had booked them into rooms at a first class hotel. Joe tipped the bellboy and heaved a sigh as the door clicked shut, leaving him alone at last. His shoulders slumped, and he pinched the bridge of his nose. Stripping off his shirt he went to the lavishly appointed bathroom where he splashed water on his face. Maybe it would energize the tired looking face staring back at him from the mirror. His plan was to order room service, go over the information he had for the next morning's meeting, and later go for a walk and give Byron a call. He knew Byron would call if he had any information, but he wanted to tell him about the live camera system he was putting in. A weak excuse maybe but he wanted to feel like he was doing something.

The unmistakable click of a door interrupted his thoughts. The bellboy must have forgotten something, but he should have knocked. Laying the towel aside Joe stepped back into the bedroom area only to be brought up short.

"Ohhh, Joe," Gwen stood, eyes glued to Joe's bare chest, "you are a strong sexy hunk of man."

"Gwen, what are you doing here? How did you get in?"

"I got us adjoining rooms in case we needed to work late. The door was open."

A form fitting cocktail dress with a plunging neckline clung to her curvaceous form. *Changing at the speed of light, amazing,* Joe blinked.

"I'm here to go to dinner. I made reservations and we don't have much time." The flippant attitude, so much a part of Gwen's personality, was missing and cocktail dress aside, Joe found himself seemingly dealing with a calm rational woman.

"I had just planned to get room service and do some work."

"Joe, I admire you so much for how hard you work but you just have to take a break once in a while. We can talk work over a good meal. Now put your shirt back on and we'll go."

Gwen waited in a chair by the table watching Joe put his shirt back on. He added a tie—the least he could do considering the fancy dress Gwen was wearing. *Maybe,* he pursed his lips at the mirror as he tightened his tie, *I've been too hard on Gwen. She does try hard, just lacks polish and experience and a sense of what's proper. I'll cut her some slack tonight, tell her she's doing a good job.*

He was smiling as he ushered Gwen out the door, and they took the elevator down.

* * *

Dinner was excellent and to be expected in this establishment. Tables crowded with tourists, wealthy locals, and government officials groaned under the weight of platters full of all manner of delicacies. Joe and Gwen had been seated at a table in a back corner that provided as much privacy as was to be had. Gwen sat close to Joe, saying that they could talk more quietly that way and not be overheard by neighboring diners.

Conversation was congenial and Joe found himself enjoying her company, like she was a different person. Apparently she was finally getting the idea about being businesslike. She ordered a bottle of wine and over his objections kept topping off their glasses. Gwen didn't bring up complaints about the office or Joe's, according to her, lack of interest in accompanying her to visit clients. They talked some about business subjects and kept things light by sharing a few childhood incidents or discussing current affairs. By the time they finished a tiny brownie with an even tinier dip of ice cream they had finished off the wine and Joe was feeling relaxed and mellow. Maybe Gwen had a point about relaxing once in a while.

Joe grinned and admitted there must be something to it and she laughed, leaned toward him and took his hand. A blinding flash of light almost caused him to tip over backward in his chair. Gwen laughed happily.

"Mr. Black. Do you have a word for the local press? Are you visiting us for business or pleasure? Will you be contracting for a big job here?"

An enthusiastic middle aged, if rumpled, reporter loomed over them. Joe ran a hand across his eyes.

"You could blind a man with that thing. We hope to do business locally but any information for the press will be issued out of our office in Anchorage." Joe rose and turning away from the man, helped Gwen from her chair and hurried her toward the hall and the bank of elevators. He had gone from being mellow and relaxed to irritated.

Gwen insisted on returning to Joe's room to complete the nightcap she claimed had been interrupted.

"All right, Gwen, just one drink."

"Just to get you relaxed again, Joe. That guy caught us unaware, but that's what we have to expect. Business like ours is going to be newsworthy you know."

"Humph." Joe tossed his jacket on the bed and took a seat at the small table, leaning back in a chair while Gwen headed for the complimentary liquor stock. She had been happy and professional all evening, and Joe decided she might shape up into a good employee after all.

Handing him a scotch she settled into the other chair and began chatting about their morning meeting, giving him advice and insight on the prospective new customer. Joe nodded, occasionally asking a question. He was just so tired. His eyes were beginning to blur and he wanted nothing so much as to go to bed. Tossing off the last of his scotch he stood up and blinking, attempted to focus on Gwen.

"We need to get to bed. We have to be up early. Let's wind this evening up."

She rose also, moving to his side.

"Of course, Joe. You do look tired. I'll see you in the morning." Watching his eyes becoming unfocused she leaned into him and brushed his lips with hers. "Good night, Joe honey," she whispered as he tilted forward. She managed to aim him at the bed before he hit the floor. She was only partially successful, and he collapsed with his head and shoulders resting on the foot of bed.

"Too bad I couldn't have gotten you into bed before my magic potion took effect." Gwen had turned the covers back and was now standing on the bed as she tugged and pulled, inch by inch moving Joe further up on the bed, all the while chatting as one might to their dog. "If you would just give me a chance I could make you feel sooo good." Deciding she had him where she wanted him, she hopped off the bed and turned to removing his shirt, pausing several times to run her hands over his chest, fingers playing over his large flat nipples. Splaying her fingers as she ran them through the hair on his chest, following it downward as it disappeared beneath his belt buckle.

She pressed her hands against his belly and kneaded softly as her eyes roamed the hard muscle her fingers felt. Smiling, enjoying what she was doing, she inserted her hands downward into his pants, her fingers curling themselves in the abundant bristly growth of curls. Closing her eyes she threw back her head and laughed.

The laughter stopped abruptly and her eyes snapped open, the instant of mirth they had held gone, replaced with a sudden intensity. At a frenetic pace she unbuckled his belt, followed by opening the zipper of his pants. A few minutes tugging and pulling had his jeans off. Back on the bed, she straddled his legs. The rough course hair on his legs rasped against her inner thigh, her muscles tightening at her arousal. She studied the mound under his briefs as if savoring it before reaching out to grasp the top of them. They came down easily leaving her to ogle his limp manhood.

"Oh, Joe. You have a beautiful specimen of a cock. Too bad you aren't awake. I could make you holler with pleasure."

Moving off his legs and leaving the bed, she finished pulling his briefs off, dropping them on the floor.

"That damn Linda has been a pain in my butt but that's going to change." She continued chatting on in the one-sided conversation with the comatose Joe.

"You and I are going to be together. I'm going to see to it." She ran her hand up the inside of his leg. "I'm going to be so happy to be Mrs. Black, and I'm going to make you happy. I am." She caressed his limp penis.

Stepping back, she hurried to remove her own clothing. Smoothing and folding her clothes she carefully placed them over the back of a chair. Once naked she went to the door and eased it open a few inches. Across the hall the photographer from the dining room stood nervously glancing up and down the hall. Seeing no one else in the hallway she stepped back and opened the door wide. He shot through it as if under pursuit.

Once in, he glanced at Joe, then Gwen, apparently unaffected by their nakedness.

"Is he out good? I don't want him waking up before we're done."

"He'll be out till morning."

"Okay." He began taking out his camera. "Tell me what you want and we'll get this over with."

"You're nervous as a cat. What's the matter? Never seen naked people before?"

He stopped and glared at her. "You're damn right I'm nervous. What we're doing is illegal as hell. I'm never comfortable doing this sort of thing. I try my best to stay out of jail and you should keep that in mind also. Now, how do you want these?"

A few minutes later his flash was going off at a rapid pace as he instructed Gwen to make small moves this way or that for lighting purposes or to attain the affect she wanted. Moving from Gwen laying full out on top of Joe to sitting up as if they were in the midst of a wild ride to her burying her face in his crotch, hair spread out to hide her face. Almost all of the shots left her face hidden or unidentifiable. Other features would leave no doubt who she was if the viewer had ever met her.

"That should do it, unless you have more ideas?"

"No." Gwen moved off the bed. "How soon can you have this for me?"

"You're sure you don't want prints or anything touched up?"

"Just a thumb drive. I can do the rest."

"I'll have it by morning."

Five minutes later she locked the door behind him and turned back to Joe. She would like to crawl back into bed and entertain herself and let him wake up beside her. But that would, she was certain, end everything, as he would no doubt be furious and probably fire her. Best to play it safe and leave him to wonder. Tonight had gone well. She could make more progress staying in his good graces. She gathered up his clothes and folding them neatly, placed them on a chair. Getting his briefs off had been fairly easy but putting them back on would be a major job so leaving him naked she just tossed the comforter over him.

Gwen's natural curiosity, added to her ulterior motives, made her dangerous. Turning her attention next to Joe's briefcase she found it unlocked and proceeded to examine its contents. Finding nothing but information on the upcoming morning's meeting, she checked his pants and jacket. Here, her interest was aroused.

What does he need a burner phone for? It had only one number programmed in it. There was no name. Her curiosity spiked. Returning to his other phone she checked everything on it, coming up with nothing informative but a few text messages to Linda with words of what could be construed as endearments scattered through them. Her eyes glittered and she bared her teeth much as a dog about to attack. Returning to the burner phone she stared at it for several minutes trying to figure out what its purpose might be. In the end she pushed the button and listened to it ring.

"Yeah, Joe?" A male voice that obviously knew Joe. She sat quietly, waiting for the man on the other end to give up some piece of information.

"Joe? You there?"

"Who is this, please?" Gwen put a light note in her voice and raised it a couple of octaves.

"Who are you? Why are you using that phone?" The voice had turned stern and guarded. The usefulness of this call was over. She disconnected. A minute later the other phone rang but the number was blocked. She smiled. She must have worried someone. But who? And why? Why did Joe have contact with some mystery man? Would Linda have known who it was? Well, didn't matter. She had the number and she'd find out who it was.

Gathering her clothes, she moved to the connecting door of her adjacent room. Leaving Joe's door ajar a half inch so she could return in the morning, if necessary, she closed hers firmly which automatically locked it from Joe's side. She smiled, thinking of Joe's confusion when he woke up.

CHAPTER TEN

There was something out there in the fog that Joe needed to grasp, but it kept eluding him when he tried to concentrate and capture it. Every time it returned it was more unsettling and irritating. Then it went away, and he was floundering in the fog. His head pounded. His teeth felt sensitive. Explosions seemed to go off in his brain. He vaguely came to realize it must be a knocking on the door. Then a voice penetrated and hands shook him, sending his head into outer space.

"Joe! Joe! You have to get up. You must have slept through the wake-up call. Come on now. You have to get up or we're going to be late to our meeting. We can't be late if we want his business."

Joe tried hard and managed to focus. It was Gwen.

"What? What happened? What time is it?" His voice cracked and broke.

"You overslept. Now come on, get up and shower." Gwen was pulling at his arm. "We don't have long. I have to go finish my makeup."

Joe groaned as he sat up and held his head with arms heavy as lead. Gwen disappeared though the connecting doors leaving them open.

The meeting. I have to get ready for the meeting. What the hell is wrong with me anyway?

He tried standing and despite his being still foggy in the head he managed to remain upright. It wasn't until he was in the shower, water beating his face as he held it up, that he realized he hadn't had any clothes on. A deep intake of breath left him snorting water from his nose.

What the hell?

Shutting off the water he grabbed a towel and made quick work of drying off. He was rapidly sobering up from whatever was wrong with him. He hadn't had that much to drink, he was sure. He remembered the wine at dinner, and he was having a drink with Gwen here in his room afterward. He had been tired, and after that photographer ambushed them at dinner they had come back here. He had a vague memory of Gwen sitting across from him talking about today's client. After that there was nothing.

Emerging from the bathroom he made a valiant effort to hurry dressing. He was still shaky, his brain a little fuzzy. Trying hard to concentrate on what he needed to know for the impending meeting, he couldn't banish the question of why he couldn't remember what happened and why was he naked.

Gwen bustled through the connecting doors, but he had no chance to question her.

"Come on, Joe. Oh good, you're ready." She brushed at a speck of lint on his jacket. "Let's go, we have five minutes before we're late."

She handed him his briefcase and held the door open. They made the meeting with a minute to spare.

* * *

The meeting had gone well, and Joe now had a better idea of what the client wanted. The man was happy enough with what Joe had to say that the meeting turned into a tour of the property and surrounding area that lasted into the early afternoon, followed by a late lunch. The deal included the architecture work also. Joe promised to get the appropriate people in as soon as possible to start work on it. Agreement was reached on a preliminary contract to be signed in a couple of days. All in all it was a successful trip as far as business was concerned.

Otherwise, Joe's mind was still in a state of turmoil as he and Gwen made their way to the heliport where one of the company choppers was waiting for them. Where had his memory of the evening gone? The last he could remember he was fully dressed and talking to Gwen. When he had time to think about it with a clear head he wondered about her being in his room this morning to wake him up. Of course there was the connecting door and he probably forgot to make sure it was locked.

When the courtesy car from the hotel dropped them off at the heliport, Joe finally had a private moment to speak to Gwen.

"Gwen, wait a minute." He set his bag down and waited as she stopped and turned back to face him.

"Yes, Joe?" Her low sultry tone hit him in the gut with the knowledge that he wasn't going to like what he was afraid he was going to hear.

"About last night – and this morning – I don't remember getting into bed. The last I remember is talking to you about today's meeting."

"Oh, Joe," she crooned, moving closer and running her hand down his arm. "You had a little too much to drink. You finally expressed your true feelings for me."

Gwen stepped closer and her low caressing voice caused Joe's nerve ends to curdle, like swallowing a sour pickle.

"You tried to make advances, but you just couldn't, if you know what I mean."

She twittered a short laugh and tilted her head coquettishly. "It's too bad you can't remember it, Joe. You had a really good time and loved what you found." She pushed her breasts out and wiggled suggestively. "We could try again tonight if you want?"

"No!" Joe's reply burst out in an explosive breath. "My clothes?" His face was red, and his voice sounded like he was choking.

Gwen's laugh rang out and Joe cringed as if it was drawing attention to this awful thing she was telling him had happened.

"Honey," she made a show of lowering her voice, "bare skin against bare skin usually gets the results you were looking for last night."

"Gwen, I never had any intention or interest in a relationship with you. I still don't."

"Joe, I have no intention of forcing myself on you. I know you like things very respectable and all. But I am sooo attracted to you, and I know now that you return that interest. I can wait for you to realize that we are good together." She arched her eyebrows. "In the meantime, should we board the plane?"

* * *

"So what are you going to do now that he's having cameras monitor everything?" Seth asked nervously.

"Not up to me. Whatever her paying me wants done." Roger's eyes were cold.

"She'll be back today."

"Good. Tell er we either need work or I need money. Men I'm using for this won't sit around without money fer long. They leave they might talk, and I can't afford no trouble."

"I'll tell her to contact you."

"Tonight. You understand?"

"I understand."

Roger rose from the picnic bench, eyes furtively doing a reconnaissance of the surrounding area. Satisfied, he pulled his hoodie down further and walked away. Seth felt his body relax like a puppet when the puppeteer puts down the strings that make him dance. Of all the scum Gwen could have picked to do her dirty work, Roger was the most dangerous. He didn't care what he did or who he killed. Seth thought of the goons Roger kept around him as escapees from a mental institution. He hoped Gwen knew what she was doing, but sometimes she seemed a bit unhinged too.

* * *

It was quitting time and Linda gritted her teeth as she shut down her computer and locked her office door. She hadn't heard from Joe and damned if she would be the one to call him. Mrs. Ramsey had been wonderful about staying the night on short notice but this was the second night with no warning. If Joe didn't contact her soon, Linda would have to stay at Joe's with the children or ask Mrs. Ramsey to stay again. She couldn't expect Mrs. Ramsey to stay with no notice all the time. Of course he might have already called Mrs. Ramsey. Normally he wouldn't do that without letting her know, but he seemed to be shutting her out of a lot of things now.

Overnight trip with Gwen with only a few hours' notice and now it's night two and not a word from him. What is he thinking?

Wallace and Seth were also heading for the door as she entered the reception room. Seth nodded and offered a quiet, "Good night, Ms. Sloan." Seth was aware of the tension between her and Gwen, and he would also be aware of where Gwen and Joe were today. That would account for his subdued attitude.

"Good night, Seth."

In contrast, Wallace's good-by was cheerful and bubbly. He was so obviously happy that Linda couldn't help but smile. Normally very reserved, he had come into the job of receptionist with no experience and very little confidence in spite of the fact he had graduated with honors from the local university. Linda had made it a point to watch his work and educate him on any process he wasn't familiar with. He was doing excellent work and she let him know it with praise when it was due. She had no doubt that his loyalty to her was above and beyond.

"Good night, Wallace." Linda smiled broadly. He was one bright spot in her operation at the moment. She headed for her SUV and home.

* * *

Mit stoically watched two men make their way along the bank of the stream. They would no doubt see the cabin. She didn't recognize them. They walked like men comfortable with walking in the wilderness. Tourists almost never got this far into nowhere, and when they did they usually flew in or came by boat. Coming from the small dock, their attention shifted to the cabin up the hill. Mit stood in the shadows of the trees alongside the cabin, sure now that she had never seen them before. She shifted the rifle she carried to cradle it along her arm, aimed loosely at the men now trudging up the hill toward the cabin. The dogs set up a cacophony of noise, challenging these intruders.

It was obvious they were not lost tourists. They moved forward with care and seemed to be looking at everything as they neared. Were these enemies of Bulls or friends? She silently corrected herself. Bull had no 'friends,' only business associates. He seldom brought anyone here. He was gone and she didn't expect him back for days, maybe weeks, he never told her. As always, she was on her own. One of them spotted her and spoke to the other. They stopped and stood watching her as she watched them. They spoke to each other but she was too far away to hear what was said. Finally, they moved toward her. Mit stood her ground, the only movement a slight shifting and steadying of the rifle so that it pointed at their midsections.

"Hello." The man spoke in a pleasant manner, not rough or angry like Bull and his friends. "We're looking for someone and we were told that a Bull Smith lived in this area and might be able to help us."

Mit said nothing.

"Do you speak English?"

She nodded.

"Is this Bull Smith's place?"

She hesitated, then nodded again.

"Is he here?"

Mit decided to talk. "No"

"Do you expect him back soon?"

"No."

The second man spoke for the first time. "Are you his daughter?"

Mit's eyes narrowed. "Wife."

Neither man spoke for a minute. "Maybe," the second man added, "we could ask you some questions. We've been walking a long way and if we could buy a meal from you we would appreciate it." They waited, not speaking or pushing her, while she thought it over.

"One dollar. Each." When they nodded agreement she motioned with the rifle in the direction of the cabin.

Seated where Mit indicated at the rough plank table, Jake Travers and Harry Conley watched Mit and made mental notes on the inside of the cabin and its contents. She had motioned for them to put their guns in a pile by the door. When they hesitated she pointed her gun at them. The look on her face left no doubt she would shoot them both without even blinking. They left the guns where she indicated and were relieved when she didn't think to check for the ones hidden in the back of their waistbands and in their boots.

This gal is like a wild animal, quiet, but wary and skittish. She's young, really young to be married to Bull Smith. She might know something useful if we can get her to put more than two words together. Harry Conley rested his elbows on the table and gave her a friendly smile.

"Do you have people live near here? Must be lonely for you with your husband gone." She shrugged her shoulders and he tried again.

"We're looking for some bad guys that we heard were up this way. Someone said your husband might be able to help us."

"Who are you?" She set two plates of stew in front of them.

Harry introduced himself and Jake. "We work for a good man that is trying to stop these bad guys from hurting some good people."

"What will you do with the bad men?"

The corner of Harry's mouth turned up. *This girl is smarter than she lets on and she talks as good as we do when she wants. And, she's curious.*

* * *

Joe pulled to the side of the road about halfway home after leaving the plane. He held his stomach with both hands while he took gentle breaths. *What the hell did I do? I've never done anything like what Gwen says we did. I think I'm going to throw up.* He let his head fall back on the headrest and closed his eyes. His stomach gave him a respite and he opened his eyes.

Groping in his briefcase he located the phone he used to talk to Byron. Could Byron do anything to help this situation? No. But he might have some idea about it and right now Joe desperately needed someone to talk to.

"Hello."

"Byron. It's Joe. I have a problem."

"Yes, you do. Have you checked the call record on that phone?"

"This phone? No. Why? What's going on?"

"I got a call on that phone last night from a woman. Wanted to know who I was, hung up when I didn't answer. I called back and someone picked it up but didn't speak and then hung up. Was that phone out of your possession last night?"

Joe groaned. "Byron, I've been a fool. Let me tell you what happened."

Ten minutes later Joe had unburdened himself about his behavior, and Byron had asked a lot of pointed questions.

"I can tell you for a fact that she drugged you. It makes me suspicious about it being purely love related, because she would know you wouldn't be able to do anything even if you wanted to. Obviously, she snooped through your things. Anything for her to find, other than that phone?

"Everything else is business information she has access to anyway."

"Okay, don't beat yourself up over this. Lots of good people get drugged by someone they trust." Byron paused a moment. "She'll try and find out who this number belongs to. Won't do her any good, all my numbers are covered. I'll get another number for you to use and call you with it. It could be she's just obsessed with you. Or it could be she's part of the larger problem you've been having. Her dad is a major criminal element on the waterfront up there we've found out and we are digging into that. I'm going to divert more effort to her and her past."

"How do I handle it with her? I feel like I want to wash my hands every time I think of her."

Byron chuckled. "Welcome to the world I deal with all the time. Keep your distance but don't give her any reason to think you're suspicious of her or don't trust her. I'll be in touch."

Joe replaced the phone and took a deep breath, testing his stomach. It seemed to have settled down considerably, and he shifted into gear and pulled back onto the road.

* * *

CHAPTER ELEVEN

Mrs. Ramsey had left dinner already prepared, and Linda only had to heat it up. The woman was a treasure, and she intended to talk to Joe about paying her more. Rather than going through the motions of the job, she seemed to really care about the people she worked for.

Linda laughed as they ate, and she listened to Art and Renee recount their day's events. At the sound of the door opening and closing, the kids were out of their chairs like bullets out of a gun. She smiled when Joe entered the kitchen carrying Renee in one arm and with the other around Art's shoulders.

Joe was smiling too, somewhat wanly it seemed to Linda. He put Renee back on the barstool she had been sitting on, and Art reclaimed his place. Linda rose, and he wrapped his arms around her so tight she almost couldn't breathe and buried his face in her hair. *Somethings wrong. He seems more upset than I've seen him in a long time.* She moved to get him a plate for dinner, but he protested.

"Just a small bite or two. My stomach is a bit off this afternoon."

"All right." She complied, and they all returned to their meal.

When the kids had finished, Linda loaded the dishwasher and finished what little needed to be done in the kitchen. The kids settled down to have him look over their homework, a job he did every night if he was there. If he wasn't Linda filled in. Tonight he did what was unheard of for Joe, he begged off.

"How about you let Linda go over that with you while I go back to take a shower and change."

In time the homework was done and approved, and Joe had reemerged in a sweat suit.

"Okay, I want to see how quick you two can do your bath and get into your pajamas. We all had a busy day and need our rest, and we're keeping Linda from getting her rest too."

Linda's internal antenna suddenly went on alert. She'd expected to stay a while and have a glass of wine with Joe and talk about how his trip had gone. It was obvious he wanted her to leave.

"Good night, you two rag-a-muffins." She tousled their hair and watched them racing down the hall. She waited for Joe to say something, and when he didn't she walked away. Pivoting at the door she gave Joe a small smile. "If you want to talk about anything you know where to find me."

Joe stayed where he was, neither approaching nor moving. His head tilted in an almost imperceptible hint of acknowledgement.   His expression was so woe-be-gone that Linda's heart turned over. *Why won't he let me help him?* She closed the door softly on the way out.

* * *

Linda dropped heavily into her chair and faced her blank computer screen. The coffee in her right hand was black and strong, and she sipped at it gingerly as the fingers of her left hand kneaded her temple and the small headache gathering there. More from habit than intention, she reached out and turned on the system.

Today was a terrible reality for her. She had not seen or heard from Joe over the weekend. If he was home they usually spent the time together with the kids. But things had been changing between them almost from the minute she landed here. Now – this morning – everything was different. If she knew why, she could cope with it, but Joe wouldn't talk to her.

She needed a plan and she needed it soon. All she had to do was think of one. What was she going to do now? How was she going to do it? When? On and on her brain whirled. Her organized nature eventually kicked in and she removed herself from the equation, for now anyway. Obviously, she wasn't getting anywhere from here in the office. Things ran smooth now. Everyone had a role and stuck to it. Except for Gwen, of course, who constantly fought any systems or control. Linda had managed to limit her to her own accounts and information pertaining to them. To Gwen's ire, no, rage, Linda corrected herself, she had no access to private company business, HR or payroll matters, or anything that didn't pertain to her narrow sales function. It was constant low grade war between them.

None of this helped Linda to know what she should do next. One thing she wasn't going to do was roll over and play dead. If Joe wouldn't talk to her then she would just have to find out what was going on some other way.

She looked up and watched Joe walking down the hall to his office. He looked toward her through the glass partitions, nodded, and mouthed "Good morning." Normally he would come into her office with smiles and jokes and conversation. Something must be terribly wrong to bring on this sudden change.

The sound of loud laughter and chatter announced Gwen had arrived a couple of moments before she hit the hallway. Bouncing past Linda's office, she breezed into

Joe's. Linda could hear the laughter and whooping. The blinds were closed on Joe's side, as usual lately, so Linda was spared watching Gwen's glee as well as having to listen to it. Then the noise changed direction, and Gwen barged into Linda's office waving a newspaper.

"Wonderful news, Linda! Joe and I had such a successful trip. We made the paper and got tons and tons of good publicity for the company and for Joe. I'll just leave the paper with you and get back to Joe. We have lots to talk about." Gwen flounced out.

Linda turned the paper over to find a large picture taking up a good portion of the front page. It showed Joe and Gwen at dinner in what was obviously an upper class eating establishment. Gwen was leaning into Joe's shoulder and looking up at him with what could only be described as adoration. A small crease in his forehead might indicate Joe was not happy with having the picture taken, but his smile was pleasant as would any businessman's be at attention from the press. Big headlines declared that "Black Capital Comes to Town."

Linda's stomach clenched, and she pressed on it with one hand to ease the stab of pain. *Joe went on an out of town meeting with Gwen. The local paper took a picture of them at dinner with Gwen looking worshipfully at him. Joe came back and not only won't talk to me but is avoiding me. He's guilty or ashamed or both. If there isn't anything to be ashamed about, he would be angry instead.*

The realization settled over her like a cold rain that any relationship she previously had with Joe no longer existed. He didn't seem to want to pursue it, in fact was moving more and more toward Gwen.

She couldn't just get up and walk away – from him – from the kids. She needed to know for sure this was what he wanted and that it was right for him. Then she would go. But Joe had other problems now with the company, and she would see him through that first. Unless, of course, he asked her to leave.

Leaning back in her chair and carefully taking a deep breath to keep her stomach down she turned her thoughts to what she could do that might produce answers that would be helpful. An hour later she closed the blinds to her office and furiously delved into a stack of folders she retrieved from the file cabinets.

* * *

"I'm leaving this afternoon. Hopefully, I'll be back by tomorrow evening." Gwen pronounced this while closing the blinds in Seth's office. She was more comfortable knowing anyone passing down the hallway couldn't observe her. Seth knew she felt this way and frowned.

"You're closing the blinds, so you must be fixing to tell me something I don't want to hear. Looks like you pulled a blind side off on Joe." Seth nodded to the paper she had tossed on his desk earlier.

Gwen threw her arms wide and with a peal of laughter dropped into a chair at one of Seth's work tables. "It was beautiful! You should have seen the look on his face the next day. Have you seen him today? Looks like a dog with his tail between his legs."

"What are you doing, Gwen? I thought the plan was to ruin Black Capital and run them out of Alaska. Then you wanted to marry him. It doesn't compute. You can't do both."

"I can if he leaves Alaska with me as his wife," she snapped, eyes glittering.

"And what about Linda? It's obvious he cares for her. She's practically a mother to his kids."

Gwen chuckled and swung back and forth in the swivel chair. "Oh, Seth, you are such a simpleton. Did you think the picture in the paper was the only one? When she gets a gander at some of the others, she'll be leaving."

Seth shook his head. "Did you talk to Roger? He's not happy sitting around."

"I talked to him. I came in to tell you I'm going to Juneau tomorrow. The Senator wants to talk to me. He's getting impatient."

"I expect he is. We're getting new contracts in here every few days. You're part of the reason for that. How's he going to like that?"

"He has his objectives, I have mine. Joe needs to think I'm his best asset in bringing in business."

"Good luck with that."

Seth watched Gwen flounce out of his work room, shutting the door just hard enough to not resonate down the hall as being slammed, but hard enough to show her displeasure in Seth's lack of confidence in her plans.

* * *

Joe had struggled all day to deal with the million and one things on his desk that he needed to concentrate on. He sighed and closed the folder containing a contract proposal. He'd try again tomorrow. If he kept at it today, in his current frame of mind he was apt to make mistakes.

I didn't talk to Linda all weekend. She's got to know somethings wrong. I need to go in and be cheerful and ask her to dinner with me and the kids. She's going to think I don't care about her. I can't let that happen. But I just can't talk to her yet, not today—maybe tomorrow. I'll think of some explanation for being withdrawn. I sure as hell can't tell her I ended up naked and unconscious in bed with Gwen. That sure wouldn't make her want to accept any proposal from me.

A few minutes later he stood at Linda's office door. Her blinds were uncharacteristically drawn, but light peeked out around the edges, so he knew she was still there. He tapped on the door and opened it slightly.

"Working late?"

Linda looked up from the computer and blinked as if she was returning from someplace else.

"Oh yes, just a few more things and I'll be done." She gave him a tired smile. "Did you need something?"

He made a valiant effort to produce a happy smile and stepped into her office, closing the door behind him. It occurred to him that everyone had started out leaving their blinds and their doors open.

"No, just wondered how it was going. Any problems? Are you overloaded?"

"I'm fine. I'll be done in a few days with auditing all the payroll records. I'll have a report for you then. I would like to ride the chopper when it takes a supply run to the sites to go over payroll procedure with the managers, just to ensure they understand the system. It will go a long way toward avoiding mistakes."

"Absolutely, whenever you're ready."

Her answer was a wan smile and a nod.

"Well." He looked around, and finding nothing else to say, came up with, "Don't stay too late now."

Fifteen minutes later he sat in his SUV at the waterfront – crying. He had never been one to cry, couldn't remember crying even as a kid. After his painful and disastrous divorce, it had been months before he had finally cried. Now here he was, crying again. He wanted to go to Linda for comfort, but to do so would hurt her and maybe end his chances of spending his life with her. Eventually he quieted, took a deep breath, and pulled out the cell phone to call Byron Marks.

"Nothing earth shaking yet, Joe. I have people on everyone as best I can. I have limited resources up there. I'm sending some people up from here, but Alaska is not an easy place to follow someone or to get information. Everyone knows everyone, and that's a double edged sword if you want to stay out of sight. But we'll find out what's going on. You know as well as anyone these things take time."

"Anything on Gwen yet?"

"Not much. Her normal routine will be more obvious in a week or so. She did meet one man at a park on the outskirts of town. We haven't been able to identify him yet, but I should have that in a couple of days."

Joe turned the phone off and drove home wondering if he was destined to fail at expanding this Alaska office. *Damned if I will. A Black doesn't fail.*

* * *

Mit knew Roger was coming long before he stepped in the door of the cabin. Bull was gone. She never knew how long he would be gone, but from talk between him and the two men with him she suspected it would be at least a couple of weeks, maybe more. She was in for a bad time. It always was when Roger came.

If her husband had been home it would make little difference. She was like a horse or a sled dog to be loaned out, a piece of property to be used by anyone Bull permitted. Her husband was bad enough when he took her to bed, but Roger was mean and crazy. He liked to hurt people. She was always afraid he would go too far and kill her or injure her so that she couldn't work. If she couldn't work, she wasn't sure what Bull would do. She would like to kill Roger, but Bull would kill her.

"Hello, whore." He swung his pack to the floor near the door. "Get me something to eat, and you damn well better have coffee."

She turned without a word and added wood to the cook stove. A makeshift table against the wall took the place of a cabinet or counter to work on. From it she retrieved a pot half full of the eternal stew that served as a meal here and placed it on the stove. She used a dipper to fill the big coffeepot from a pail of water. She added coffee grounds and set it on the stove next to the pot of stew. Roger had taken one of the rickety chairs and turned it backwards. Out of the corner of her eye she could see him straddling it. When she turned away, she could feel his eyes on her back as if they were hot embers from the fire pressing against her flesh.

When the stew was hot, she filled a tin plate and poured a large tin cup full of coffee, placing both in front of him. Her effort to stay out of reach came to nothing. He grabbed her, pulling her onto his lap and painfully squeezing her breast. Holding her on one leg, he ate the stew with one hand and pawed at her with the other. She knew from past experience that to attempt to move away would throw him into a rage. His hurry caused him to be sloppy, and stew dribbled down his chin. He laughed and kissed her. When the stew was gone he pushed her off his lap.

"You got thirty seconds to get naked and get in bed."

Mit hustled off to the walled off corner that served as a bedroom. Obedience wouldn't save her from the pain she knew was coming, but it might save her life. Being stoic was her only defense.

It was worse than she'd expected. After brutally taking her, instead of leaving for his own place that she knew was only four hours away, he pulled a bottle from his pack. Then began her long night of hell. By the time he ordered her to get up and fix him breakfast she was desperate for him to leave. Blood oozed down from between her legs, and the pain from the damage there was such that she limped badly. Her right arm hung limply at her side. It was wrenched, but she intended him to think it was broken. Bull would not be happy if she were damaged too badly.

Roger was hung over and impatient with her slow pace. As soon as the coffee was ready she put a half cooked piece of venison on the tin plate and set it in front of him. A couple of bites of the half-cooked meat again enraged him, and he threw it at her. She cringed for a blow, but he must have looked at her and decided he had done enough. Better to let it go than have an argument with Bull. He swore, and picking up his backpack, slammed the door on his way out. She continued to cower until she was sure he was gone.

When she felt sure he wouldn't be back, she straightened up and grit her teeth. If she stayed here she would die sooner or later. If she tried to leave Bull, he would kill her. The nice men that had come by were trying to arrest her husband, Roger, and their men. If she helped them, Bull and Roger would kill her. It seemed to be her destiny to die.

Accepting that as her fate, she decided on revenge as her only option. Heading outside, again limping and dangling her arm in case Roger was higher on the mountain watching the place, she made her way to feed and water the dogs. At the last cobbled together shelter in the row she fed the dog, and while he ate she shuffled to the back of the shelter and sat down. Removing a rock she pulled out a carefully wrapped phone the men had left her. They'd showed her how to use it to reach them. She hadn't said she would, but last night had made up her mind for her. They had programmed their number in it, and she touched it like they told her to do.

* * *

CHAPTER TWELVE

Joe greeted Wallace with what he hoped sounded like a cheerful good morning. He was, in fact, feeling better about things. Byron would gather information sooner or later that would solve these problems. He was convinced now that Gwen was a part of it in some way. He just wished he could be done with her, but Byron said not to rock the boat until they knew what was going on.

Linda was already in her office, and the blinds were closed. That made Joe uncomfortable as she usually had everything wide open, smiling and waving to everyone as they came in. Seth's blinds were open, and he was at his drafting tables. Gwen's blinds were closed, and the light was not on. She apparently was not in yet. He was glad of that and with a small smile tapped on Linda's door and went in.

"Hard after it already?"

"Just routine work. I have a couple of files ready for you." She picked the folders up and held them out.

"All right." Joe took the folders and stood, holding them, feeling awkward, not knowing what to say. "Is everything okay? Any problems?" He noticed she looked tired and had dark circles around her eyes.

"I'm still going over things." She spoke wearily, and her shoulders slumped uncharacteristically. "I'll give you a report as soon as I'm done. As for problems, I don't know. You're the one to tell me that. Do we have problems?"

"I'm still looking into things too. Hopefully, everything will be cleared up soon." Her shoulders seemed to sag a tiny bit as she studied him. "Yes, hopefully."

"Why don't you come to dinner tonight? The kids were asking where you were."

That brought a smile, and she murmured an acceptance. Joe hoped it was one small step back to normalcy.

* * *

Gwen crossed the Senator's office like a boat under full sail. Her dark blue

83

business suit would have pegged her for an up-and-coming executive aimed at the glass ceiling had it not been for its hugging her figure more like a wet suit than a business suit. Lack of the customary silk shell worn under it allowed the plunging lapels to showcase her cleavage. The use of a barely existing lace bra was revealed when she circled the Senator's desk and bent low to kiss his cheek.

"Hello, big guy. Have you missed me?"

The Senator eyed the bra and cleavage displayed for his benefit and gave her a wry smile.

"Still wearing expensive underwear, I see. You pay for that with Black's money or mine?"

"Is this one of your grumpy days? I would think you would be glad to see me."

"What have you been doing besides drumming up business for Black? You are supposed to be getting him and his company the hell out of my state."

"Well, -- Big Guy." Gwen spread her arms wide and drew her words out as if explaining something to someone not quite bright. "I have been working on it, and it's coming along fine, thank you very much. He has had trouble on every site and several times on some."

The Senator's eyes turned cold. "Don't give me crap, Gwen. I know exactly what has happened at every one. You think I wait for you to tell me? All you have been so far to Black is an inconvenience. You can't even get into his bed. Now I want results. You go see Roger and come up with something that will make them turn tail out of Alaska, you hear?"

"If you want things that big, they will get media attention."

"What the hell do I care? If they get bad PR, the better it is for us."

"All right. I'll see that things start happening."

"Good." He nodded to the man standing by the door. "Show Miss Smith out." He watched her stomp toward the door. "Oh, Gwen!" He called. As she turned a pouty face to him he pointed a finger at her. "You want to marry Black or be his whore, I don't care either way. But you do your job for me first and you remember to keep your mouth shut. You have one foot planted in this and always will have. Don't make the mistake of forgetting that."

* * *

Linda laughed and gathered both Art and Renee up as they threw themselves at her. She carefully kept her eyes off Joe as she fielded questions from the kids about where she had been and why she hadn't come over for the weekend. Mrs. Ramsey had left dinner for them, and the kids informed her that Joe wasn't as good at dishing things up as she and Mrs. Ramsey were. Joe, who at the time was attempting to get the meal from the kitchen to the table, rolled his eyes. Linda laughed and went to rescue him.

The meal went well and conversation was pleasant, focused mostly on the kids and school. All seemed to be going well, and Art was finding his niche on the soccer team. Renee had a group of friends and was full of news about their girl chatter.

Things fell into their normal routine as Linda finally rose to clear the table and clean up from the meal. The kids went to bathe, and Joe silently joined her cleaning up the kitchen. The silence was deafening and made Linda want to scream.

"Have you told Mrs. Ramsey that Josie will arrive Monday?"

Joe looked up in surprise. "I didn't know she was coming Monday."

"Oh, well she is. You remember Mrs. Ramsey is going to care for Seyma?"

"I do remember all that. I just didn't realize she would be here so soon. Have you made all the arrangements for her with Ashton?"

"Everything's ready for her. She's going to try and line up some suppliers here in Alaska. She's allowed herself two weeks, but thinks she can do it in less."

"Good." Joe opened a cabinet door and set the clean plates back where they belonged.

"Her decorating service has been well received. I understand they are going to start recommending it more to the new clients and for large projects especially." Linda dried her hands on a dishtowel.

"I hadn't heard that. I haven't been in touch with the home office and what's going on as much as I should. Seems like I've been fighting one fire after the other ever since I got here."

"We used to talk about things. Would you like to talk about what's going on?" She stood holding the dishtowel, gripping it as if it might escape

"You have enough on your plate. You don't need to listen to my problems too. Are you getting along all right in the office?"

Linda sighed and turned away. "I have the daily routine under control. Contracts are a problem and cause extra work. You will have to deal with that sooner or later. In the meantime I'm still working on the back payroll records but should be done with them soon."

Linda noted Joe gritted his teeth at the mention of contract problems, aka, Gwen. She folded her dishtowel and hung it over the rack. When a few seconds passed and Joe didn't invite her to join him for an after dinner drink, she said goodnight and they parted politely.

Across the hall in her own apartment she settled in alone with a large glass of wine. She went over every word of the evening. He was so preoccupied he had forgotten Josie was coming. Things were going from bad to worse, and she didn't know how to help him. And what was worse, she didn't think he wanted her help. Tears mingled with the wine.

* * *

"About time! Where the hell have you been? I've been waiting for thirty minutes, I was about to leave." Gwen glowered at Roger.

"We need work or the deal is off. You promised enough work to make a lot of money. I want work, or I want my money."

"You're about to get work, lots of it. I'll tell you what I want done and approximately when I want it done. Tell me if there is any problem and how it's going to be taken care of. I'll have to make arrangements around it. If you need anything, tell me."

Roger grinned and leaned over the picnic table in the little used park.

"About time."

* * *

Josie smiled broadly when she spotted Linda at the edge of the crowd. She waved as best she could while juggling a large tote bag, an infant seat, and managing a stroller with a rambunctious toddler between three and four years old. The wave was interrupted abruptly when her suitcase came into view on the baggage conveyor belt. She somehow managed to dash through the crowded melee of people and with a last minute lunge grabbed it by a corner just before it moved beyond her reach.

Linda came to her aid in time to retrieve a second piece just rounding the end of the circle. Once all the luggage was pulled off and they moved to the periphery of the now thinning crowd, the two women came together in a tight happy hug.

"I'm so happy to see you," Linda laughed, eyes bright.

Josie recognized it was tears giving Linda's eyes that bright and shiny look. Linda must be lonely up here, more than anyone realized.

"I'm thrilled to be here. This is so exciting."

"I'm parked just outside. I can't wait to get home and get my hands on this beautiful child." Linda bent over the stroller, smiling at Seyma. "Let's get home and pop open a bottle of wine to celebrate your being here."

Driving into Anchorage, Josie was engrossed in the passing surroundings.

"So tell me all about being here. Do you like it? Is there a lot of difference in living up here?"

"Oh, wow, where do I start? Let's get you settled, and we'll talk about it all later. There's so many different aspects to it."

"Linda, I don't mind my department footing the bill for a hotel while I'm here. I didn't intend to intrude on your life by staying with you."

"You are not intruding on anything, Josie, and I'll hear no more about it. I'm looking forward to having someone to talk to. I want to hear all about the decorating department and how it's going. I can't wait to see what you do with the units here in Anchorage. Someday Black Capital will build a permanent complex here and you will be able to do that also."

"I can't wait to do that. I have yet to do a Black Capital building, and I'd really like to show my stuff on something like that."

"From what I've heard your 'stuff' is pretty fantastic."

"So far everyone has been happy with my work." Josie nodded. "But, every new job is a whole new deal. What I did on the last job has no influence on how much people like the next one."

"I think I understand that more than I'd like to." Josie caught the undercurrent of the comment as Linda wheeled into the underground parking of the apartment building.

An hour later Josie reclined at the end of the couch in Linda's apartment. She held a cracker covered with cheese spread in one hand and a wine glass in the other. Seyma had run and played with a surprisingly emotional Linda. It had been a tiring flight and Seyma was as exhausted as Josie felt. A few minutes of play, something to eat, and a few more minutes of rocking and Seyma was out for the count. She would probably sleep until dinner. Josie hoped so. She wanted Seyma to be rested and happy for dinner across the hall at Joe's where Linda had told her they were to eat.

Something didn't seem right. Linda was different—yet the same. She seemed tense, and Josie hadn't missed that Linda had yet to mention herself and Joe in other than a work related topic. Josie had been a victim of spousal abuse and she was sensitive to the negative vibrations coming from Linda. She and Joe had been considered an unshakeable couple before moving up here and everyone had expected a wedding soon. As far as Josie knew there was no word of that happening floating around. Linda had always seemed to her to be the type that could handle pretty much anything thrown at her. Could living up here be so bad that it caused this change in her? Josie suspected there was more to it.

Linda came in and lowered herself into a chair and finished off her glass of wine.

"I'm going to go in for the last hour at work. That will give you a chance for a long relaxing bath and even a nap. When I get back we'll go across to Joe's for dinner. Mrs. Ramsey is a great cook and it will give you and Seyma a chance to meet her before you leave her there tomorrow."

Josie frowned at Linda. "I was right, wasn't I? You have tons of work and I'm interrupting and making it harder for you."

"No, I don't, and you aren't. I just have some things I had Wallace snag for me, and I want to pick them up before they get distributed or disappear. I won't be gone long."

An afternoon bath and nap was a luxury Josie hadn't indulged in for a long time. As she drifted off with Seyma sleeping peacefully in the crib next to her bed, Josie couldn't help but wonder about what Linda had said. She had someone named Wallace 'snag' something for her and she wanted to get it before it got 'distributed or lost?' None of that sounded like an office of Linda's. She was looking forward to dinner, maybe some of the odd things she saw here would become logical to her. She closed her eyes and drifted into blissful sleep.

* * *

Josie rode to the office with Linda after depositing Seyma with Mrs. Ramsey. Seyma had immediately taken to Mrs. Ramsey the evening before and Josie felt she could go to work with no worries about the home front. The plan was that Joe would meet her at the office and she would follow him to the apartment complex in the van he had rented for her. He would introduce her to Ashton Baxter.

Linda gave her a quick tour of the offices and the conference room that would be used as Josie's office while she was here.

"Maybe you can do a few things for this place while you're here." Linda spread her hands in an all-encompassing gesture.

Josie laughed and turned her attention from inspecting her temporary office to Linda.

"I think you did just fine. You have excellent taste. If you ever want to quit working for Joe, I'll be glad to add you to my department—assuming they continue it."

"Thank you for the compliment."

Josie caught a shadow and an almost imperceptible frown crossing Linda's face as she turned away for a second.

"From what I hear," Linda turned back, a bright smile had replaced the frown, "you're doing very well, and your services have received rave reviews. I'm expecting them to make your department larger and permanent."

Josie couldn't help but beam. "Oh, Linda, I hope so. That would be so wonderful. I know I can make a living at decorating but this would be a *personal* success. Like I did something myself and it was good." She ran her fingers over the highly polished conference table and was silent a moment. "You know my history. Sometimes it's easy to fall back into the old pattern of thinking I'm not capable. Confidence is a fragile thing."

Linda wandered to the end of the table and slowly sank into one of the chairs ringing it. "I do know. Life is fickle with our self-esteem. Sometimes, no matter how good you are or try to be it just isn't enough."

Josie waited for more, hoping Linda would confide in her. But after a moment of silence, Linda slapped her fingers on the edge of the table and stood abruptly. "In the meantime we just keep doing what we are good at and hope to find our place in this crazy world."

Josie laughed. "Right you are. I saw a coffeepot in your office. Let's go—"

Josie was thrown forward by a deafening boom shaking the walls and rattling the glass in the interior windows. She grabbed the edge of the heavy table, shocked and taken unaware. Linda had already jumped to her feet, immediately knowing trouble had struck again. She ran to the door and down the hall to the front of the building. Josie followed, completely at a loss as to what was happening.

Josie heard voices, the draftsman and the receptionist. Both were headed out the door. Linda ran to catch them, Josie at her heels. Joe was just exiting his SUV in front of the door. To his left, racing at breakneck speed toward him came a woman in hysterics, screaming at the top of her lungs. Behind her a car was on fire, or what was left of it. Large parts of it lay nearby. The woman literally threw herself into Joe's arms.

"Joe!" She kept screaming. "Hold me Joe! Don't let them hurt me, Joe. They know if they hurt me, they will hurt you because you care so much about me! Oh, God, Joe, hold me!"

Joe's arms were wrapped around the woman tightly as he tried to calm her. He looked back toward them, an unreadable expression on his face. Josie looked around in astonishment. Linda stood as if she had been punched in the gut, white as a sheet.

The short receptionist called Wallace approached Linda. "I've called 911. They're on the way."

Linda seemed to snap back. "That's good. Thank you, Wallace. Ms. Darnell and I will be in my office if we're needed. Would you call Ashton Baxter and tell him our plans are uncertain for the next hour or so. I expect Ms. Darnell to be going to the site but will be delayed until this is sorted out."

As they turned to reenter the building Joe caught up with them, guiding the still upset woman with him.

"The police have been notified," she informed him.

"Good. Gwen this is Josie Darnell. She's here to work on the decorating of the apartment complex. Josie, this is Gwen Smith, our entire sales department at this time."

Josie held out her hand and struggled for a reply. *What do you say to someone you meet just after their car blows up?*

She didn't, in fact, have to worry about it as Gwen started bawling again. Lowering her voice between sobs she begged Joe not to leave her, to stay with her when the police came and that she couldn't possibly meet "Linda's little decorating friend" right now.

Josie stood, mouth open, until Linda took her arm and tugged. Back in the office Linda made coffee and bade Josie sit in one of the comfortable chairs facing the desk. Linda joined her.

"What's going on, Linda?"

"We aren't sure. We have experienced a lot of vandalism problems at all the sites. We had one case of vandalism here when we remodeled but nothing since. We aren't sure why it's happening, at least I don't think we are. Joe hasn't brought me up to date on it in a while."

"Who is this Gwen woman?"

"She's Joe's saleswoman. She was hired by Donald Larson when he opened the office originally."

"I see." Josie did see all of it now, above and beyond Gwen being a saleswoman. She understood now the sad and withdrawn look Linda wore when she thought no one was watching. Her guess was that Linda would return to the home office in time. These other-woman situations never turned out well.

Linda discarded her paper cup and headed for the office door.

"Gather up what you need, and you can follow me over to the project. I'll introduce you to Ashton. That is unless the police need us, and I imagine we can be interviewed later. I'll let Wallace know."

"Linda!" Josie stopped her. "If you want to talk I'm here."

"Thank you." Linda made no effort to pretend she didn't know what Josie was referring to. "Maybe sometime. Not now."

* * *

Ashton Baxter was a pleasant surprise. Josie's reception by construction personnel was usually some degree of surly, contemptuous or dismissive. Ashton, on the other hand, was pleasant and friendly and rather than seeming to resent her, seemed to get the idea of what she was doing and why. The fact that he was young, strong, had a physique borrowed from a Greek god with a face to match, and a head of thick reddish brown hair all helped to enhance his likeability.

Linda did the introductions and left, exhorting Josie to stay in touch and call if she needed anything.

Ashton discussed her needs with her and then took her on a tour of the complex. After she made a decision on where she would start, she found to her surprise that Ashton intended to work with her. She nervously moved from one foot to the other while she held a leather bound folder against her chest with both arms as if it were a shield.

"Honestly, I don't need help. I work alone all the time. You must have misunderstood what they told you."

"Nope." He sounded matter of fact. "I understood perfectly, but as you probably realized this morning, there are some problems going on. This is the one project that hasn't yet had a major problem, and I intend to keep it that way until it's turned over to the owners. I also intend to keep you safe. So just get used to me because we're going to be fused at the hip while you're here."

"Is it really that bad? That car this morning might have been a mechanical malfunction. You hear of that happening." Josie moved down the hallway with Ashton.

"I'm afraid it was no accident. There have been some others—one put a man in the hospital. I know Mr. Black is working on trying to stop it. I just hope it gets taken care of soon. In the meantime I have around the clock guards, and I intend to personally be your guard."

He grinned mischievously, and Josie was shocked to find her heart pounding. In all the time since her husband died that had never happened. She ducked her head and changed the subject to what information she needed to gather and how she planned to do it. If he was going to shadow her, he had just as well help. The idea gave her a warm feeling.

* * *

"Listen, Alfred, I voted on your bill and even put money on the line on some of your projects and sites. I haven't seen a dime back and I haven't seen anything happening with your construction company. I even saw one where this Black Capital is going to get the job. What the hell is happening?" The tall, thin man in spite of his expensive hair stylist and an expensive suit still looked more like his itinerant fisherman father than a member of the state legislature.

"Calm down, Walter. You know that construction company is in my cousin Josh's name. I can't be there in the office and run it personally. I'm a state senator you know, and I do try to discharge my duty as best I can."

"Right on all counts except for discharging your duty. Now cut the crap. We've backed each other up on this kind of stuff from day one. We both know the score, and we both have things to cover up. Now I want to know what is happening to my money and when I can expect some return on it."

The senator snorted and mashed his cigar stub into the outsized ashtray. "Okay, truth is it has taken longer than I expected. This Black Capital bunch has deeper pockets than I thought, and they seem willing to absorb some losses and move on. Then one of the people I put on it has been slow to move. I hope I got that sorted out a few days ago."

Walter sat, elbow on the arm of his chair, chin resting on his fingers. His black eyes dared the senator to look away. A grin began to seep out around the grim set of his mouth. "And you would be talking about Gwen. I saw the picture in the Juneau paper."

"Yeah, well, you know Gwen. Now she has some idea she wants to marry this Black guy and go back to the states as his wife when he gives up here. Problem is, he don't seem to be too interested, and she's trying to bring in customers to be important to him. Customers, I might add, that should be going to Josh's business."

"That girl's as crazy as her old man. You need to do something about this or you're apt to end up with a big problem."

"I talked to her the other day and things are stepping up. She has some good help and I told her to get them moving."

"Help?"

"Rodney Cane."

Walter jumped up, throwing his hands in the air. "Rodney! Rodney! The Rodney? I thought that bastard was dead?"

"Everyone seems to have thought so, but apparently not. My guess would be Bull's had him hid out up in the mountains. She lured him out with money, my money, and a lot of it by the way. I told her she better be showing some results."

Walter retrieved his hat from a rack where he had laid it and jammed it on his head. "I'm leaving here. I know nothing about this and don't want to know. If I eventually make money on our deal, all's well and good. If I don't I'll consider myself lucky to not be associated with it. One thing I'll tell you right up front, Alfred. I will not be investing in another deal with you. I have spent my life distancing myself from my own disreputable family and their friends, and I'll be damned if I get brought down by yours."

* * *

CHAPTER THIRTEEN

Joe tried all morning to find a time to talk to Linda, but between her taking his place introducing Josie to Ashton and Gwen hanging on his arm like a shirtsleeve, there had been no chance. He tried talking Gwen into taking the day off and going home to lie down. She wasn't having it. Finally, after getting her involved in a project that Seth was working on, he managed to find Linda alone in her office.

"I've been trying to get a private minute with you all morning."

"You've had your hands full." The statement dripped with the hint of sarcasm. Not something Linda usually let herself resort to.

"I know, I know. What could I do? She has a right to be upset."

"Who would want to blow up her car?"

"I have no idea. I can't help but think it has something to do with our problems, but why target her?"

Linda shrugged her shoulders.

"Did you get Josie settled in?"

"Yes. What an introduction to our new office. We'll see her at dinner tonight."

Joe nodded, stood uncertainly for a minute, and when Linda encouraged no more conversation, left the building before Gwen could attach herself to him again. He told Wallace he was out to lunch if anyone called.

A detour around the drive-thru at Burger Wonder equipped him with a burger and fries and some sort of weak liquid meant to be a soda. His drive ended at the waterfront where he arranged his burger and fries on a picnic table in a way he could eat one-handed and then took out the cell phone he used to call Byron with the other.

"Byron, you won't believe the latest."

"Actually, I already know about it. The man I have shadowing her saw the whole thing."

"Did he see anything that will help us?"

"Not that we didn't already suspect. What he did see is Gwen reach in her purse and glance back at the car. I would bet money that if you searched her purse right now, you would find the device that set off the bomb."

"So why don't we tell the cops?"

"Because that might nail her for blowing up the car but it won't tell us who or what is behind all these attacks against the company. I seriously doubt she'll tell us."

"So why would she blow up her own car?"

"My guess would be to make you feel like her protector. I've done a lot of investigations and I can tell you that some people can get obsessed with someone, and there is no limit to the lengths they'll go to."

"Wonderful. That makes me feel better. So what do we do now?"

"It's up to you, Joe. We can tip off the cops before she leaves the building and has a chance to ditch the detonator or we can hold off and keep working at it and hope that something she does will tip us off to more. If we wait, it leaves you vulnerable to more attacks and problems."

"And if we don't wait?"

"We may never find out or it may take a long time. Longer than you're going to want to pay me for. It's got to be your call."

Joe hung his head down over the picnic table and rubbed his forehead. He took a deep breath and looked out over the bay. "Okay, Byron, we wait and go for the big fish. Let me know if you find out anything."

"Joe?"

"Yeah?"

"You sure you don't want to let Linda in on this? She could be a big help to you."

"No! The less she knows and is involved the safer she and the kids are."

"Okay."

* * *

Rodney sat in front of a large tent cleaning his guns. He was dirty, vulgar, uncouth, and unkempt, but his guns were always polished and oiled to a degree that would have passed any military inspection. He was alone. The three men usually with him had chosen to lie low in towns or homes of family or friends until called for their next foray against Black Capital.

Patting his rifle lovingly, Rodney slipped it into its scabbard. He would leave at daylight to meet Gwen near Anchorage. He had time to make it down to Bull's and spend the night with Mit, but that might not be a good idea. He had hurt her pretty bad, and he doubted she was back to normal yet. He also suspected Bull might be back, and he would be pissed if Mit was hurt bad enough to keep her from taking care of the place and the dogs. He'd stay away for a while. Getting in a ruckus with Bull would mean giving up his security at this location, and he didn't want that.

His thoughts turned to Gwen. She was finally coming up with work for him and his men. She'd paid well for what they'd done so far but this would bring him some serious money. He picked at his teeth with a fingernail and grinned. This might bring him enough to buy a good fast boat and get him back into the smuggling business. In a bigger way this time. Drugs were the big thing now, and they meant big money. Big money would make him a big man. He tipped his head back and laughed long and loud at the sky, much like a wolf howling at the moon.

* * *

Josie packed the last of the paperwork in her briefcase and straightened up to face Ashton.

"I guess that's it. I'll be back in a month when everything is delivered and all the units are finished. It shouldn't take but two or three days to put it all in."

Ashton hooked his thumbs in his pockets and leaned against the door frame. "I'll look forward to that. You coming back, I mean, not the furnishings."

Josie felt the heat creeping into her cheeks. She couldn't remember when she blushed last—high school maybe? "Thank you. Don't flatter me too much or I'll get over confident and not do a good job." Her effort at deflecting the direction of the conversation was clumsy at best, but Ashton let it pass.

"Come on, I'll walk you to your car." He took her arm and they moved off toward the exit.

She drove away, reluctant to leave, and that gave her pause to think about a part of her life she had intended to put behind her, the part that included a man. Ashton had invited her to dinner a couple of days ago, and she had surprised herself by accepting. She tried to convince herself it was more of a business dinner, but she knew better. Ashton was adept at putting her at ease and before she knew it she had let him crack the wall of privacy she kept around herself. Not that she had spilled her guts, mind you, but she did let him know she had been treated badly, and that experience had left her preferring a quiet social life. So now she knew she wasn't immune to being attracted to a man. Tomorrow she and Seyma would fly out early and be home by the end of the day. She could get back to business without distractions.

* * *

95

Bull Smith watched the bundles of lumber and building supplies swinging out from the ship to the dock. It had been a while since he'd received any. With all the new security and Gwen not having access to the ordering, they had to quit purloining Black Capital supplies. It had made a nice addition to his smuggling income, although it wasn't smuggling. It was out and out theft.

He was hoping to squeeze a bit more out of it before it all fell apart. Gwen was going to lose this one. He didn't know if she would go to jail or manage to wiggle out of it, but he did know she was out of control on this deal. She had never done a deal this big before and when the Senator decided to use her it went to her head. Everything worked fine until the older guy running things retired, and she got a look at that rich good looking Joe Black.

"Humph." Bull watched the bundle being maneuvered onto the flatbed truck and the crane releasing it. *I tried to talk sense to her till I'm blue in the face. She'll just have to learn the hard way.*

Bull headed for his old battered pick-up. He had a lunch meeting to pay Seth for information, and he didn't want to miss it. If he could get an occasional tip on incoming supplies from him he could still milk this a while. And this arrangement with his nephew had the added advantage of dealing with someone with a practical grasp of the situation. Seth was careful and all about the money, worth ten of Gwen, but unfortunately Gwen was his daughter. He would protect her as long as he could, but if it looked like she was going to take him down with her he'd cut her loose, family ties or not.

* * *

"Linda!" John met her as she ran from under the downdraft of the helicopter that had brought her to the White Mountain project. "God, it's good to see someone beautiful from the land of sanity." He swept her up and swung her around.

Laughing out loud she held onto him as he set her down. "John, you are so good for my ego."

"How are you Linda?" He squinted his eyes a bit. "You look tired. Is Joe working you too hard?"

"Just a lot of work to get done. I'll catch up eventually."

"How about some breakfast? They still have some left from the morning's chow line."

"A mug of coffee and a real breakfast might be just the ticket. My usual breakfast is a roll and coffee at my desk."

He took her arm and steered her toward the big tent that acted as a kitchen.

"At your desk? You used to have breakfast in the company cafeteria with Art and

Renee and made sure they ate every bite of it whether they wanted to or not. If I think about it for a minute I can probably quote that "eat healthy" lecture they got with it. Who sees that they eat right if you're sneaking a roll and coffee at your desk?"

Linda gave what she hoped was a pleasant smile as he guided her to the cafeteria style line that had only a few breakfast leftovers at this time of morning. She filled her plate and followed John, who carried two mugs of coffee, to a bench in the almost empty tent.

"They have a wonderful nanny called Mary Ramsey who feeds them and takes them to school and then picks them up and cooks them wonderful dinners. She has raised her own family of five and is unbelievably good with the kids."

"When do you get to spend time with them?"

"I try to see them for a few minutes a couple of times a week."

"I see." John's expression went blank, and he blew on his hot coffee before taking a hurried sip.

"So, to what do I owe this enjoyable but unexpected visit?"

"I'm finishing up one of the jobs that needed to be done to get things up to date. I've gone over the payroll back to when the office opened. I suspect most of the men don't check their payroll slips that carefully. Most people don't. Those that do, reported the errors and had them corrected. I've brought checks for the errors that shorted some checks, plus interest." Hopefully, all the men are still here. I'd like to deliver the checks in person along with an apology for the mistakes. Sort of an employee relation type of thing."

"I'd expect some to be gone. You know how we've been plagued with turnover. Anyone still here is going to be happy as hell and love you for correcting it. You'll be the resident angel around here." John leaned on his elbows and cradled his coffee mug in both hands. His voice turned somber. "We've had a lot of bad news and problems since this site opened, and any good news is welcome by all of us. As for me, I'm just glad to see the office finally working smooth. I can't tell you how happy I am that you're in charge."

"Thank you, John. I'm glad you approve." Linda pushed the hash browns on her plate around in a distracted way. Looking up, she found John sipping his coffee and watching her. Obviously, she wasn't doing a good job of covering up her nervousness.

John set his coffee mug aside and clasped his hands in front of him. "All right, Linda. What's going on? I want to know why you don't see the kids but a couple of times a week, why Joe isn't here with you, and why you look so tired and stressed out."

She pursed her lips for a moment, and then her shoulders dropped as she gave a weary sigh.

"Just between us, John?"

He nodded. "Just us."

"The office was a mess when I got here. I have everything running well now with a couple of exceptions. Then there were these problems and accidents. I know Joe has been trying his best, and he's worried about it, but I'm out of the loop. He doesn't tell me anything, not a word. And then there's Gwen."

John winced and looked down at the table. She stopped a minute before continuing in a low voice.

"I've had to battle her for my own office. Joe says she's important to bringing in new business, but she makes mistakes on contracts and he lets it slide. This payroll thing was her fault; she was doing payroll then. I've fixed it, and I've locked her out of the payroll system, but now I need to start on the contracts. I know I'll find mistakes, and Joe and I fight every time I mention something she does." Linda's shoulders slumped. "It's like I stepped onto the plane in California in one world and when I got off the plane I was in another. I don't know people here, but you I know, and we've worked together. I'm afraid Joe has developed feelings for Gwen. So, I need to know what you know, John. Please. I can't fight what I don't know about, Gwen or these other problems Joe won't talk about."

John frowned, his lips clamped together hard. He stood up so quick his chair almost overturned. Snatching his coffee mug and then Linda's, he stomped away. By the time he returned with full mugs for both of them he looked calmer. He set her mug in front of her.

"I don't know what to say about the company problems. It has to be someone that wants to do serious damage to us up here, because almost every site has had problems. It can't be some disgruntled individual I wouldn't think because of the kind of stuff that's happened. It would take some deep pockets to do what's been done. I have no idea what Joe is doing about it other than we got an extensive security camera system. He plays his cards close to the chest as you of all people know."

"I don't understand." Linda leaned in on her elbows with her mug gripped in both hands. "I've always worked with him on problems before. Everything was fine until the kids and I got here. Joe was here for two weeks before we arrived. So what changed? He doesn't even spend a lot of time with the kids, a couple of hours in the evening if he isn't out of town and sometimes he's gone part or all of the weekend too, always checking a site or seeing a customer or something. He doesn't tell me much about where he's going or why."

"Linda, this is none of my business—you know—about Gwen. But she practically ran things when Donald was here. If you had a problem, you weren't going to get much help with it. It got to where Donald wouldn't even take your call or call you back. Then Joe took over. I hoped it would get better. It has. I can call Joe if I have a problem and he'll try to fix it. I don't have payroll complaints every payday anymore, thanks to you, and I'm getting my supplies on time and what was ordered. I seldom deal directly with Gwen now. This project is pretty far along to need to coordinate with her. We don't like each other. I watch my back with her. I don't know if she goes with Joe to all the sites or just this one, but she is almost always with him. Maybe she thinks I'll complain about her—which I have."

"Yes, she goes with him almost everywhere. They did a weekend together in Juneau not long ago." Her eyes met John's and held. "I guess I'm just in denial."

He reached across the table and took both her hands between his, holding them firmly.

"I honest to God don't know anything. But I will tell you, because I think you need to know, that before Donald left there were rumors and whispers that Gwen was sleeping with him. Maybe that's her MO. I don't know. I can't say if the rumors are true. But my gut tells me that woman is bad news."

Tears began to gather in Linda's eyes, and she looked down at the table and blinked them away.

"Thank you, John." She took a deep breath, stood up, and forced a smile. "Let's go get these checks passed out."

* * *

Senator Alfred Robard and his cousin Josh sat at a back table in a dark BBQ joint that enjoyed a certain amount of popularity in Juneau. Mid-afternoon was quiet with only a handful of customers in the waterfront area. Each had plates loaded with a giant bun topped with a large mound of dark red BBQ overlapping the sides. The Senator had removed his suit coat and placed it on one of the unused chairs. He took his time tucking several paper napkins around his collar and where possible down the front of his shirt.

"Why bother? You know you're going to get it on you anyway."

"Not this time."

Josh rolled his eyes and dug his knife and fork into the juicy pile of meat and bread. He inhaled, chewed slowly, and closed his eyes.

"We need to do this more often."

"We aren't doing this for fun. We're here because I don't want to talk about this around my office. And while everyone knows you're my cousin, I don't want to be more visible than normal. So, what's so urgent you called me?"

"I've been telling you for months that we've been losing business to Black Capital ever since they came up here. Well, now I'm telling you we are going to fold soon if things don't turn around. All I'm getting are small cut rate jobs and they don't add enough to the bottom line to keep us going. Now, what are you doing, if anything, about it?"

"I told Gwen to step it up last time I saw her."

"What, exactly, have I missed that she is doing to make it better? I haven't heard of any of their projects having problems lately, and I haven't seen any sign of them packing up and going back where they belong. All I see is her bringing in more clients that should have been ours. *And*, I might add, one of the big ones just hit the paper with a big cozy picture of her and Black down here to talk to the customer, who is a buddy of yours if I remember correctly. *Right under your nose, Alfred.* I need some help here, and I need it soon or it isn't going to be just my bank account that suffers. Remember you're a majority owner in this too."

The senator grimaced and put a hand to his ample belly.

"My ulcer is acting up and you aren't helping it any."

Josh cut further into the BBQ and forking it into his mouth, studied the senator while he ate.

"Okay, I know something has to be done." The senator conceded. "I've been hoping she would get going on this, but looks like she's too enamored with this Joe Black guy. I'll get on it today."

"See that you do. Both our bank accounts depend on it."

* * *

Rodney stood partially behind a tree and watched the worksite across the narrow valley. Three men had similar positions nearby. They blended in as only native woodsmen, born and raised in the elements, could do.

He raised a pair of binoculars and squinted in concentration while studying every angle he could see from his current position. It wouldn't do to be seen now. After the accident with that construction worker and all the other problems, security was tightened and a hunt would be launched for anyone seen nearby.

It was bad enough they had installed the twenty-four hour live cameras. Yesterday he'd picked up the blueprints showing their locations and wiring. He would have to disable those. So far the most effective way seemed to him to be to take out the man monitoring them and just turn them off. If they had to kill him that was all right. The four men discussed the project before them and where they could strike that would render the most damage. The ultimate aim was to destroy the entire thing. After a while they moved back and began to circle the project site to study all sides of their target. When he thought he had all the information he could get, Rodney motioned for them to head back into the forest.

"We'll bring in our supplies and cold camp a couple of miles away. I don't want someone taking a walk to stumble onto us. After midnight we'll set it all up as soon as everything's quiet. I want to trigger it about 4:00 A.M. if we can. Chances are they'll all be in deep sleep and by the time they get their heads clear to what's going on it will be too late to stop it. Once we set it off we're out of there."

* * *

"Is everyone gone?" Gwen glanced up and down the hall before entering Seth's office.

"Everyone left. We're alone."

"So, what was so important you had to have me come in for?"

"I don't want to be put in the middle of this business anymore. I've known about it, and I've covered for you, but I'm not going to be part of it. I wasn't asked to be and I don't get paid for taking risks. I have a good job here until you put them out of business, and at that time I would rather look for another job than go to jail."

"What put a stick up your tail? Everything was fine up to now."

"I'll tell you what. I was stopped, waylaid better describes it, by Rodney a couple of days ago. Demanded, demanded, mind you, that I get him a copy of the cameras and wiring we just did at the White Mountain site."

"Did you get it for him?"

"Are you kidding? Does anyone ever not do what Rodney says? Damn straight I got it for him. But Gwen, I do not want to be put in that position again. You understand?" Seth was yelling.

"What in the hell do you expect me to do about it?" Gwen yelled back.

"I don't know what arrangements you have, but you see to it that I'm left out of it, you hear me? Only thing I've done wrong is being related to you!"

"Don't be such a baby. This will be over soon. I'll talk to Rodney when I see him."

"And when will that be?"

"I don't know. I have to go to Juneau tomorrow. The great man calls." Gwen made the reference with heavy sarcasm.

"Is something about to happen at the White Mountain site?"

"I don't know and from your rant I take it you don't either. Just tend to your little drawings and keep your mouth shut."

Gwen flounced out, followed three or four minutes later by Seth.

It was a good ten minutes before the door to a storage room opened and Wallace emerged. He'd needed to pick up the keys to a company vehicle and had come in to hear an argument going on. Hoping to avoid embarrassment he slipped into the storage room where the keys were kept and closed the door. The argument accelerated and turned to shouting and as he listened Wallace instinctively froze against the wall and worried about them hearing his heart beat or his labored breathing. Suddenly staying out of sight involved much more than embarrassment.

He'd recognized who Gwen was when he'd come to work here. The daughter of the criminal boss Bull Smith. Wallace's mother had said that Wallace had a third cousin that had been sold to Bull Smith for a wife. Not much was known of her since. When liquor flowed, bad things were sometimes whispered about his daughter, Gwen. Wallace hadn't suspected Seth was related to her though. He knew, without a doubt who the Rodney they were talking about was. "The Rodney" that scared the shit out of even the criminal world. But then Rodney wasn't just a criminal, he was crazy.

He retrieved the keys he needed, locking the storage room as he left. He checked the parking lot to be sure he was alone before leaving.

It was 4:00 A.M. before he fell asleep. What should he do? Linda had shown such faith in him when she hired and trained him, and this job was the answer to a prayer. He owed her his loyalty. He thought of talking to Joe who was, after all, the owner, but Joe seemed to be close to Gwen. He even argued with Linda about her. If he shared what he had heard he could end up dead and maybe some of his family as well. He had grown up on the wrong side of poverty and was all too familiar with the criminal element over a wide area of the state. He knew what these people were capable of. He decided to just watch everyone and see where that led him. After all, he didn't really know what was going on, anyway.

CHAPTER FOURTEEN

A restless breeze kept the trees dancing in the moonlight. Black silhouettes twisting and turning over four black silhouettes of the men moving like ghosts through them. They all wore black and carried black backpacks filled with supplies. Each carried a handgun and a rifle. Any shiny part had been removed or painted black. Faces and hands were also blackened. At the edge of the forest, where they would head down the slope to their target, they put down the rifles. They'd pick them up on the way out—and use only if necessary. It was supposed to appear like an accident. But things could go wrong and Rodney was a careful if brutal criminal.

Motioning for the others to wait, Rodney faded into the trees and began to circle the project. His objective was the small temporary structure erected as an office. The security cameras were going. Hopefully, the man monitoring the screens would be tired and drowsy. Rodney had the instincts of an animal, and he moved slowly from one black shadow to another, at times crawling on his belly if his gut didn't feel right about something or he felt the hair coming up on the back of his neck. Any animal mother would have been proud to have a son with his stalking skills.

He crouched next to the wall at the side of the building, listening for any sound that didn't belong to the night. He'd hoped to do this at 4:00 A.M. but caution had slowed him some and he was now running thirty minutes late. A small feeble light shown around the door to the office. He had no idea if the door squeaked or not, but he had to assume it did.

Lowering his backpack to the ground, he reached into it and came out with a plastic bag containing a large rag, a small bottle, and a mask that would cover his nose and mouth, much like a doctor might wear. Putting on the mask, he poured the contents of the bottle onto the rag. Dropping the bottle into the plastic bag he fisted the rag into a wad and with one sweeping survey of the surrounding area ran the eight feet from the corner of the building to the door. The door squeaked only a little and taking large rapid strides he was inside in a matter of seconds.

The security man, hearing a slight noise at the door, looked up smiling, expecting an early riser come to shoot the breeze while waiting for the cooks to start coffee and breakfast. He jumped from his chair at the sight of a man, black from head to foot with only a white mask over his face, barreling toward him. Barely upright when he was body slammed into the wall and a rag rammed against his mouth and nose, his brain never had a chance to register what was happening before he slid to the ground. Rodney resisted the urge to crush his skull against the floor but Gwen said the senator wanted it to look like an accident. Like something that could be blamed on Black Capital being careless. So instead he knelt and held the rag against the man's mouth with one hand and pinched his nose closed with the other. When he was certain there was no pulse he grinned. No pulse, no identification, no knowledge anyone was here.

His first objective was to turn off the cameras so the others could start their work.

He clicked a small mouthpiece twice, then whispered. "Move in."

He moved the body back to the desk and placed an ashtray next to a stack of papers he gathered from the other desk in the office. Retrieving his backpack from where he'd left it outside he pulled out a liquor bottle and poured it liberally over the body. He then doused the stack of papers and surrounding area. A container of heating oil for the stove stood in the corner. He turned it over and let it spread over the floor. It should look as if a drunk employee set it on fire when he dropped a cigarette or dozed off at the desk.

Satisfied with his preparations, Rodney turned his attention to the others. Back at the door he checked the area again and saw no sign of anyone and hearing nothing that alarmed him he whispered into the tiny mouthpiece.

"Everyone ready?"

Smiling at the affirmative answers, he turned back and tossed a lit match onto the top of the desk. Once he saw the first flicker jump he vanished out the door, moving quietly but rapidly back toward the trees. By the time he was halfway past the main structure he saw flames beginning to climb from the window of the office building to the roof. Then he saw the flicker of a fire in the interior of the building. Two others spaced far apart were soon visible. Reaching the meeting place and retrieving his rifle, he was joined in seconds by another man.

"You take care of that well?"

"Yeah." The other man chortled. "They're out of business for a while."

Rodney saw the other two men coming up the slope. Daylight was beginning to break now and even with their black camouflage they could be seen. A shout was heard from below, and they went down on one knee to watch what they had wrought.

Men poured out of the improvised bunkhouse and noise erupted as they began attempting to put out the fires. Rodney smiled. His job here was done. Gwen said the big man didn't want anyone hurt—too bad. He might even ask for a bonus for this one. He stood up and motioned to the others.

"Let's go. We're done here."

* * *

Griffin Stein was an early riser, usually the first one up. He liked sitting and watching the dark as it turned to early morning sunrise. He was pulling on his boots when he realized he smelled a trace of what sure smelled like smoke. He grabbed his hard hat and jacket and hurried out of the bunkhouse. The first thing he saw were flames coming out the windows of the office and climbing the walls.

"FIRE! FIRE! OFFICE ON FIRE!"

He ran toward the now almost engulfed office, to be met at the door by a blast of heat that forced him backwards, followed by a wall of flame that burnt the hair off his arms and face.

"Jeff! Jeff!" He cried out even though it was obvious there wasn't going to be an answer. Men arrived with hoses and buckets. John Everett appeared beside him pulling him back.

Two co-workers, Allen and James, arrived. "It's too late, it's too hot. There's no way we can get in there. Come on back now before it collapses," they urged Griffin.

Another shout went up. "Fire! In the main building!" That was followed by another call. "More fire at the south end!" Then someone yelled, "There's no water pressure!"

John felt a chill go up his spine in spite of the heat from the burning building. The next second he was running toward the separate building that would house the garage and workshop areas of the resort and where the control room for the electric and water was located.

Fire was casting a glow at the rear of the building. John jerked the door open and was met with a thick tumbling cloud of black smoke. Flames winked through it, engulfing the ceiling. A blast of flame exploded, driving John and the two men with him back.

"We're going to lose the generators. No way to get them out of there. With the electricity gone the well's gone."

He turned back, waving the others back with him. The fire was spreading rapidly with little opposition. Men had spread out with what fire extinguishers they had and were trying to do what they could. Others had buckets of water from the big water tank but it didn't begin to be enough to help.

"Push it back onto itself where you can," John yelled, running into the midst of the donnybrook. "Cut off any beams you can, push anything back into the fire that you can. Concentrate on keeping new spots from catching."

Men nodded and spread the word, working frantically to try to stop it, slow it down, anything they could do. John moved from one group to another, all frantically trying to stop the fire's progress. Thirty minutes after the discovery of this disaster, they weren't even holding their own against the fire. Without water they were limited to trying to keep what was already burning from spreading. The biggest hot spot was proving hard to control and John sweated alongside his men to contain it.

A shout went up next to him. A flaming truss they had been trying to tip back into the fire was stubbornly leaning in toward them, threatening to come down on the two men trying to hold it. They were trapped under it, not able to get out of the way quick enough to avoid being buried under it as it came down and not able to push it back. Taking in the situation immediately and ignoring the shouted warnings, John ran forward with a long 2 x 4 to help stabilize the beam, wedging it higher on the apex of the truss.

"Out! Out!" He shouted at the two men.

Needing no encouragement, they leaped and scrambled clear of the falling debris. John wasn't so lucky. The minute the men were no longer holding the sides of the truss the weight on the burning and weakening timber was too much for the section John was trying to prop up. It separated and the flaming timber fell. He had no chance to get completely out from under it and it came down, barely missing his head but taking him to the floor as it slammed against his lower back and came to rest on his legs. He screamed as the fire ate into flesh and set his clothes on fire.

Men jumped forward with anything they happened to be holding and while some pried the burning timbers off his legs other hands gripped his arms and pulled him out of range. Others were already wrapping coats and shirts, anything they had around him to smother the flames. They carried him out and away from the danger area and laid him on a patch of grass. Squatting around him, they looked helplessly at each other.

"Has anyone called the office?" Griffin asked.

Nobody knew. Griffin leaned over John who lay pale and still.

"John! John! Can you hear me?" John opened his eyes and seemed to have difficulty focusing. "Did you call the office, John?" John continued to gaze at him. He tried again. "John, did you call the office?"

John continued to gaze at him, then opened his mouth and tried to speak but produced nothing but a groan. He tried again as Griffin leaned in putting his ear close to John's mouth.

"Call Joe," the faint whisper came. "Phone. Back pocket."

"Right." Griffin reached under him, sliding his hand down into the back pocket, feeling for the phone, trying not to disturb him. Once he had the phone he moved away from John, out of hearing distance and checking John's contacts, touched the number for Joe.

*   *   *

The phone rang fifteen minutes before Joe's alarm was set to go off. His first coherent thought when he looked at the clock was that a call this early was not a good thing. He was right.

After listening to Griffin's account of what had just happened, he shoved the shock he felt to the back of his consciousness and took charge of his thoughts.

"Call 911 now and get a plane on its way to pick John up. Ask them what to do for him until they get there. He's bound to go into shock. I'm on my way."

His next call was to Mrs. Ramsey, who would be there shortly anyway, but he wanted her to hurry. He couldn't wait long. He dialed Linda's number, and she answered in a sleepy voice that made him think of how she looked lying in bed, hair tousled, lips swollen with sleep. He batted that image to the back of his brain. He had serious things to think about.

"Linda, I just got a call from White Mountain. They had a massive fire and John has been hurt. They're calling for a plane to get him out of there. Apparently, we lost everything, and they think Jeff Cotton, the man who monitored the cameras, is dead. As soon as Mrs. Ramsey comes, I'm leaving."

"I'm going with you."

"Linda, you don't need to go."

"I know I don't. I'm going anyway. I'll meet you at the door." She broke the connection and Joe was left to call the pilot of the helicopter and let him know his plans for the day had just changed.

*   *   *

Griffin was on the phone in seconds with the emergency number, and a plane was dispatched. A medic called Ray was added to the line. He calmly but quickly asked questions. Griffin put the phone on the speaker so they could all hear.

"We won't know until we can get a picture of his back if that is serious or not, so we have to assume it is until we know. Is he on his back?"

"Yeah, he's flat on his back."

"Okay, keep him stabilized, and if you move him try to find something to keep him laying flat, like a door or something. The less you move him the better until we know more."

"We can do that."

"You say the burns are all on the legs, and it didn't get to the groin area?"

"That's right."

"What about his feet?"

"His boots are burnt a bit on the outside but he wasn't in the fire long enough for it to burn through it looks like."

"Good. We'll leave them alone until the medics get there. Now I want you to *carefully* cut his pants off. Cut the outside seam and open the pant legs up. Okay? Let me know when you're done. I'll wait."

Griffin turned to the others. "I don't have no scissors. Which one of you has the sharpest knife?"

"I got one sharp as a razor," a man stepped up.

"One of you help him. Try to hold that material up a little so he don't cut John by accident."

Another man came forward and both knelt beside John. They worked with care and took their time. Finally, they laid the pant leg open. John's legs lay on top of the material and the smell of burned flesh mixed with the smell of smoke. Looking at the burned flesh, some of the men swore and crossed themselves, some closed their eyes, some groaned involuntarily and a couple started to take a deep breath, only to quickly cut it off rather than inhale the smell of charred flesh.

Griffin returned to the phone. "We got them cut off, still attached at the back."

"Good, leave them until you move him. You can cut them off then. We don't want dirt in the burns. Do you have water?"

"We got any water left?" Griffin raised his eyebrows at the others.

"There's a few cases of bottled water in the kitchen."

"Go get a couple of cases." Two men hurried off.

"We're getting it," Griffin said into the phone.

"You need to move him after you use the water. Do you have something to put him on where he won't have to be moved off it again?"

"We need a door. Take the one off the bunkhouse if you have to." More men took off at a run.

"Now after you pour that water on him, we want to cover the burns up with clean material, soft if possible. Got anything like that?"

Griffin relayed the information. One man spoke up. "I got a couple of clean t-shirts that might work." Others spoke up with "Me too!" "Yeah, I got one of those." They were dispatched to get them.

The water was stacked close by, and men arrived with a door. In a couple of minutes men were back with hastily grabbed t-shirts.

"All right, Ray. How do we do this?"

"First I want you to open a few bottles of that water. Then look his burns over, and pour it gently over them. Look for anything that doesn't belong there like ashes, a piece of something, anything that isn't burned flesh that could cause infection. If you see something flush if off carefully, no big blasts of water. Okay?"

"Yeah, we got it."

"Go ahead, I'll be right here to answer any questions."

Griffin pointed to a couple of men. "You two, grab those bottles. You heard what he said on how to do this."

The two men nodded and moved up on either side of John. Both wore serious expressions, one frowning in concentration, the other with his mouth drawn into a tight line.

Griffin bent over John, who lay with his eyes closed. "John, you with us? You ready for this?"

John's head moved in a barely perceptible nod. "I been listening." His voice cracked.

The two men began slowly pouring the tepid water from the bottles over the burnt legs. Agonizing moans came from between clenched teeth as John arched his back. Other men clasped his hands, and he gripped like a woman in the throes of childbirth. Then it was over.

"I don't see anything else." One of the men sat back on his heels, wiping sweat and grime from his forehead with the back of his hand. The second man followed suit. "Me neither."

"Okay." The medic on the phone had been listening. "Have you guys seen how they lift people onto ambulance beds or transfer them in hospitals from one bed to another? Put the door next to him. Then I want you to get on either side of him and put your hands, and arms if necessary, under him and lift him enough to move him over onto the door. When you lift his legs have someone cut those wet pant legs off while you have his legs up if possible. That will save him the pain of doing it after you put him down. And those boots are probably heavy so if someone could lift his feet at the same time it might save him some pain."

Starting to operate as a team, listening to the medic give instructions, three men moved to each side of John and the man with the sharp knife moved close. Others moved the door as near as possible to his side.

"Slow and careful," the medic's instructions came over the speaker.

The men nodded as if he were standing there. One looked around at the others. "On three," he began to count. At three they lifted him slowly up, and the man with the knife moved swiftly to reach under John's legs and slice through the back of the pant legs. Then John was on the door, and they moved it away from the wet area where they had flushed his legs with the water.

Griffin spoke into the phone. "He's on a door, and we cut the pant legs off. What now?"

"We need to protect his legs from anything floating around in the air. You need to wrap his legs loosely in the t-shirts. The softer the better."

They set to work, eliciting more loud groans from John. It was obvious he was getting tired. Even his groans were weaker. When they had done the best they knew how they turned their faces to Griffin.

"His legs are wrapped. What now?"

"Keep him warm but not hot. I'll be staying on the phone with you so watch him and let me know if anything changes. The plane's on the way. A prayer might not hurt."

Griffin set the phone down. "Two of you stay with John. The rest of us need to go see what our situation is. I expect Joe to be here soon and with John out of it we need to be able to tell him where we stand."

* * *

CHAPTER FIFTEEN

Linda rolled out of bed already pulling off her pajamas. She was into jeans and boots and shirt in five minutes. Glancing in the bathroom mirror, she ran a brush through her hair. Grabbing a jacket and her purse on her way out, she opened the door to meet Joe coming out of his apartment across the hall. Mrs. Ramsey could be seen behind him still removing her coat. They hurried down the hall together as Joe gave her all the information Griffin had given him.

"You don't have to go, you know." Joe hesitated as they reached his SUV.

"Oh no, Joe. I just saw John the other day, and we've both worked with him for years. He's a friend, and *I'm going.*"

The SUV sped through town on the way to the heliport while Linda called Griffin. The plane was on the way to fly John out to a hospital. They had done what they could for John with the medic's instructions. Now all they could do was wait for the plane. She relayed the information to Joe.

When the chopper was a few miles from the site, they passed the plane carrying John going in the opposite direction. They approached the landing, and Joe was speechless before breaking into a stream of swearing.

Linda gasped, hardly able to take in the devastation below. Just a few days ago she had looked down on a beautiful site. Now it was a black blotch on the landscape—the only structure standing was the makeshift bunkhouse and attached kitchen.

Emerging from the chopper they were met by an older worker who seemed to be in charge during the disaster.

"Mr. Black. I'm Griffin Stein. Nobody knows what to do now."

"How's John?" Joe,'s agony was channeled into those two words.

The older man shrugged his shoulders. "Burnt his legs pretty bad. He's conscious, in a lot of pain. We did what the medic told us but didn't seem to be much we could do."

Joe nodded. "What the hell happened?" Griffin told them what he could of the fire, how he had been the first up and found it. How it seemed to explode in three or four places. The office was too far gone to save, and the control room burnt and they lost the generators and the wiring which put them out of both electric and water. Without water they hadn't been able to fight the fire. He told them that most of all they were sure that Jeff Cotton was dead in the pile of blackened char and ash that used to be the office. He told Joe how John had been hurt helping two other men get out of harm's way.

When he finished, Joe's shoulders slumped. "Show me," he said grimly. The man moved off with Joe, Linda trailing behind. An hour later they stood in front of the office. Linda had tears running down her cheeks. Griffin had left them alone to go for a bite of the breakfast the cook had prepared for the exhausted and discouraged men.

"What are you going to do?" Linda looked into Joe's tortured eyes.

"What can I do? We'll eat this project. My manager is hurt, no telling how bad. It's sure he won't be back to this place. I don't have an experienced man to put on a project this large, even if I go through the home office. They have a lot going on. Everyone is on a job. Even if I had a manager," he paused, "a man is dead this time. I may not even be able to keep a crew here—or at any other site for that matter."

"It's not like you to just give up."

"What in the hell can I do?" Joe answered angrily. "I can arrange to take the hit this time and I can talk to the client and see if he will give us another chance— although I wouldn't if I were him. But where in holy hell would you like me to find a competent construction manager?"

"You're overlooking the obvious. You grew up doing this. You were educated to do this. You had the best example to follow and emulate. You're no stranger to a set of blueprints or a hammer and saw. I don't know if the customer will stick with us or not, but the best way for you to keep a crew is to show them you'll work right beside them as long as you're needed."

Joe listened and marveled at how Linda could always go to the core of a problem. Somewhere along the way he had quit thinking of himself as competent at anything. His mind went to work. *Could I pull it off? Would the men buy in long enough to get it rebuilt? Will the customer give me a chance to make it right?*

"There's a lot we'd have to do. We've got to clean the site up and start from scratch. There's the matter of building materials. We had all kinds of trouble getting what we needed before. Now I need it overnight. And people. I need lots of help and we've had trouble keeping enough men as it was." He sounded thoughtful as he spoke, all the while studying Linda.

Wiping her eyes and cheeks of the tears, she gave him a tremulous smile. "You used to have a pretty good girl Friday. If you wanted to use her, she could probably help with a lot of that."

Joe smiled for the first time that day. He pulled her into his arms and buried his face in her hair.

"Oh, Linda --". He choked and couldn't continue.

They clung to each other like drowning people clinging to a life raft. Linda looked up at Joe through tear-filled eyes.

"If we're going to do this, we ought to start making a list."

Joe laughed, picked her up and swung her around.

Two hours later, Joe had called the client and received his blessing. He then put together a couple of lists of what he would need to do first and what he would need to do it, Joe gathered the tired and dirty crew together in the tent. He couldn't do anything without them.

"You guys take a seat. I've asked the cook to make coffee and whatever snacks he can manage, so if you want something go get it and then we'll talk." Everyone moved off to the serving counter. A few took cheese and crackers or sandwiches and almost everyone took a big mug of coffee. Linda took a seat next to where Joe stood waiting. When everyone had settled again and turned reddened eyes toward Joe, he began.

"You all know we've had problems, not only here but at other sites. Probably someone wants us out, for whatever reason I can't guess. I've heard rumors of bad luck hanging over us and such. This was not bad luck. Bad luck didn't start all these fires at once in four different places. We had a security system monitoring things live with a man on it 24-7. My guess is there's a reason why he didn't raise an alarm, and we'll find out after they're able to get to the body. Someone out there, someone human and nasty, wants to do us harm and show we are not a good bet to do business with."

Joe paused a moment before resuming. "We are working on finding out who is involved in this, and in time we'll stop it. It reached a new level today. A man died. A Black Capital man died. We won't let that go. We will find them. We are the best, and we deliver and make good on what we do. I just talked to the client a few minutes ago and have his blessing for an extension to get this done. The cost will be swallowed by Black Capital. What I need is a good crew—that means you guys. We're going to pull out all the stops in getting what we need in here to clean up and start over. I'm going to put out a call for men. If I don't get enough here in Alaska, I'll go south. There are always construction men willing to go anywhere for work. You'll have all the help I can get. What I want you to do now is have your coffee and think about it. Do you want to stay on? If you don't, I understand, no hard feelings. If you have any questions ask them now."

A man at the end of one of the tables spoke up. "You going to replace the security system?"

"I'm not only going to replace the security system, but I'm going to put men on the ground patrolling this place day and night." Several men nodded in agreement.

Another hand went up. "With John gone, who's going to take over?"

"You're looking at your new project manager. As soon as Linda takes off after this meeting, we'll get together and outline the way forward. Anyone who decides to leave will be going out with her now, so you won't have much time. Any other questions?" No one spoke up, so Joe turned to Linda. "Anything you have to say, Linda?"

Nodding in the affirmative she rose, facing them. "Everything was destroyed in the office. Luckily, we don't keep much on the sites that goes back over a couple of weeks. About the only thing was payroll for the last week or so. If you have your last pay stub hang on to it. I'll send someone out here to do the office function. He will meet with each of you and take down the hours you worked since your last paycheck. So try to remember and jot it down. I'll try and have someone here right away. Everything to do with your pay or supplies other than construction materials will be handled through him." Linda stepped back and nodded to Joe.

"Linda and I are going to get a coffee and a sandwich and give you 10 minutes. I'll need your answers then. I know it's not much time to think about it, but if we're going to move on with this project we need to get started." He took Linda's elbow and steered her toward the counter. When Linda left thirty minutes later, not a single worker had opted to leave with her.

* * *

Wallace was listening to muffled screaming coming from Seth's office. Gwen had come in late, as she often did, so was the last to hear about the fire. After screaming at Wallace because he couldn't give her information he didn't have, she retreated to Seth's office and slammed the door.

The direct line to Wallace blinked on his phone console and he picked it up. It was Linda.

"Wallace, here's what I want you to do. Get whatever you need in the way of clothes and personal items together. You're going to be at the White Mountain site until the project is done. You'll go out with the chopper late this afternoon. I need someone to take your place right away. I know I will have to train them, but see if you can find me someone that could learn and do it temporarily. I want them today if possible. Try and bring anything you are working on up to date but if you can't don't worry about it. My office and all your access is to stay locked to anyone else until I get back. We are leaving now. Any questions?"

"Ms. Gwen is here. She's in shouting at Seth now because she didn't know what was going on. What should I tell her?"

"Nothing. I'll have to deal with her when I get back."

The line disconnected and Wallace thought about what was happening. *It must have been bad for them to be sending him out. What happened to the man they had?* He reached for the phone and started calling. His mother would gather up what he needed and bring it to him. He instructed her to put it in his car, not to come inside. He didn't know what was happening, but he didn't want to have to explain anything to Gwen or Seth. His second call was to a girl he knew, Lela Sams. They had gone to school together. She was the half-breed daughter of a prostitute, and if life was hard for most of the native kids, hers was ten times worse. In spite of her circumstances she somehow kept trying to better herself. In spite of graduating high school with excellent grades no one wanted to hire her, and she worked harder at menial jobs to survive than anyone Wallace knew.

After putting everything in motion, he turned to his own work and quickly began bringing it up to date. He made a list of notes for Lela, a sort of cheat sheet. Linda would be busy and training might be limited, and he wanted Lela to be successful. A door slammed, and Gwen emerged from Seth's office, storming up to Wallace at the reception desk. Seth ambled in behind her.

"Where is Joe? I need to talk to him, and I keep getting no answer."

"All I know is that Joe and Linda are at the site. Maybe they have their phones off for some reason. I don't know."

Gwen swung around to Seth. "I need to get to Joe and find out what is going on."

"All the choppers are going to be out."

"I'll rent one."

"You can't be serious? How ridiculous is that going to make you look?"

Gwen gave the closest thing to an animal snarl possible for a human and stomped back to Seth's office. The door swung shut but not before Wallace heard her say, "He should have told me when it would be."

* * *

Linda came briskly in the front door. Her first words to Wallace were to inquire where they stood for his job. He assured her his clothes were in a bag in his car, and the girl he recommended was waiting outside in his car also. He hadn't wanted to explain her presence to the others. The daily work was caught up.

"Good, get her in here, and I'll see her in my office. Then I need to talk to you. Spend the rest of the day training her on basic things like the phone and doing whatever I may need until it's time for you to go."

Linda hadn't unlocked her door before Gwen stormed out of Seth's office demanding to know what was going on. Seth followed her.

"We called Seth. I'm sure he filled you in." She unlocked the door and led the way into the office. Moving behind her desk she faced the others. "As for any changes there are going to be some. There will be a major push to clean up the site and began rebuilding. John Everett is badly burned and we have no information on that yet. Jeff Cotton is believed to be dead in the remains of the office building. Wallace will be going out to the site, and I will train a replacement for him. Seth, you can expect to field a few possible changes or redos. Joe will talk to you about anything he needs. We are going to try and stay on top of this as well as any other projects we have going. That may or may not mean overtime for you. Gwen, you are to continue to work on your accounts and try to keep things running as smooth as possible."

Gwen's fists clinched and her face turned red. "Who are you to be telling me what to do? Where is Joe? I need to be with him to help with this. Is he at the site? I'm going out there right now."

Linda's eyes narrowed, otherwise she seemed calm.

"No, you are not going to the site. The chopper will be loaded to capacity and have no room for unnecessary cargo. Joe does not need your help to shovel ashes or dig a dead body out of them. You are needed to keep your part of the business running smoothly. Now get out of my office. I have work to do."

When Gwen showed signs of arguing, Seth hustled her out. Linda turned to the phone. Her first call went to Mrs. Ramsey. The kids were taken care of. Linda sighed. *"Note to self, give Mrs. Ramsey a big bonus."* Wallace came in with an attractive native girl. She looked Linda right in the eye and nodded but her nervousness showed. Wallace introduced her as Lela Sams.

"Lela, I'm sorry I don't have time to talk to you now, but as I'm sure Wallace has explained this is a difficult time. Wallace will show you the phone and the basics of taking care of the calls. Don't worry about not knowing how or what to do. I will show you, I promise. Welcome to Black Capital."

"Thank you, Ms. Sloan." The girl appeared torn between embarrassment and elation. Wallace led her out.

Linda's next call was to Billy Black in California. It was a minefield trying to explain it all to him without also explaining that she knew very little about what was really going on. He would expect her to know. In the end she rushed through the call with the request that he put out an inquiry as to how many men would possibly want to come north for a project if that became necessary. Then there were calls to employment agencies and construction unions in Alaska, to the security company, to suppliers for the list of items Joe had compiled that he needed immediately on the return flight if possible. Not a word or a minute was wasted. This would be her routine every day from here on out until the project was done.

By four o'clock there was a scramble of deliveries at the heliport to be loaded on the chopper. She sent Wallace on his way and asked Lela if she could remain a while and talk to her. She introduced Lela to Gwen and Seth, receiving a derogatory snort from Gwen.

* * *

Joe felt productive for the first time in weeks. He had some of the men take what unused material they had on hand that hadn't been consumed in the fire and start on a small, simple one room building to replace the office. It would sit well to the side of the old one. The destroyed building was still surrounded by law enforcement and someone from the coroner's office. It would probably be tomorrow before it cooled enough to retrieve what was left of the body.

He sent a full third of his men to bed, explaining that there would be security people arriving the next day but tonight they would, working in pairs, have to handle it themselves. The men were tired and filthy from fighting fire since dawn. A small rivulet made its way down the mountain about a half mile away. It was small, not much more than enough to get your feet wet but it was water and it was clean. They made their way to it and managed to wash off the main layer of grime. "Damn," commented one man who had spent several years in the army. "Never thought I'd have to do guard duty again."

There was quiet talk as they straggled into the sleeping area one by one. What had happened was serious business. Everyone was uneasy. They were surprised, to say the least, that the new big shot, son and part owner of the company was going to step into John Everett's shoes.

"Hope he knows what he's doing," one commented.

"We'll know in a couple of days."

"If he don't, I'm outta here," someone added.

"He probably has a big fancy degree but being able to read a blueprint don't mean he knows shit about doing real construction."

That was answered with several grunts implying the affirmative as those who could slipped gratefully into sleep until time to patrol for the night.

Joe gathered the rest of his crew and put them to salvaging what hadn't been damaged and cleaning up what had cooled enough to deal with. He located John's bunk and found an extra hard hat and gloves, which he donned. When he had everyone working at all they could do for the day, he quietly joined one of the groups working to pull the burnt and partially charred lumber out and away so that gradually the site would return to bare, and they could start again.

Men exchanged glances and a few raised eyebrows. Some nodded and gave him a hint of a smile. Joe wondered if they were smiling in welcome or amusement, waiting for him to fall on his face. He hadn't felt like he had to prove himself since he was thirteen, and Billy sent him up on a roof with a nail gun.

Well, He smiled to himself, *Linda thinks I can do it and that's all that counts.* He set to work with a will.

Everyone worked late and had a filling if not excellent meal considering the cook was working without a water supply. As they finished, the sound of the chopper coming in could be heard. Joe smiled. This, to him, marked the beginning of recovery. His improving disposition took a dive when the first one out of the chopper was Gwen. Rushing up and throwing her arms around him in front of everyone she turned on the tears.

"Oh, honey, I was so afraid for you! Nobody in that bloody office told me what was going on until I got to work. I would have been here with you. How awful for you to have to take care of this alone." She looked up and blinked through her tears. "Oh, my darling, you're all dirty! You haven't been helping cleanup, have you?"

"What are you doing here, Gwen?" Joe put his hands on her shoulders and firmly moved her back, breaking her grip on him.

Gwen put forward a wide-eyed earnest look, and Joe picked up on the smirks of some of the men who had come to unload the chopper.

"I'm here for you, Joe. To help you. Whatever you need me to do."

"All right, Gwen. You can start by getting back in the chopper and handing anything you can out to these men. Understand?"

"Of course, Joe." She moved back to the chopper with a determined look.

Joe turned to Wallace, who had stood aside quietly while Gwen made her entrance.

"Mr. Black, Ms. Sloan said I was to set up in the mess tent until I had an office. I'll start in the morning bringing things back up to date."

"Good, Wallace. I assume you have an update for me on what's on board and what I'm still waiting on?"

"Yes, Sir. Here's a list of what we brought. Mostly supplies and parts for repair. A small temporary generator is crossed off, it had to be offloaded. It should be on the morning flight. Ms. Sloan was still having deliveries arriving as we left."

"The generator? Damn! We need that generator. Why was it offloaded?"

Wallace shifted from one foot to the other. "Umm, well, Sir, we were at the weight limit, and the pilot said we couldn't go over. It was unloaded so Ms. Smith could come."

"She had equipment we need offloaded? So she could come out here? Didn't anyone object?"

"I believe, Sir, Ms. Sloan told her at the office she couldn't come, but at the chopper she was the highest level in charge."

Joe looked down at Wallace. "I see. Very diplomatic of you, Wallace. Go on now and get settled in. Ask the men where an extra bunk is."

"If it's all the same to you, Sir, I brought a sleeping bag and I'd like to sleep by my work area."

"Up to you." Joe motioned a man over. "Help Wallace carry his office machines down to the tent."

Joe turned his attention to the list and the unloading of the chopper. The men made quick work of it. Gwen managed to ease herself out of working at it and plant herself close to Joe who was helping unload. When it was empty Joe spoke to the pilot.

"Come in the morning as soon as you can get a full load. You may be making three trips a day for a while." Joe glanced at Gwen who was trying to hold his arm. "Ms. Smith will be going back with you. It's already late. I suggest you get going."

"What! I absolutely am not going back!" Gwen seemed shocked he would suggest it.

"Yes!" Joe's tone brooked no argument. "We have no place for you here and nothing for you to do. You go back and tend to what you are supposed to, which is our customers." Joe picked up the bag she had sitting beside her and tossed it back on the chopper. Turning back he took her arm and helped her back up. His last view of her as the chopper rose was a furious face.

* * *

"Don't you bring trouble here, you understand?"

Mit stirred the pot of stew as she listened to Bull talking to Rodney. It had been two days since Rodney and his men torched something that apparently had to do with Gwen.

"We hit and were gone before anybody knew what was happening. I'm still supposed to be dead. You got nothing to worry about." He laughed. "Nice piece of change for this job. Your gal and her congressman pay well."

Bull scowled. "I got a bad feeling about this. It's all going to turn to shit and blow back in our faces if she ain't careful. She's as crazy as you are and I'm going to get caught up in it sure as hell."

Mit didn't understand what it was all about, but she was pretty sure it had to do with what those men, Jake and Harry, had come here for. She would call them again on that phone. But not right away. Patience was her only protection, and she would wait until she knew everyone was gone and it was safe. She ladled up two plates of stew and set them on the table, followed by big mugs of coffee out of the big tin coffeepot. Then she left the house and went to feed the dogs. As she worked her way down the row of kennels, she kept glancing at the last one. Once at it she was almost afraid to glance behind it. You never knew who might be watching, and behind this one was buried the dangerous phone. The phone that could bring her help and rid her of Bull and Rodney—or get her killed.

* * *

CHAPTER SIXTEEN

The senator sat swigging heavily sugared coffee and staring across his desk at his cousin, who kept laughing and waving his hands around in the air as he talked.

"This is great! I couldn't believe it when I saw the paper this morning. Gwen finally came through. Now we have something to go after them with. I sent two salespeople out this morning to talk to possible prospects, and I'm going to send Barney to talk to the ones signed up with Black Capital. With this kind of shit happening they are likely to break their contracts. And guess who they will go with?" He reared back in his chair laughing.

"I'm not amused, Josh. A man died and they know someone set the fire. That makes it murder and arson. It was sloppy. It was supposed to be just a fire. I was afraid from the start that Gwen couldn't keep Rodney in line."

"Yeah, too bad about the dead guy, but what's bad publicity for them is good for us. What does Gwen have to say about it?"

"That worries me too. I haven't been able to get her; she's not returning my calls."

"Call her old man, see if he knows what's going on."

"Are you nuts? You, me, Rodney, and Gwen are the only ones who know about this—unless she's told Bull, which I wouldn't be surprised at. Walter pulled out of our arrangement as soon as I told him she had enlisted Rodney's help. Rodney needs to disappear permanently. I thought he was dead. He should have stayed dead."

"Well, whatever, it can't do anything but good for Alaska Construction Co. We've been bleeding money and only getting the jobs that can't afford Black. We can't last another six months without some new contracts. So it's just in time for me. You're the one brought in the looney woman and her crazy sidekick, so you'll have to deal with them."

The senator's face screwed up in a sour scowl. "Thanks for the sympathy. You wouldn't be so desperate if you'd got rid of that money pit you call a wife when I told you to."

Josh raised one eyebrow. "Not a bad idea, wives do have a way of getting old and bossy. I can't afford a divorce now though. I don't suppose you could see your way clear to a loan for that could you?"

"Oh, for--." The senator studied his cousin and concluded he was, for once, serious. "Check with a good lawyer and see how much it will cost and we'll talk. But get a good one, we don't want to screw it up and have her walk away owning Alaska Construction, okay?"

"You got it." Josh bounced out of his chair and waved as he left the office.

The senator took another swig of his now cold coffee, made a face at it, and sat back wondering how long it would be before he could get Gwen on the phone.

* * *

Linda sat on the edge of a chair beside John's bed in the burn unit of the hospital. She suspected he was in more pain than he let her see. He was groggy from medication but able to focus enough to communicate with her. The first thing he had asked was about the site, and she had just updated him on what was going on there. When she told him Joe was taking his place, he closed his eyes and lay still for a moment. Then a crooked smile formed.

"Wish I could see that." He spoke so soft it was almost a whisper and then stopped for a few seconds. "When he was a kid," he paused and took several breaths, "he was a whiz with a nail gun—ran around on the roof like a monkey."

Linda smiled at the picture that brought to mind. The nurse appeared at her side indicating it was time for her to leave. She hadn't been able to see him the first night, but she had persisted tonight. John, also, had kept asking for her or Joe, so they had relented and given her five minutes. She had stretched that into ten already so she squeezed his hand, promised everything was going forward, the project would go on, and she would be back every day they would allow her to come.

Driving home, Linda's body told her it was tired, but her mind was wired and wanted to do more. She stopped at her apartment and gathered up clothes and necessities for the night and crossed the hall to Joe's apartment. She had come by earlier to see Art and Renee before they had to go to bed. They had accepted the fact that their father would be gone for some time stoically, but Linda knew them well enough to see through that to their disappointment. Art, she thought, was the more affected of the two. He was doing well and making a place for himself on the soccer team, and Joe's presence at the games was, no matter how Art tried to act like it wasn't, a very big deal to the boy.

She let herself in quietly so as not to wake the kids or Mrs. Ramsey, who would be staying overnight as long as Joe was working at the site. Linda herself would stay here also until Joe returned. Mrs. Ramsey could feed them, take them to school and back, and see they sat down and did their homework but they needed someone every night who they knew better. Someone who loved them, could cuddle Renee, read to them, and share their day. Linda had been athletic in school and knew her way around a soccer field, so she could talk about it with Art, but what he wanted was his father to see and appreciate how good he was and share it with him.

The four bedroom apartment left Linda with only Joe's bed available. She opened a drawer and laid her undies in it—next to Joe's. Spreading her fingers she lightly ran her hands over the top of the drawer's contents. Emotions churned until she closed her eyes and swallowed hard. Snatching her undies out, she shut the drawer and put her things on a chair.

She had come to Alaska hoping to share Joe's bedroom. That hadn't worked out because of Gwen. The last time she thought it would happen had been cut short by Gwen. Linda knew in her head that Joe had to leave that night, it could have been some disaster. Still in her heart Linda couldn't help but feel that Joe let it happen. With this latest disaster he had turned to her again like he always had. Gwen hadn't been called or involved. He had hugged her hadn't he? If she helped him pull this off, they would be close again, wouldn't they? She had no doubt at all that Joe could do the job at the site if she could get him the supplies he needed without all the problems they had before.

Showering and slipping into a nightshirt and one of Joe's bathrobes, she went to the kitchen table and opened her tablet. She marked off what she had gotten done, marked the things she wanted to follow up on, and ranked all of them from urgent to needed, listing questions she had for Joe or any suppliers. An hour later she closed the tablet. The bathrobe overwhelmingly smelled of Joe. Pulling the overlarge robe up loosely around her, she closed her eyes and buried her face in it lapels, inhaling deeply.

I'm tired. I need to go to bed. I don't want today to catch up with me tomorrow.

Her mind now becoming as tired as her body, she slipped into Joe's big bed only to find that it too smelled of him. Closing her eyes, she tried to imagine he was holding her again like he had at the site. She slept through a night of restless dreams and couldn't remember them in the morning.

* * *

Joe meant to call Linda and let her know what progress there was, but he had no time or place for a private call. The progress they had made seemed small. They had the temporary generators hooked up while they waited for the large permanent ones. They now had the precious water that had been needed so desperately during the fire and could also keep food and drinks cold and have light where they needed it. Wallace had power for the office machines he had brought, and they could now recharge their cell phones. Joe felt it would be at least two weeks before they could begin to rebuild. So he guessed there was progress, he just wanted it to be more.

Linda knows how it is out here, so she'll understand, and I'll be talking to her in the morning about supplies anyway.

There was one call he had to make no matter how late or tired he was. Walking up the hill he sank down on the ground and pulled out the cell phone he used to talk to Byron.

"Damn, I'm glad you checked in."

"Sorry it's so late Byron. Hard to find a place to talk here."

"I heard about it. News is spreading like wildfire. What can you tell me?"

Joe started at the beginning and passed on all the information Griffin had given him. Then he told Byron about going ahead with the project and the extra guards he had coming, ending with the fact that he was going to be the site manager now, so his presence at other sites would be minimal.

"What about Gwen Smith? Has she been to the site?"

"She came out after it happened. She thought she should have been called out first with me. I sent her packing back to the office."

"Well, make nice, can you? We're onto a lead that may take us to who did this. I also have a connection that makes me suspicious, but I need more on it. Can you keep her happy without having her out at the site all the time? I want her free to lead us to anyone involved."

"Crap! I can't hardly bring myself to be civil to her."

"Yeah, I know, but we don't want to tip our hand right now. By the way, I have some of my men spotted around at all the sites with the security men coming in. You put a strain on the men available at the security companies." Byron's chuckle was loud and clear on the line. "They must have wondered if you thought you were calling the National Guard. Made it easy to send men up to take the jobs. This was a big attack, and while I would think things would settle down for a while you never know. Also keep in mind that if I can put my men in the security companies so can they."

"Great. Now I have guards guarding the guards. Anything else I should be doing?"

"No, I think you're all right. I'll call you if I have anything, but keep in touch with me in case I can't reach you."

Joe made his way back to drop wearily into his bunk. He was in good shape but it had been a long time since he had put in a day of hard labor. His muscles ached and he was sore in places he had forgotten you could be sore. He smiled as he drifted off thinking of holding Linda in his arms and of how she thought he could do this.

* * *

"No! God dammit, girl! Don't you give me any of that fantasy shit you have in your head. None of this right time, opportunity, he's getting discouraged, trust me, shit. I need them folding up their tent and moving back to California, you hear me? And no more of this shit with Rodney either. I specifically told you everything had to look like an accident or caused by something they did. Now we have a dead man and multiple fires, for God's sake!

Senator Robard was spewing spittle and Gwen wanted to wrinkle her nose and make a face but he was enraged and she knew enough from the days when she was his mistress that this was not a time to irritate him.

"I'm really sorry. I really, really am. I did tell him, and I had no idea he was going to go off the deep end like that."

"Apparently you didn't tell him in a way he understood. Perhaps you were too busy with your fantasy to make yourself Mrs. Black to concentrate on what you were supposed to be doing."

Gwen opened her mouth, but he held up his finger in a threatening gesture. "You of all people should understand how serious it is that the law is now involved. That they have a damn reason to be involved. They've pretty much ignored all the other calls from Black Capital as minor stuff, mostly caused by the outsiders themselves. That won't fly with this, and they will go back and maybe take a look at some of that other stuff too."

"I know, Alfred." Gwen tried her contrite act. "What can I do to try to clean up this mess Rodney made?"

"I'm not sure what you can do at this point. One thing you have to do or else is get Rodney under control. You should have let him stay dead like everybody thought. Anything else that is done is to look like an accident—no exceptions! You got that?"

"Yes, Alfred, I do, and I will get Rodney under control. I promise."

"Now, pay attention to what I'm about to say." The senator folded his hands in a grip so tight his fingers turned white. "If this causes me trouble or something like this happens again or if your fantasy of being Mrs. Black gets in the way of getting Black Capital to fold their tent and get out of Alaska, I will put you in the same category as Rodney and deal with you accordingly. Do you understand me?"

"Yes, Alfred."

"Now get out of here and stay in touch every couple of days. I want to know what's going on."

Gwen managed to nod and stood on legs that she hoped he didn't realize were wobbly.

She made her way to a restaurant near the airport and ordering a drink, took a table in the rear. She was in a rage and knew she had to calm down and make a plan before doing anything. The senator being so pissed off was a serious thing. She did not underestimate his willingness or ability to do whatever he had to do to protect himself and his reputation. She had to somehow find a way to shut down Black Capital. Then she had to somehow get Rodney under control. She still needed him, but he would have to follow orders. She signaled the waitress for another drink. Rodney could only be kept under control by something he wanted badly. She would have to think about that.

Third on her list, only because if she didn't accomplish the first two she might end up dead, was how to become Mrs. Black. Joe wasn't falling for her charms as she had expected. Even the night in Juneau had driven him away instead of bringing him closer as she intended. Now the fire had made it hard for her to be near him at all. Her lips curved into a snarl as she thought about Linda being at the helm in getting supplies to the site and managing just damn near everything. She should be the one doing that, not Linda. She was pushed back to finding new clients and new projects. Well, she would just have to be more forceful in obtaining more contact with Joe. And Linda had to go. If it weren't for her, Joe would turn to Gwen in a second. She threw some bills on the table and left the restaurant much calmer than she had come in.

She would take her rented chopper—all the company choppers were in use ferrying supplies to the burn site—and go back to the office. Then she would start to put her new plans in operation.

* * *

The dogs' restless movements and small noises told Mit that someone was near. She waited like a stone statue in the shadows under a tree next to the cabin. If it were friends of Bull or some of Rodney's men they would have come right in, not bothering if they made noise or not. The men waited and, unknown to them, Mit waited for them. She had nothing on her side but patience. If the men in the woods were thieves or some of the criminal types hiding about, they might be here to rob Bull's hideout. Crossing Bull Smith would be a dangerous thing to do, so if that was their goal they would without a doubt kill Mit. Her eye caught sight of them in the brush, making their way toward the cabin. It was the men on the phone.

"Stop!" Mit's voice challenged them from the side of the cabin.

"It's okay, Mit. It's Jake and Harry." Both men stepped into the open.

After a few seconds Mit appeared and made a motion with her rifle toward the cabin door. If they could come, then others could come and she didn't want them seen here.

"Why you here? Bull could come any time. Rodney at his camp with men. Can come any time. You must go, quick."

"I understand," the man named Jake said. "What you have told us on the phone has been helpful. But we need more to put them in jail. We want to set up a recorder to record everything said in this cabin. Okay? Can we do that?"

"They find it, I die."

"I understand how dangerous this is for you. We'll install this where they won't find it. Something bad happened. A bad fire. A man died. We believe Rodney is the man who did it, but we need proof." They waited for Mit's answer.

Mit had been afraid when they left the phone but Rodney hadn't known about the phone and he had hurt her anyway. She was always in danger. Would she be in anymore if she let them do this? Making a decision or taking a stand on anything was something that had been beaten out of Mit a long time ago, and facing a decision like this made her feel dizzy.

"We'll hide it good. I promise." Jake spoke softly, as if he understood what she was going through to do this.

"Okay, but have to hurry."

Mit put her rifle on the table for the first time. She watched the men go to work searching the cabin for likely places to hide this thing they brought. They asked her questions about where Bull would likely never go to find anything unusual. Finally, they decided on a shelf high on the wall over the area Mit cooked. One of the men pried off a piece of bark from the end of the shelf in the spot they wanted to put it. Then he made a tiny hole in the end of the shelf and placed a small thing they called the 'mike' in it. They put tacks into the bark piece and placed it back over the mike. The tacks held it out from the mike so that something they called 'reception' wouldn't be bad. They placed a device inside the shelf at the back and placed a strip of bark in front of it. It would never be noticed unless the shelf was searched. They told Mit that it would start when it heard someone talking and stop when they quit talking. It ran on a battery, they said, that would last for many hours. They would be able to hear what was said now, they told her. Then they were done.

"Wait." She motioned them to stay inside. Taking her rifle she went out and walked along the dog houses, scanning the surrounding area as she walked. Nothing seemed wrong and the dogs had settled down. She turned and motioned the men out. They started to thank her, but she motioned them on impatiently.

"Go! Not on trail! Through trees! Always through trees." Her urgency transmitted itself to them, and they ran quickly to the security of the forest.

Mit watched them go. She had no faith in these strangers, these white men from that other world she had once hoped to join but had never got to venture into. She would help them because they were enemies of Bull and Rodney, but she didn't believe they could take them to jail. They would be killed trying, and she would be found out. It wouldn't matter. She was going to die anyway. If Rodney didn't come someday and kill her, Bull would get mad like he sometimes did over something she did or didn't do, and he would beat her to death.

Her feet padded lightly on the cabin steps as she returned to make a pot of stew in case someone came.

* * *

CHAPTER SEVENTEEN

Joe straightened up from where he was working with a group of men building frameworks. The debris was mostly cleared away, and Joe hoped to soon be setting up the new frameworks. Time and men had been devoted to getting the basics going again. Then there was the small building to serve as an office for Wallace and the newly arrived security team to work out of.

Joe wiped his brow with the back of his hand as sweat trickled down his neck. He was getting into the swing of labor work again. It had been a while, but he could still cut it. The men had been wary at first, watching his every move. But they soon found out he could hold up his end of any beam, wield any piece of equipment they had with efficiency, and in general knew what he was doing inside and out. By the third day he was accepted as one of them with only a slight deference to his being not only an owner of the company but also the site boss.

He paused, cocking his head a bit to listen. The chopper was coming in with the morning load of supplies.

"Sorry, guys." Joe held up his hand up in a departing gesture. "Choppers coming in. I'll be back when I get today's shipment checked in."

A flurry of nods and murmurs answered him, and he turned away, looking toward an open area where a make-shift heliport made do until a permanent one could be constructed when the main lodge was finished. It would be the only way in or out of the lodge other than on foot or dog sled in the winter. Ducking into the office building, Joe grinned when he found Wallace holding out the ledger Joe used to check in the supplies and keep track of what they still needed. Wallace grinned back.

"I heard it coming too. Figured you'd be along in a minute."

Joe was standing at the edge of the cleared area as the chopper swung around and sank to the ground. The pilot cut the power and the rotors began slowing until they finally eased to a stop. Following the pilot out was Linda.

Joe's heart jumped in his chest and he ran across to meet her. She looked fresh and beautiful, and he was so happy to see her he didn't know what to do. Grabbing her up and hugging her tightly, he never wanted to let go. Then realizing he was dirty and sweaty and making a spectacle of himself, he let her go and stood drinking in the brightness she brought with her. A burst of laughter bubbled up her throat, and she took his face in her hands eyeing the sweat and the dirt on it.

"My goodness. You really are a construction worker. They haven't thrown you off the job yet?" She teased.

He threw back his head and laughed out loud for the first time since the fire had happened and maybe for a long time before that.

"I've lost weight. I sleep the sleep of the dead at the end of the day. My muscles have quit complaining, and the men seem to think I know what I'm doing. I can work as hard as they do, and they see to it that I do."

He put his arm around her shoulders, and she put hers around his waist and hugged him. Reality set in as the pilot approached, and they moved apart self-consciously. Joe remembered he still held the spiral ledger in one hand and opened it. A half dozen men were headed toward them.

"I'll have to get the men started unloading this," he told Linda, sounding regretful.

"I know. I need to talk to Wallace. I'll be with him when you're done."

Joe grinned and turned to the pilot and the open doors of the chopper. "So what did we get this load?"

It took a little less than an hour to unload everything and set it aside. Joe gave instructions where to put it and what to do with it. He sent the pilot to the kitchen tent for lunch and went in search of Linda. She was, as she had said she would be, with Wallace and was all smiles. She said goodbye to Wallace and they left the office.

"He must be doing a good job the way you're smiling." Joe guided her toward the newly cleaned site.

"Wallace has turned out to be excellent help. He's done an exemplary job of picking up the reins here. That's one area I don't have to worry about."

Joe's brows furrowed, and he paused in their walk. "What do you have to worry about?"

"It's been like pulling teeth to get some of the supplies, and I don't understand why. I wanted to talk to you about that. I know some of them have what we need, but they tell me they don't have enough or it's in 'reserve,' whatever they mean by that. It's been a struggle to keep the chopper coming with a full load. I'm wondering if we shouldn't order some of this from out of state. I know we have what we need back in California or if we don't we can get it overnight. Then if we have it flown up here we can keep moving forward. Otherwise you're going to be sitting here with men and guards and nothing to work with. I know it adds to the cost but --- "

"They're telling you they don't have it?" Joe's brain seemed to spin as he put this new development into place.

"Yes," Linda waited, knowing he was processing what she had told him. Then he dropped a bombshell.

"Can you have Gwen call them?" he mused.

Linda stiffened, and her smile disappeared.

"No. I have not seen Gwen since the day of the fire. I have no idea where she is or what she's doing. You know as well as I do that she does not work *with* anyone."

"You're right. I'll talk to her when I can. In the meantime get the home office to help us out and send what we need. Cost is not an option. Getting this project done and having it be spectacular is. If we can do that, it will go a long way toward restoring client's faith in our producing even with a disaster like this."

"All right. I'll get on it as soon as I get back to the office. I'll go see if Jones is finished with lunch and ready to head back."

"Linda?" Joe's plan of showing her the accomplishments he was so proud of disappeared while he watched her back as she walked away toward the food tent.

"Damn." He hurried after her. He knew what it must have been. He shouldn't have mentioned Gwen. But he had no idea what the situation at the office was and while Byron was investigating her she might possibly be a help in loosening up the supply chain. Well, nothing to be done now. Hopefully it would be all over soon and Gwen would be out of his company and out of all their lives.

* * *

Gwen paced the cabin and the trail in front of it. She had arrived at daybreak in a rented chopper. She was furious that all the company choppers were busy ferrying supplies to the White Mountain project and none available for her. She had tried to send Mit to fetch Rodney, but Mit had refused to go. Mit had no right to refuse anything she was asked to do, and Gwen was furious at her. She was furious at Bull for not making Mit go. Rodney must be rutting around after Mit, and Bull must know it. Bull had finally agreed to go himself, but now time was slipping by. She was paying the pilot of the chopper by the hour, and he was just waiting around running up a bill.

Where the hell are they? If I didn't need that son-of-a-bitch so bad I'd shoot him myself. She clenched her fists and kicked out at one of the dogs as she passed. A vague sound reached her ears from up the trail and her eyes glittered. That was them. Now she could get this taken care of and get out of here.

The two men emerged out of the trees on small scruffy ponies and pulled up next to the porch. They dismounted, and Bull led the ponies off. Rodney stomped up the steps to the open door.

"Mit! Get me a beer out here." He looked Gwen over with a look that she could only describe as distasteful. Mit came to the door and handed him a beer. "So what the hell's so important I have to hustle down right now?"

"Took you long enough. You think I don't have anything to do but wait around all day for a screw up like you?"

"Careful who you call names. The only man in the state that doesn't know you're a slut is your Black guy and even he don't seem to want you."

"You filthy bastard. I told you to make that fire look like an accident, and what do you do? You set several fires at once, and you killed a man. The law's involved now, and who knows what they'll come up with?"

Rodney's face twisted into a nasty lopsided grin. "You think you can do it better, you go do it."

"The senator was mad as hell. With the law involved they may trace it to you or one of your guys. What if one of them gets arrested for something else, and they turn on you? He was furious at me for hiring you."

Rodney gave a loud laugh. "The old bull of the herd mad at his little cow, is he? Don't worry about him. I know him. He's no different than me cept he likes to dress up and be a big shot. Under that suit and those expensive rings is just another waterfront street fighter."

"Listen, you idiot. He happens to be the one paying for all this, and if you want to make any more money you damn well better start doing what the hell I tell you."

"You saying you got another job for us?"

"Thanks to you we have to back off some, but the senator wants Black Capital out of business and out of here, and he's tired of waiting. They hired so many security men that all the sites are going to look like a military compound."

"We can handle that."

"Not that way! Haven't you heard a word I said? It can't look like someone did anything, you understand?"

"Sure, I got it. What you want us to do?"

Twenty minutes later Gwen tromped her way to the chopper and the waiting pilot. Rodney and Bull stood on the porch, watching her go. Rodney took a swig of his beer.

"That kid of yours is dangerous, Bull."

"Tell me something new why don't ya?"

Mit also watched from inside as the chopper lifted off. She wondered if the little box thing the men had put in to record what was said in the cabin had been able to hear what was said just outside the open door.

* * *

Joe gritted his teeth as he watched Gwen deplane from the just arrived chopper.

She was showing up every other day or so and once had come on an afternoon flight and had, unknown to Joe, sent the chopper back without her. She excused her actions saying she wanted to spend the night with him. It had caused a lot of inconvenience in finding her a bunk and making it private. Four men had spent the night in sleeping bags on the floor to arrange that. Joe had made sure she understood that was never to happen again. She had let it be known that she wanted to share Joe's bunk and tried to pass it off as a joke, but everyone knew it was no joke. Joe was extremely embarrassed and would have gladly sent her off to walk through the wilderness to get home but for Byron's caution about keeping her happy for now.

"Joe, honey." Gwen hurried up to him and despite his defensive movements managed to get her arms around his neck and attempt to kiss him. That he did manage to avoid by leaning back far enough.

"Gwen, what are you doing here again?"

"Well, of course I'm here to see you. You know that. I'm so completely in love with you, Joe. I just can't stand to be away more than a day or two. I don't know why you can't let someone else work here and come home where you belong."

"Don't talk silly, Gwen. Are you keeping up with your own work?"

"Of course I am. I have some ideas we can talk about, preferably in bed."

"Gwen!" Joe grimaced. "You know I don't want any relationship other than business. And I don't want to hear any more remarks of that kind."

She tossed her head and patted his arm as if dealing with a petulant child.

"Of course, Joe. But keeping that kind of desire bottled up isn't good for you. So whenever you want to relieve a little stress I'll be here for you."

"Oh for--," Joe growled. "What do you want to talk about this time?"

He started off for the office, leaving Gwen to follow. She smiled like a kid about to get candy and hurried to keep up with him.

In the office he set up two folding chairs. Wallace sat at a small table with his computers and a man from the security company sat in the corner facing four screens that showed all movement surrounding the site. Joe smiled and nodded to them while Gwen pointedly ignored them.

"All right." Joe sat down opposite Gwen. "What do you have?"

"I thought we might talk about some prospects I could check out. I have a few names here."

"Are these people that have contacted us?"

"No, I don't have any of those. I do have some that I could approach if you want."

"So you really have nothing to talk about and made this trip for nothing?"

"I have a lot to talk about, Joe." Gwen's eyes narrowed. "But it's a bit personal. Perhaps we should go for a walk unless you would rather talk here." She glanced sideways at the other men, then raised her eyebrows at Joe in a questioning way.

Joe rose to his full height and glowered at her. "Come on then, let's go for a walk and see what you have to say."

Stopping several hundred yards up the hill and away from the site Joe gazed out over it all.

"So what do you have to say, Gwen?"

"We need to come to an understanding about this, Joe. I'm desperately in love with you, and I know you have feelings for me too. You just have to give this a chance and quit fighting your feelings. We could be so good together. I could help you run this company and be a real asset. I would make you so proud of me, my darling."

Joe rubbed a hand across his face, and his shoulders slumped.

"Gwen, I keep trying to tell you, and you just refuse to listen. I do not care for you in that way. You are my employee and a good sales representative. You are not a potential lover. You are making your feelings public to the point that it is embarrassing and gives people the wrong idea. You have to stop this and concentrate just on business."

Her lips compressed into a thin line. "You are embarrassed that I show you affection in public? That I bare my soul in devotion to you and your company? That I care about nothing but you?" She bristled indignation.

"Gwen I—"

"Never mind!" She cut in, speaking over him with finality. "I will continue to serve you devotedly until you realize you love me."

Putting her back to him, she marched back down the hill. Joe followed, boiling with a mixture of dislike for her, wanting to fire her, and heeding Byron's caution of keeping her happy until they could determine who she was working with.

By the time they walked back to the site, the pilot was ready to start the return flight to Anchorage. At the chopper Gwen turned to Joe with a wide smile on her face. Before he could ward off her advance she had her arms around his neck and was kissing him briefly on the lips.

"Don't worry, Joe. In time you'll come to realize you love me."

She spun away toward the chopper, leaving Joe watching it rise in the air while he ground a perfectly good surface off his teeth.

* * *

"I can't hardly stand it. I want to start getting everything put in place and see how it looks." Josie chattered on to Linda as they entered Linda's office. She and Seyma had arrived from California early that afternoon. Linda had picked them up, and after they deposited Seyma with Mrs. Ramsey they had come to the office so that

Josie could pick up a vehicle for the time she would be here.

"It's like this with every job I do. Until I see how it looks when it's finished, I can never be sure I did it right."

"It's going to look wonderful." Linda laughed as she pulled a set of keys out of her desk drawer. "How long do you think it will take to get it finished?"

"I'm hoping no longer than a week. Ashton said he could get me all the help I need from the workers now that the project is about done."

"Sounds great. That's one project that has gone fairly smoothly. Looks like we may be able to turn it over to the client soon."

"Are you still having problems? I heard all about the fire at the White Mountain site."

Linda shrugged. "I would assume we still have problems but nothing since the fire—yet."

"What does Joe say?"

"Joe doesn't say anything to me except to order this or that." Linda jerked her head slightly in an 'oh, well' manner.

Josie paused, then grabbed the keys. "I think I have time to run out to the project and take a look at what's been delivered. I can't stand it, I'm going to go. Want to join me?"

"Wish I could. I can't seem to catch up now between the regular office work and staying on top of supplies for Joe at White Mountain. You go on. Just be careful. I can't help but feel another shoe is going to drop one of these days."

Josie pulled up to what would be a manned security gate when the project was done. At present it was closed off with construction gates and guarded by two men patrolling the entryway. She recognized neither of them, and they called Ashton to announce her arrival. The gates were immediately opened, and she drove around the curving drive, arriving at the wide welcoming entrance where she found him coming out to meet her.

Forgoing a business like handshake he swept her up in a bear hug. She laughed, aware of the pleasing flush spreading over her.

"Beauty has returned to my dreary jobsite." He held her out at arm's length, grinning.

"You flatterer. I just got in today and couldn't wait to come see what has arrived and how it looks." She turned to the car and retrieved a large portfolio folder.

Taking her folder in one hand he used the other to take her hand and led her in the big front doors.

"Oh, my." Josie stopped and made a complete turn as she admired the lobby. "Oh, Ashton, this is absolutely beautiful." A small frown caused her forehead to furrow. "Maybe I didn't make the décor in the units elaborate enough to match this."

"Don't be silly. I saw those workups, and they were beautiful. The furnishings we have received already are gorgeous. We unpacked some of it, but I wasn't sure where all of it went so I didn't have anything placed yet. Now that you are here we can get started."

"I can't wait. Do we have time to do some this afternoon?"

"I have some men still working on a few finish items. I can have a couple of them help, and then tomorrow I'll call some in just to work for you. Where do you want to start?"

"I guess I better take a look at what I have to work with."

* * *

CHAPTER EIGHTEEN

Seth poured a scotch for himself and one for Gwen before settling into his arm chair with a tired sigh.

"I'm tired of all this push to get everything done—again—so damn fast. I'm having trouble keeping up. But," he lifted his drink to her, "I have news for you since you weren't in the office today."

"I was at the site consulting with Joe." Gwen sipped her drink.

Seth chuckled. "You mean trying to screw him don't you?"

"Fuck you, Seth," she replied grimly. "What's the big news?"

"Josie Darnell is back to finish the job on the apartments. The furniture and all the other stuff is being delivered. She'll be working out there all week." Seth put his feet up on the coffee table and swigged some more scotch.

"That bitch. Finishing the decorator job is the last of that project. They'll be ready to turn it over to the customer. If I could just figure out a way to get someone in there. Joe has so many guards working all the sites it's like he's guarding Fort Knox.

"You really aren't as smart as everyone gives you credit for you know, Gwen."

She was stung by the look he shot her, somewhere between a grin and a sneer.

"So how would you do it, Mr. Bigshot?" Her voice was stone cold, her expression showed no emotion."

"They'll be delivering furniture and other items every day this week." He sat sipping his drink, watching what he had just said sink in. She started to smile.

"And I suppose you know who is delivering it?"

He smiled, then reached in his shirt pocket for a folded piece of paper. Holding it between two fingers, he flipped it to her.

She studied what was written on it, gulped down the last of her scotch, and headed for the door.

"Gotta go." She slammed the door behind her.

* * *

Josie chattered on at dinner, keeping the kids occupied and listening to their stories about school and Art's soccer team. It didn't take her long to realize that Linda was anything but happy and that her mind was focused only halfway on the dinner table talk. There was trouble in paradise all right.

The next morning she kissed Seyma goodbye and left early for work. She wasn't surprised to find Ashton at the site before her. He put four men completely at her disposal. Spreading her drawings and plans out on a counter in the lobby, they checked each piece that had been delivered. She directed them what unit it needed to go to. They made good time, and when it was all where it belonged she went to the units and set them to placing the furniture and putting up paintings and wall hangings.

Before they were through, she got a call from the front gate that another truckload of furniture had arrived. Leaving the men to continue with their work, she went to the lobby to meet the truck.

"You have plenty of help today." Josie commented pleasantly to the men, noting there were four of them.

"Only for this morning." One of them answered good-naturedly. "There's another truckload to come this afternoon and these two will be on their own for that one."

They labored carrying in couches, chairs, tables, beds, and other pieces one by one. Then one of them, a tall rough looking sort, approached her with a winning smile.

"We can take these to where you want them to go if you want."

"Oh my God, that would be wonderful. You're sure you don't mind?"

"Naw, all part of the job."

Josie turned in time to see two of the men scowling at him. She started to say it was all right if they didn't want to, and then decided it was best to let it lay as it was and let them work it out amongst themselves. Going to her lists she began telling them where the various pieces went. The tall man put a sticky tag on each piece with the unit number for where it belonged. When everything had been tagged the men started moving it, piece by piece, to where it was to go. Josie returned to oversee the work her men were doing.

She had revised her estimate of a week to finish up, but if things kept going this well she would come close. She was pretty sure they could start on the truckload being delivered now before the day ended. She couldn't be happier except when Ashton came around to take her to lunch. She objected to leaving work but he insisted on her taking a break to go with him to an eatery several blocks away and relax for a few precious moments.

Leaving by the front entrance, Josie was surprised to find the delivery truck already gone. They must have really hustled to get everything where it went so fast. But they had another truckload to bring today, so that was an incentive. She hoped they got it all in the right units. She was a big believer in the saying 'haste makes waste.'

In a booth toward the back of a small mom & pop café they looked at each other over a couple of tall glasses of tea. Ashton would have preferred a beer, he replied in answer to Josie's question, but he was, after all, working, and he would never drink on the job.

"You're an unusual man, you know that? You fit right into Black Capital."

"That's one reason I chose to work for them. They have a reputation of being honest. They're carrying that to the extreme with the White Mountain project. They're eating all the cost of rebuilding. I don't know of any other outfit that would do that."

"I know there have been a lot of problems at the sites, but I don't know much about it. Why do you think someone would hate them enough to do something like that?"

"It's not hate. It's business. Damages at all the sites, difficulty getting supplies, rumors about them, unexplained accidents, now a man has been killed. My guess is that someone wants them out of business. I'm sure Joe is working on finding out who's behind it."

"I hope so." Josie thought for a moment about how Linda should, but didn't seem to, know what was going on. Was Joe trying to figure it out, or did he already know? He was managing the site now, so she wouldn't see him while she was here. She would like to talk to Linda about it all, but Linda didn't seem to want to talk. Still she felt Linda needed to talk about it. Something wasn't right.

"You've done a fantastic job furnishing this project. I hope you realize that."

Smiling, Josie hugged her shoulders in a shrug. "I'm glad you think so. It was so generous of Billy to give me this chance, and I really want it to be a success. I've been doing it almost three years now, and I think it's going well."

"I'm sure it's been a great success." Ashton leaned back as the waitress set their lunches down.

Talk turned to their lunches and condiment choices and smoothly moved on to other light topics. Before they knew it the time came to return to work. Both left the café smiling.

* * *

By late afternoon Josie was beginning to see how much they would finish today and that gave her an idea of how long it would take to finish the entire job. The delivery men bringing the furniture and other items up to the various units they belonged in had been a great help but she couldn't count on them wanting to do that again. They had assured her when they brought the afternoon delivery that they didn't mind taking the items to the units where they belonged. She had looked out a window earlier and the truck was gone, so they must have hurried to finish.

She went back to the first unit she had started on that morning and began a tour of the apartment, checking off each item on her list, standing back and studying the room. She wanted it all to look perfect. Finally, she was confident that every item to go in that unit was in place and looked good. She was able to check the unit off as completely furnished.

Wanting to cross off the ones that were complete as soon as possible, she crossed the complex to the second apartment they'd worked on. It would have been nice to do all the ones on the same floor and wing at once, but the furnishings weren't delivered that way, so she placed what she could. Many units would sit partially done until everything arrived. The second one she checked was larger, more expensive, and beautiful. It had a large panoramic window in the living room that someone could stand at and see for miles. Josie had taken great care in ordering the right items for this one. By some miracle everything, including wall hangings and paintings, had arrived. She spent an inordinate amount of time checking this one out and looking at the effect each piece had on the whole. In the end she was extremely pleased with the results and wished that she could see the reaction of its future occupants when they first saw it.

She heard some of the men leaving. It was past time to quit. She had to lock up, and while she wanted to play with Seyma some before her bedtime, Josie was also caught up in the thrill of seeing the results of her work. She would take just a peek at the next unit on her list. If she remembered correctly, they did not yet have everything needed for that one, so she could check it quickly and still have time with Seyma.

She took the elevator down to the first floor level and hurried along over the luxurious carpeted hallway. Mind on the décor of the next apartment she was checking and thinking herself alone, she rounded the corner where the hall changed direction and bumped hard into a man coming from the opposite direction.

Her first scream, as she recoiled from him, was the scream of surprise and fright when one is severely startled. The second scream was longer and louder and was a scream of terror as the man jumped toward her. There was no third scream because he slammed her hard against the wall and had a hand over her mouth.

"Scream again and you're dead." He held a long, nasty looking knife in front of her face. "Understand?"

She managed to move her head in a semblance of a nod, and he lowered the knife.

"What are you doing here?" She asked the tall rough delivery man who had volunteered to place the furnishings in the units.

"I'm here to blow this place up. We thought everyone was gone. What the hell are you doin' here?"

"Working late. What do you mean blow this place up?"

"Just what I said. Anybody else here?"

"I don't know."

"Fuck. This was workin right good until you turned up. Wasn't anyone supposed to get hurt. Now we got another body turning up."

"We could dump her at sea or take her up in the mountains and leave her for the bears," a second man spoke up. He was wearing a large backpack that Josie assumed was heavy because he kept shifting it on his shoulders.

"No. You and I can get out of here without being seen but we'd never get her out too without being seen. She'll just have to have got trapped here when it burned down."

"No, please. I won't say a word to anyone, I promise." She knew as she was saying it that it was no use. She had been a timid, abused, and frequently beaten wife a few years ago. She knew that anything she said would make no difference. He was going to kill her. Even if she could get away from him, which she doubted, she couldn't outrun him down these halls. If she could make it into one of the units, she might be able to lock the door against him. She would have to have a good head start to get in the door and close and lock it. That left fighting back against that nasty looking big knife. But she wasn't that timid wife any longer, and she had to try something.

"Come on, move." He pushed her on down the hall. Midway to the end he stopped and kicked the door to one of the units open.

He flung her across the room. She landed hard against a trio of large iron wall ornaments and screamed in pain. Sitting on the floor, she hugged her knee, sure that it was broken. Blood was soaking her torn pant leg. Anger began to mix with her fear. She had been treated this way before, been married to a man like this, and she had survived. She didn't see much hope for escape here, but she wasn't going to go quietly. She choked back her sobs.

"This is as good as any of them. Let's get this done."

The second man set to work unloading his backpack. The tall man prowled the room, occasionally looking out the window. She wondered if one of the guards would see him. Probably not. They would be watching for trouble from outside the site, not inside the building.

The door still stood open. She wondered if she could escape that way while his back was turned. His gaze kept flicking back to her. She would have to get to her feet, and she wasn't sure how bad her knee was hurt or if she could walk on it, much less run. Still, it was the best idea she had.

Glancing back and forth from the door to her captor, she caught a movement in her peripheral vision. Watching closer she saw Ashton looking around the edge of the door. He gripped a gun with both hands. Then his eyes settled on her. Taking advantage of the two men's lack of attention on her for a moment she looked to the door and mouthed, "Bomb." Ashton nodded once that he understood.

Josie tried to straighten her knee and found it didn't move without excruciating pain. Putting both hands on the floor and shifting her good knee until her weight rested on it, she began to raise herself up.

Sensing her movement the tall man turned and sneered. "Think you're goin somewhere?"

"I can't. I think you broke my knee." Josie straightened up, letting him see her pain and think she couldn't move at all. She wasn't sure what she could do either, but Ashton was here now, and she would sure try to help him. Putting her hand on top of a heavy iron cross about two and a half feet tall—one of the hangings she had fallen on—she braced herself like it was a cane.

"Won't be making no matter to you. Only place you'll be goin is when this thing blows you away."

"Sounds like he's more dangerous than you are." Josie hoped Ashton understood what she was trying to tell him.

The tall man laughed. "Don't you believe it, bitch. I'll be the one to cut your throat before we go."

Josie gripped the top of the cross with both hands and tried to lean against the wall. She was beginning to shake. He turned back to the other man.

"How long? I want to get this done."

"Give me another ten minutes. You're the one wanted to finish it here."

"I didn't want to finish it here. I just didn't want us to blow ourselves up getting it in here."

He paced back to the front windows, his tension palpable. Josie held her breath as Ashton stepped softly across the entryway until he could see the second man working at the bomb in the back of the room. He raised the gun, took careful aim, and fired. A neat hole appeared in the side of the man's temple and he collapsed over the device he was working on.

A howl of fury rang through the room as the tall man's body hurtled through the air from the window at the front of the room. Ashton tried to swing around to bring the gun in line with the attacker coming from behind him. He was a second too late, and the knife caught his arm, opening a long deep gash. The body slam and the knife slash was enough to send the gun flying across the room. Ashton was holding the arm of his enemy as the raging man attempted to slash at him again. Blood flowed from the open wound on Ashton's arm as he desperately attempted to use it, but it was little use against his assailant.

Josie's heart slammed inside her chest. Watching the struggle, almost without thought, her grip tightened on the iron cross, and she put everything she had into swinging it at the tall man. One side of the crosspiece caught him in the back of his right shoulder, and not only did he drop the knife, but his whole arm dropped useless at his side. Ashton grabbed for him but he twisted and slipped out of reach. In a second he was through the entryway and out the door. By the time Ashton reached the door and scanned the hallway the man was gone. He turned back to Josie, pulling his phone out with his good hand.

"Police will be here in a minute. I sent a text so I wouldn't have to talk. They'll get an ambulance for you. My God, Josie, your leg. You lost a lot of blood! Can you walk? Oh, honey, I'm so sorry. I should have stayed right with you but I thought you were going home." He wrapped her in his good arm where she began to cry and shake. Cupping his good hand behind her head he held it firmly to him.

"Hush," he whispered in her hair. "Hush now, sweetheart. You're safe now. We'll get you to a doctor soon."

"You need a doctor more than I do," she sniffled. "We need to wrap your arm and stop that bleeding."

Before he could answer a pair of the company guards ran in the door. "Jesus!" one said taking in the dead man and all the blood on Josie and Ashton.

Sirens sounded outside.

"Did you get the one leaving?" Ashton asked the two guards.

"Nobody saw hide nor hair of him. He could still be here hiding somewhere. We'll have to do a search."

"Every corner, every cabinet, every inch of this place," Ashton replied.

A couple of minutes later the police were there, took a quick statement from Josie as to what the dead man had been doing, and called the bomb squad. Everyone was taken to the parking lot, well away from the building. An ambulance had been called, and medics examined Ashton first at Josie's insistence that his was the most serious wound. They put a temporary wrap on his arm and declared he would have to go to the hospital. Cutting the leg off Josie's pants to better see what they were dealing with, they then informed her that she also would be going to the hospital for x-rays and possible surgery on the knee.

Both answered all the questions the police had at the time. They were told they would be questioned more later. Ashton called several men in to help his guards and the police search the area, promising to be back as soon as they let him out of the hospital. The bomb squad was still closeted in the room when the ambulance pulled out.

Ashton called Linda first and then Joe. He was on the phone with Joe while they admitted him and the doctor stitched him up. It took a long time and a great amount of stitches.

Josie was in x-ray when Linda arrived at the hospital, so she barged into the emergency department, much to the nurse's displeasure. They were still sewing Ashton up. He was on his phone.

"Linda just walked in, Joe. I'll give you hourly updates as soon as I get out of here." He listened a few seconds. "Right, okay." He handed the phone to Linda. "He wants to talk to you."

She took the phone and stepped to the back of the room out of the way.

"I just got here. Josie's in x-ray. I haven't talked to Ashton yet. I'll call, I promise." Linda disconnected the call and gave the phone back to Ashton.

He repeated in detail the information he had already given the police. He had given Joe an abbreviated version earlier. Joe had sounded beside himself, but Ashton argued that he should wait a few hours before leaving the White Mountain site without a manager—even for a short while.

He finished telling Linda everything he knew as the doctor finished sewing him up. He was instructed what not to do with the arm, which was pretty much everything for a few days. Work was not an option for two or three days, and after that he was to do nothing with the arm for another week.

"That's a bad cut, and if you don't want to end up right back here you'll take care of it," the doctor cautioned. "Here's some pills for the pain. They'll help you sleep tonight," he added. "You have a ride home?"

"I'll take him home," Linda said. "Can he rest here while I see Ms. Darnell?"

"Sure, just let the nurse know when you leave."

Linda left to check on Josie's progress and found her being fitted with a knee brace.

"We stitched up the cuts," the doctor volunteered. "They were superficial so they shouldn't be a problem. The knee just had a bad twist. She'll have to use crutches for a while, give it time to heal. Absolutely no weight on it if you don't want problems in the future. I had the nurse make you an appointment with Dr. Taylor for Friday. He'll let you know if you can quit the crutches or not."

"That's going to slow things down some," Josie complained when the doctor had left the room.

"You can stay at Joe's apartment, and Mrs. Ramsey can help you. After the doctor sees you Friday you can make plans for work."

"Not a chance! I'll just be slow, and someone may have to help me, but that's better than having the whole project on hold waiting for me. How's Ashton's arm?"

Linda relayed his condition, finishing just as the nurse came in with crutches for Josie. Another nurse followed with a wheelchair. They made sure the crutches fit

Josie's height and that she was adept enough at using them. Then they declared her ready to leave.

Ashton had been given a pain pill and was sleeping quietly. They woke him up, and there was a confrontation over his needing a wheelchair, rules or not. He conceded when he saw Josie was upset. They enlisted the night guard at the emergency entrance to push his wheelchair.

Linda hurried off to bring her SUV to the entrance while the small caravan of a nurse carrying crutches, a nurse with a wheelchair, and the guard with a second wheelchair made their way slowly outside to the pickup area. Once they were both loaded into the SUV, Linda asked Ashton where he lived.

"At the site. I have a cot set up in the manager's apartment."

"You can't stay there by yourself," Josie protested.

"Yes, I can. The cot is comfortable, and there's a bathroom. I even have a mini-fridge. Besides, there are several guards on duty round the clock if I need anything."

They reached the site, and after being let in by the guards at the gate, Linda drove right to the front entrance. Two guards met them there and stood by while Ashton insisted on taking no help getting out of the vehicle. Refusing to let Linda escort him inside, he did concede to letting the guards go with him. In a few minutes, Linda had left the site and was headed home.

"You have bigger problems than anyone lets on, don't you?" Josie questioned Linda.

"Yes, we do."

"Want to talk about it?"

"I don't know what to say. I don't know much about it. Joe won't talk to me except to do this or do that. Everything's different up here."

"And the difference is Gwen?"

"I think so, yes. I thought the fire had brought us closer together, but she has been going to the site every couple of days. She even spent the night once."

"I'm sorry, Linda. If you ever need me, I'm here for you."

"Thank you, Josie."

No more was said. They reached home about 2:00 A.M. Linda helped the exhausted Josie navigate her crutches into the elevator and down the hall to Joe's apartment. Mrs. Ramsey heard them come in and insisted she would see Josie settled in bed and for Linda to get on to her own bed. Linda kissed Josie goodbye, and they shared a tight hug before she left.

After extracting a promise from Mrs. Ramsey, almost making her write it in blood, that she would wake Josie at her regular time, Josie gave herself up to deep sleep. Linda, on the other hand, in spite of the hour, lay awake thinking about the day's happening's and what tomorrow might bring. Would this bring Joe home, even for a few hours? Eventually she too, had to give in to the tiredness of a stressful day and night, and she slipped into fitful sleep.

* * *

CHAPTER NINETEEN

D amn!" Joe disconnected the call. Josie and Ashton, both in the hospital. They could have been dead. Another body, even though it was one of the bad guys this time, on a Black Capital site. *Josie was family, for God's sake! What would he ever tell Kate, Josie's mother and his own stepmother, if he let her daughter get killed? Couldn't he protect anyone up here?*

His inclination was to call a chopper right now and fly back to Anchorage, but he didn't dare leave here without someone in charge. He never knew when or where they would strike next. Linda had said they would both be going home after the doctors finished with them. Not a whole lot he could do if he did fly back. Linda would keep him up to date.

He walked away from the little office building, and when he thought he was far enough that anyone lingering in the dark wouldn't hear him, he called Byron.

"Sorry to wake you up, Byron."

"Me too. I just got off the phone with my man at your site. I heard what happened. How are they?"

"At the hospital. Not fatal, thank God. Linda said they'll be going home tonight when the doctors release them. What did your man say?"

"He's one of the guards. They had no idea what was happening until they heard the gunshot. Seems the one that got away was one of the men delivering Josie's furnishings earlier in the day. I can only assume they stayed in the building when the truck left. I'm sure the police will be all over the delivery company. I'll make sure to stay on top of what they find out."

"Are we getting anything, Byron? This can't go on forever."

"As a matter of fact, we are. One of the most unlikely sources has turned out to be a good one. I've expanded my search to Juneau."

"Juneau?" Joe was silent a moment. "Does this have political connections? We didn't have any problems with the business licenses or any of the paperwork when we came up here."

"Um. Well, I have some ties to people there that I'm working on. It's all forming up into a big spider web of people connected to each other. The big challenge now is for you to be able to keep your operation up and running until we tie it together."

"Okay. I'll do it if it kills me. Talk to you later."

"Joe?"

"Yeah?"

"We are making progress. I'll let you know as soon as we can nail something down, okay?"

"Okay, Byron. Thanks."

* * *

Josie sank wearily down on a dining chair that the men had just brought up. After the attack they had put pressure on the delivery company, and everything had been brought by the end of the week. Ashton brought in extra men to get it distributed throughout the building and to help with what Josie needed done. She could no longer do some of the things she normally would, seeing to pictures that needed adjustment on their hanging and rearranging decorative items. One man seemed to have a knack for the more delicate work, and she singled him out to be her shadow. Ashton came in and pulling up another chair, joined her at the table.

"You look tired. You should take a day off and rest." He smiled. "I don't think insisting on working through the weekend was one of your best ideas."

"I know. I would love a day off, but I just can't. I was hoping to be done by now or at least soon. It will be a big load off Joe to have this project done and turned over to the client."

"True. But you can't keep driving yourself or you won't be able to work at all. You should have waited a few days to come back to work."

Josie crossed her arms and leaned on the table. "Look who's giving that advice." She laughed.

"Okay, got me." He grinned. "So how close are we?"

"My part?" He nodded. "I think with the extra help you gave me, if I keep at it I can finish in a couple of days. Problem is I have an appointment to have my knee looked at tomorrow, and that will take half a day. So I'll say I should finish up about three days from now."

"That quick? Wow! I'm impressed."

"Well, we will still need to have the place cleaned, you know, vacuuming, washing the windows, things like that. We don't want to spoil the effect by having dirty windows or baseboards or footprints on the carpets from movers and such."

Ashton thought a moment. "Are you done with all the units on the top floor?"

"All but one. Why?"

"If you could finish up that one unit, we could get some housekeepers in here to work on the top floor while you finish the rest. It would put us ahead some. My men are about done with all the little finish jobs. I could see us being ready to turn this over sometime next week."

Josie smiled, and her eyes lighted up, causing Ashton to smile.

"Why don't you call Linda and have her get us some housekeepers in here tomorrow if possible."

Josie gave him a wide grin and reached for her phone.

* * *

Exactly a week from Josie and Ashton's conversation Linda put a call through to Joe.

"You have to get someone to oversee that site for at least a day. Ashton says the Eagles Peak site is ready to go to the client tomorrow, if they want it. But we need the good publicity, a ceremony, the paper, you know the drill. You need to be here for that, whenever it is. Probably best if no one knows you will be here until the last minute, but we can't have that and publicity too. You can fly right back out after it's turned over."

"This is good news. I need to call the client, but I'll need them to coordinate with you on the details. What about some kind of reception after the ceremony?"

"I'll check with the customer and see what they would like. I imagine they will want the good publicity also." Linda paused. "How's it going, Joe?"

"Better than I expected. We're moving rapidly and I think we'll beat the winter. You've done a fantastic job getting us everything we need up here. I appreciate it." He stood listening to the silence on the other end of the phone. His expression was pensive. In time she answered.

"Thank you, Joe."

* * *

Joe wiped the sweat out of his eyes and stood back to observe their progress. He *was* pleased with the way things were coming along. Everyone understood how important it was to rebuild. If they had doubts at first, his presence had driven it home.

He moved back and walked far enough away to make a call and not be overheard. He knew he was driving Linda and Ashton crazy with his constant calls, but he couldn't help it. It took two days before the client could come with the manager of their new facility and tour it. Joe was a nervous wreck. He had Ashton put an extra round of guards on, making it three times what would normally be used. It was vital they get this property turned over to the owners without another problem. He had Ashton send any men no longer needed there to the White Mountain site if they wanted to come. That helped Joe considerably. He had been working short-handed at this site since the beginning.

"To say they were delighted is an understatement," Linda told him. "It's beautiful, and they expect it to fill up in record time." Decisions had been made to locate the reception in the public room, and Linda took a list of people the client wanted invited and added it to a short list she and Joe had compiled of people they felt it would be beneficial for Black Capital to have present.

Joe was chafed by all of it. *Damn it all, anyway. I'm the head of the company and I should be the one there dealing with the customers.* He had to admit that his team, Linda, Ashton, and Josie, were doing a great job. The fact that Josie had finished the job on crutches and Ashton with an arm almost useless while it healed made him even more impatient that he was stuck at White Mountain.

Every day seemed like an eternity to everyone involved with the Eagles Peak project, but there was nothing much to be done to speed things up. It took time for invitations to go out and be returned and arrangements to be made. That time was a problem for him in more ways than one. Every day Gwen inserted herself into the plan for the celebration in some fashion. She couldn't be excluded from the event because she was the company salesperson. *At least so far.* Joe gritted his teeth. She had on more than one occasion called the client and suggested changes to the plans already made. It had made for confusion and the chance of things not getting done in a timely fashion.

Gwen was still coming out to the White Mountain site every couple of days and making a big fuss over Joe. He made a supreme effort to get a grip on his temper and spent half a day cajoling her into leaving it all to Linda. She consented through tears as she snuggled up to him to be comforted for the imagined slight to her position and authority. When he finally got her on the chopper headed back to Anchorage, he was more tired than if he had been putting up trusses all day.

Josie was staying until the celebration instead of going home and coming back. She was off the crutches now and wearing a brace as well as doing some physical therapy. She rested, spent time with Seyma, went to the office, and helped Linda with anything she could. She had dinner a couple of times with Ashton, always to discuss business.

The day of the ceremony dawned clear and bright, foretelling a beautiful day to come. Joe had flown home late the night before leaving Griffin in charge with instructions to call at the slightest thing that might be cause for concern.

"Good morning, Joe." Josie was up early feeding Seyma.

"Good morning, Josie. Looks like we're going to have a good day to do this."

"Dad!" Art came barreling down the hallway. He and Renee had been long in bed when Joe arrived the night before, and Art was bouncing off the walls to find Joe home this morning. "Are you home for good? Can we stay home from school today? When did you get here?"

Renee came running after hearing her brother. She was screaming with excitement but instead of questions, threw herself into Joe's arms.

Joe laughed as he swung her up in the air. "I probably will have to go back to the site." He answered Art. "I got home really late, almost the middle of the night last night and no, you cannot skip school." He hugged them both.

Breakfast and getting the kids ready for school was a scramble. They were much more interested in their father than getting ready to leave. Mrs. Ramsey patiently and forcefully moved them along, and then after extended hugs and kisses it was time to leave. Quiet descended on the apartment broken only by Seyma's quiet playing with her toys in the living room.

"I know you're relieved to get this over with." Josie commented as she straightened the kitchen.

"You have no idea." Joe sighed and settled at the kitchen bar with a bowl of cereal.

"Do you have any clue who is causing all this trouble?"

Joe sighed and studied his spoon a moment. "I'm working on finding out. I hope to get it solved soon."

"Good. I've never seen anything like this before." Josie wiped a plate dry and placed it on a stack in the cabinet. "Joe?"

"Yes."

Josie turned around, dishtowel in her hands and leaned back against the counter. "Why isn't Linda happy? What's happened to her up here?"

Joe stopped eating, and looking down he pinched his nose between his eyes for a moment. "Linda is, isn't... ah, hell. I don't know what her problem is. I have to get ready to go."

He left the kitchen abruptly, and Josie heard the door slam to his bedroom. "Wow. Guess I ruffled some feathers," she spoke softly. "Come on Seyma. You can play while you watch Mommy get ready to go to the party."

* * *

By eleven everyone had arrived, and the stage was set for the big handover. A caterer had everything set up in the public room and was ready to feed the crowd when they were ready. Tours had been given beforehand to those interested in one. A newspaper reporter and his photographer and a local TV station had set up in the spots they thought would give them the best coverage.

Joe decided it was time and exchanged a look and a brief nod with Linda. They moved in unison to gather the crowd together, get the owners and new manager in place, and get things moving. They had done this many times in the last few years and needed little if any communication on what was needed. Gwen had been a flighty and noisy presence the entire morning. Joe had managed to avoid her as much as possible.

Introductions were made, and Joe gave a brief speech about what a pleasure it was to work for the client. Then the client gave a speech of thank yous' and symbolic keys were presented. A yellow tape was cut that had at the last minute been fastened across the doorway. Afterwards the client launched into the advantages of his new luxury apartments and what they offered. He eventually introduced his new manager and advised everyone that informative pamphlets were to be had on tables in the public room. When he had run out of things to expound on he urged them on to the public room for lunch.

At that point it was done. Joe felt a ten ton load lift off his shoulders. He knew Linda, Ashton, and Josie felt the same way to some extent. He looked around smiling happily, looking for Linda in the crowd and was suddenly enveloped in a huge hug— by Gwen.

Kissing him on the cheek she laughed and spoke loud enough for the media, who had not yet moved inside, to hear easily. "Oh, Joe, I'm so proud of you and to have been part of this project. You're just wonderful."

Joe stiffened and firmly moved her backward. "That's enough, Gwen. You hear me? You're making a scene, and it's to stop now. Understand?" He turned and moved away only to see Linda watching from near the doorway. When she saw him looking at her she turned and followed the crowd inside.

His shoulders slumped. For a few minutes he had been happy, proud of this achievement and wanting to share it with Linda. It was Gwen, he knew that. Why was Linda so damn jealous of her anyway. Didn't she trust him? And why in hell couldn't Byron get some information on this case so he could get rid of Gwen? A member of the crowd came up and began babbling about how nice it all was, and he pasted on a plastic smile and pretended to listen. That took just enough time for Gwen to reappear.

Taking his arm with one hand she extended the other to the person babbling to him. "Hello! I'm Gwen Smith, Black Capital's sales manager. I'm so glad to meet you," she simpered. "Isn't it all just so wonderful? All due to our handsome boss, don't you agree?" She beamed up at Joe.

"Thank you for the good words." He turned his plastic smile on the person. "Gwen will tell you about her part in it. I have to check on the reception."

He found Linda, and they exchanged congratulations, heartfelt if somewhat chilly. Josie crossed his path looking happy and pleased. Finding Ashton he motioned him to the side.

"Is everything done here?" Joe asked.

"I made sure of it. I've even turned the keys over to them. Didn't want anything hanging fire here so to speak. As soon as we get the caterers and the public out of here and clean up after them we're done. They're keeping some of the guards and bringing in some of their own. The rest of the guards have already got word this is their last day. The manager will be staying here tonight and opening the place tomorrow. I tried to cover every angle."

"You've done an exceptional job, above and beyond for the entire project. I assume you want to stay on, in spite of all that's happened?"

"I do. I hope you have a place for me. My arm will be back in shape soon."

"As a matter of fact, I do. Bring your things and meet me at the helipad tomorrow morning for the flight to White Mountain. I want you to be the site manager there now that you're done here. I'll fly out with you and show you what I want you to be aware of and why. Then I'll fly back tomorrow night."

"I appreciate the confidence. Thank you very much. I'll try and do a good job for you."

"You already have or you wouldn't be going to White Mountain." Joe shook Ashton's hand firmly.

* * *

The old fishing trawler rolled gently as the sea water undulated beneath it. Rodney waited in the bow while another man eased the old boat closer to a sleek little yacht. A ladder was lowered, and the trawler drifted close enough to gently bump the yacht. Rodney grabbed the ladder. The trawler moved off but remained close enough to make contact in a few short minutes if necessary.

Rodney surveyed the deck around him and the luxury it represented. The captain moved forward. "This way, sir."

A few steps down and Rodney was in an elegantly appointed main salon with large spans of windows overlooking the sea. Plush couches and chairs circled it. Occupying a large swivel chair and holding a drink in one hand, Senator Robard appeared to be every bit the wealthy society statesman. Rodney knew better. Even now Alaska was not overpopulated, and when he had been a kid it was even more sparse. While not in the same group of kids, he and the senator had certainly known each other. The senator's roots had been only marginally better than Rodney's, and both had grown up well versed in the ins and outs of illegal deals. Their contact had lessened as the senator's ambitions increased and had become nonexistent when he decided to enter politics.

Rodney grinned. "Long time, Alfred." He looked around the room and spotting the bar went and helped himself.

"Help yourself, Rodney." The senator spoke with the familiarity of an old acquaintance.

Rodney took a seat facing the senator. "You've come a long way. Looks like you done right good for yourself." He stopped and took a drink, studying the glass with appreciation. "Damn good taste in liquor too." His eyes swiveled back to the senator, and his grin disappeared. "All these years you been on top of the heap and doing good. Now you send for me. Must mean you got a serious problem to be calling me. Want me to guess what it is?"

"You're obnoxious, Rodney, always were. Yes, I got a goddamn problem."

"Wouldn't have if you hadn't let Gwen get into it. She's got the hots for that Black guy. She ain't going to let anything bad happen to him. Thinks he's going to marry her and carry her off back to California. She's a nut case. What's worse is you can't depend on her. She'll start out in one direction and then get a bee in her butt and go off some other way. That's dangerous, Alfred."

"Tell me something I don't know. Okay, here's the story. My cousin can't compete with this Black Capital outfit. I've sunk a ton of money in his business the last few years, and he's about to belly up. Gwen was supposed to see that Black Capital had problems up here and lost so much money that they'd go back home with their tail between their legs. Was working pretty good with the first guy, but then he left and this one showed up. He's part of the family, and he's been a hard nut to crack. Then Gwen got the hots for him and thinks he's going to marry her. Jesus! Why would anyone marry her?"

The senator finished off the last of his drink and pulled out a cigar. When he had it lighted to his satisfaction, he leaned his head back and focused on Rodney. "I can't wait any longer. Now the law's involved in the fire at White Mountain. They finished the apartments, and that's now out of their hands. You screwed up on both of those."

Rodney scowled and leaned forward in his chair. The senator held up his hand, palm out, stopping Rodney's retort.

"I know it's not a piece of cake doing a job like that, and things go wrong. But it has put me in a precarious position. I still need something done about this guy and his outfit, and I need it done soon. You're still the best out there. So do you think you could try once more to get it right?"

Rodney studied the senator with a sour expression. "Is Gwen involved in this one?"

"*Gwen?*" The name carried disgust. "She's not involved in anything on this anymore. I'm washing my hands of her, but I can't tell her that or she'll turn on me and tell this Black character everything. Like you said, she's not dependable and she blows both ways in the wind."

Rodney stood and went to the bar where he poured himself another drink. The senator joined him and did the same. They returned to their seats, and Alfred watched Rodney process the information.

"Yeah. Okay. I'll do it. What did you have in mind?"

"Nothing fancy this time. Just shoot the son-of-a bitch. But make no mistake, I want him dead."

"What if there's accidental casualties?"

"Long as it don't come back on us I don't give a damn."

Rodney nodded. "This is going to cost you a bundle, you know?"

"How big a bundle?"

"Enough to set me up with a fishing operation and a boat to import goods. I plan to be a power on the docks."

"You trying to muscle Bull out of that spot?"

"Maybe. Bull's getting old."

Alfred held his drink up to Rodney. "You just do a good job for me, and you'll have your boats." They drank to each other, and Rodney climbed the steps back to the deck where the captain walked with him to the rope ladder. Rodney waved to the man in his trawler, and it eased closer. His descent was quick, and he jumped the last few feet to the trawler's deck. Turning to the yacht as the trawler swung away and increased speed, he smiled and gave the man standing in the yacht's wide windows a salute.

* * *

CHAPTER TWENTY

Gwen watched her father's cabin turn from a tiny speck below her to normal size as the chopper descended to the small clearing in front of it. She hated this place and the memories of growing up here, but it was remote and relatively safe, which, considering Bull's line of work, could be important. She wondered why Bull—she never called him father—spent so much time here. She had often thought maybe he kept a large cache of money or something valuable here but had never been able to find anything tangible to support her theory. Of course there was Mit, but he could have a woman like Mit anywhere he went. Then again, she did serve to keep anyone from snooping around and finding anything when he wasn't here.

Leaving the company pilot, who she paid well for these little private trips, to stretch his legs and wait in the shade of the trees near the chopper, she strode off to the cabin. Inside she found Bull at the primitive table studying a spiral bound ledger book.

"Counting your money?" She took a seat across from him.

"Have to keep track of things or you end up with nothing to keep track of." Bull slapped the ledger shut. "What do you want, and how did you know I was up here?"

"You weren't anyplace else so you had to be here. As for what I want, I would like for that scum Rodney to do what he claims he can do. He's screwed up and failed on both the last two jobs, and they were important ones that could have ended Black Capital or come close to it. I don't know who else to get, and I don't know how to make him deliver what he promises. I don't have much time."

"Mit! Bring a beer." He looked at Gwen. "Want one?" She nodded. "Bring two." He ordered. Mit sat two cans on the table and returned to the stove.

Bull leaned the chair back on its back legs and gave Gwen a knowing look. "I told you he was crazy and couldn't be trusted. But no, you couldn't be told a damn thing. Now you know I was right. You can't make him deliver on his promises unless he wants to. He don't have to have a reason not to. He's crazy, you get it? He does what strikes him at the minute and to hell with the consequences. As to who else you can get, I couldn't tell you. As to your time problem—that sounds like Senator Robard is getting impatient."

"He's not happy with Rodney."

"I'll bet he's less happy with you. He thought you could do the job, and you went and got big ideas about some rich bigshot marrying you. You got your priorities screwed up, and now you're in a bind."

"Everything was going fine until Rodney screwed up. I just need to show old Robard some progress, and he'll settle down."

"Don't you count on it. That company of his cousins is big and about to go under, and he owns a big piece of that pie. A lot of building going to be done here in Alaska the next few years, and he wants to skim the cream off that."

"You don't have to tell me about other companies. I know more about them than you do. I work with them, remember?"

"You're a disappointment, Gwen. You had a lot going for you, could have made something of yourself. But you have no common sense and even less self-control. You're going to get pulled under on this one. Robard will throw you to the wolves without a thought."

"I'll take care of Alfred. Is Rodney up in his hole of a camp?"

Bull shook his head. "Nope. Not that I know of, and there's no reason I wouldn't. I did hear he took a trawler out the other day. He's been around the docks a lot lately. My gut tells me he wants to get into smuggling in a big way, be a big man on the docks."

"You don't mean replace you?"

Bull pursed his lips and nodded. "Possible. He's got no common sense either. I'll keep an eye on him."

Gwen sighed. "Damn. If you see him in the next couple of days tell him I need to talk to him."

Bull nodded. "I'll do that." He studied her carefully. "Gwen?"

"Yeah?"

"You never did listen to me, but I'm going to tell you the most important thing I've ever tried to tell you." He waited a minute for her attention to focus completely on him. "This thing you are involved in has the potential to go really, really bad. I will not be dragged into it because you're my kid. I will not bail you out of this in any way. You're as bad as Rodney, and you can't be relied on. You've gone nuts over this Black guy, and it's going to get you put in jail or worse if you cross swords with Rodney. And I cannot help you."

Gwen's forehead wrinkled in a frown, and she scowled at Bull. "Can't or won't?"

"Same thing. I've done a lot of stuff over the years that could have put me away for a long time or even on death row. But I was careful and protected myself and used what you and Rodney are lacking—common sense. You think all this over carefully before you go do something else hair-brained."

Gwen slammed the beer can down on the table and stood abruptly. "You go to hell. I don't need you. Someday you'll be the one crawling to me for help."

Bull shook his head and watched her toss her head and walk out the door.

Gwen motioned to the pilot that they could leave, and as the chopper rose she thought back to Bull's face as she left. It was hard, the look that had made hardened criminals back off from trouble with him. Yet, had she seen just a touch of sadness or disappointment under it too? One thing she did know. He meant what he said. He had never cut her or anyone else any slack over the years, and he wouldn't start now. She only had one way left that she could see and that was to get Joe married and tied to her. She would start working on that as soon as she got back to the office.

* * *

Bull listened to the chopper lifting off. He could picture where it was as it moved further away by the diminishing roar of its engines. This thing Gwen had gotten involved in was going to go down bad. She was going to get herself killed messing with Rodney. He supposed he should feel some sadness, but he'd known long ago that Gwen would never be anything but trouble. Made him glad he didn't have any other kids—that he knew about anyway. Of course if Rodney got her killed he would have to kill Rodney. That was a matter of retribution, of honor, an eye for an eye.

He walked to the door and leaning one hand on the doorframe stood looking out at the woods. "Mit! Beer."

She padded softly to his side and handed him the beer. He looked at her as if she had just materialized out of thin air. Her eyes never met his, and she turned and padded back to the stove where she seemed to spend all her time. When she wasn't at the stove she was with the dogs.

"At least you're one that don't give me no trouble. Wonder why you haven't spawned any brats? Native brats wouldn't have caused me near as much trouble. Gotta say you turned out good. You work hard. You train the best dog team in Alaska even though we don't run them."

"If something happens to Gwen, and Rodney bests me, you'll be a wealthy heathen. That is if you can find the money. I've got it in banks all over the country. That'd be a joke wouldn't it? All that work over all those years. and I got all this money, and then it goes to the state cause nobody knows it's there." He took a long swig of his beer. "Can't tell Gwen I got it though. She'd go bananas to get it right away."

"Hey, Mit!" he hollered. She turned from the stove, face expressionless as always. "You understand this?" She nodded. "Yeah? What am I talking about?"

Mit frowned, thinking. "Gwen—money?" She met his eyes now as if waiting for him to praise her.

Bull sneered and shook his head. "Stupid heathen. You aren't as smart as those dogs you take care of." He let the empty beer can fly hard at her. It was a common occurrence and she ducked, letting it just miss her.

He snorted and laughed, then turned and walked out of the cabin, throwing over his shoulder as he did, "Put my pack together. I'm leaving."

She hurried to do as she was told and carried it out to him where he already had a saddle on his horse. He seemed distracted, probably because of Gwen. He tied the pack on and without a word to her rode away. How long he would be gone or where he was going was not information for her and never had been. She turned and went back into the cabin where she watched from the window as he disappeared down the trail leading into the woods and on to what Mit thought of as the outside world.

It wasn't until she turned around that she spotted the spiral ledger still laying on the table. Cold fear flooded her. He would remember and be back. Would he beat her? It wasn't something he ever let her pack for him. She didn't want to move it, but it couldn't lay on the table for long. What if Rodney or someone came by and it was there. She didn't want to touch it but she would have to if he didn't come back soon. She would hide it until he did came back.

She alternated looking out the door or window for him to return and circling the table as if it were a snake ready to strike. This was information about his business. The men that had come here were interested in Bull as well as Rodney. Would they like to see this? They weren't here. Maybe she should call them. The phone was still hidden behind the last doghouse. But what if he came back while she had it out? She continued to circle the table.

She stopped suddenly. She wanted out of this life, and so far these men that had come were the only chance she had found. She wasn't sure if helping them would set her free or get her killed, but she needed to try something. Gathering up her courage she headed out to feed the dogs. At the last doghouse she moved behind it and dug under the leaves and debris and then lifted the flat rock under it all. There was the small waterproof pouch that contained the phone. Shadows of the evening were darkening around her as she sat against the trunk of a tree watching for any sign of movement or sound around her. Then she touched the pre-programmed number the men had put in the phone and listened as they had taught her. It was answered immediately.

"Hello, this is Harry."

"This is Mit."

"Mit, what's going on? Are you all right?"

"Bull left. He leave book about his business on table. Forgot it. He come back when he think of it. You want to see? You come?"

"How long until he could come back?"

"Few minutes, day or two, don't know."

"We can't get there that soon. Mit, the phone you are using will take pictures. Remember we showed you that?"

"I not know how to do that."

"Can you take the phone, and I will talk you through how to take a picture of every page. Okay?"

Mit was silent. She didn't think she could do it.

"Mit? You still there?"

"Yes."

"Will you try? I will talk you through how to do it step by step. All right?"

"I try. Wait." She quickly scattered the leaves over the hiding place and ran back to the cabin. "Okay," she spoke into the phone. "What I do?"

"How many pages are there, Mit?"

She carefully counted them. "Twenty-one, both sides."

"Twenty-one pages with writing on both sides?"

"Yes."

"Wow, okay Mit here we go." He carefully walked her through how to do it and then she hung up and tried taking and sending the first one. Then she called him back.

"Great, Mit. That one came through just fine. Now hang up and do five in a row and then call me. That way if there is a problem with them coming through I can help you with it. Okay?"

"Okay." She went back to work. Working slowly and constantly repeating the instructions to herself, it took her two hours to finish. She was drenched in sweat by the time she was done.

"That all," she told Harry.

"Mit, you have no idea how important this is. We are getting good information from the other machine too. This should be over soon. Now you go hide that phone and do whatever you have to do to protect yourself. Okay?"

"Okay." She hung up and taking a small oil lamp, made her way into the now dark night and down the familiar pathway to the last dog house. Leaves rustled as she frantically cleared the hole out and replaced the phone in its pouch. The rock followed and then the leaves and sticks, and she convinced herself no one would ever suspect it held a secret beneath it. Putting the lamp out she made her way back in the dark and slipped into the house.

A cold sheen of sweat clung to her, and her heart pounded. Had she done it? Was Bull out there watching her, about to burst in and beat her up, kill her when he found out what she was doing?

She couldn't leave the book on the table, so she slipped it under the mattress. She would tell Bull she hid it there in case someone came. Then she herself slipped into bed and lay there racked with fear listening for any unusual noises that might be Bull.

* * *

Miles away in Anchorage, Jake and Harry sat pouring over the photos she had sent.

"I'll send these to Byron tonight. That will start his day off right when he comes in tomorrow. This doesn't really help us with the Black Capital investigation but it's a nice bonus." Harry was pleased with himself.

"Yeah, but we're getting some dynamite stuff off that recorder. I just hope they don't find it or our little gal is dead."

* * *

It was barely noon when Mit heard the pounding of horse's hooves coming up the lane. It would be Bull, and the fact that he was running the horse told her how upset he was. She stood at the stove and unnecessarily stirred the stew. When he burst through the door she turned.

"My book!" He yelled, his face a thundercloud. "Where's my book?"

"Under mattress." She struggled to look calm and stoic.

He rushed to the bed and flinging the mattress in the air grabbed the book. "Did anyone see this?"

"No one here."

His shoulders slumped in obvious relief. "Fix me a plate of stew and then go tend to my horse. I'll give him an hour or so and then I gotta go." He tucked the book inside his shirt.

Mit went to do as she was told, trying to control the trembling in her hands.

* * *

Linda switched on her office light and crossed the room where she dropped heavily into her desk chair. Her clothes were perfect, and her makeup had been applied with care. As far as her exterior appearance she was exquisite. But looking more closely, her makeup didn't completely hide the dark crescents under her eyes and in this early morning hour, alone, she allowed her shoulders to slump as if their weight was too much to carry.

She had texted Joe and asked him to stop by the office this morning before heading out by chopper with Gwen to meet with a prospective customer. He had replied that he would but hadn't said what time. Heaving herself to her feet, she went to the filing cabinet and pulled the Carmody file. Feeling the need for a jump start this morning she inserted a coffee pod in the machine on the counter behind her desk and watched the dark liquid pool in the cup. She took her first sip just as she heard the front door open and close. She glanced at her watch, only twenty minutes until 8:00 A.M. Must be Joe. None of the others would usually come in early.

A few seconds later Joe entered, carrying his own coffee mug. "You've been working late a lot, and you're in here early again." He sat on the corner of her desk. "I'm not aware of anything we have going that should require you working extra hours." His voice sounded puzzled and a bit wary, she thought.

"That's why I asked you to come in this morning. I'm about to make you aware." Her voice was controlled, no hint of emotion as she reached for a file laying on her desk. "This is the Carmody file."

"We start that project Monday. What about it?"

"It has several miscalculations. We need to rewrite it and have the customer sign a new accurate contract." Her eyes challenged him.

"We can correct our copies and adjust it as we go along. Customers expect some changes."

"And if anything happens and the customer ever sues, he has a signed incorrect contract from us." She rose and walked to a file cabinet and put her hand on top of it. "It isn't the only one. I've gone back to the beginning when this office opened. Eighty percent of them have errors that could cause legal problems."

"You're going to so much trouble because Gwen wrote up the contracts." He slammed the mug down, sloshing coffee over the desk. He stood and faced Linda, feet apart, ready for combat.

Linda's jaw clenched and nostrils flared. She moved gracefully back to her chair behind the desk. "That's all then. It's my job to make you aware of what's not done correctly. I have nothing else. Thank you for coming."

Joe turned on his heel and strode out, slamming the door behind him.

Linda sat stiffly at her desk and listened to Joe stomp down the hall and out the front door. She had been sure he would have been appalled at the contract situation. Joe was a stickler for doing things right. Instead he was angry with her. She wished Joe's father, Billy, would make a visit to this office. But he was obviously taking a hands off approach. Giving Joe a chance to sink or swim by himself. Then again, Linda began to finally face the painful fact, what could even Billy do about the fact that Joe was in love with Gwen?

A tear escaped and began to trickle down her cheek at the same time she heard the front door open again. That would be Seth or Lela coming in for work. She quickly grabbed a tissue and blinking rapidly, dabbed away all evidence of the tears. Linda Sloan didn't cry, she reminded herself—ever.

* * *

Joe stomped all the way to his SUV and sat with his hands gripping the steering wheel in a death grip. How could Gwen have been so careless as to put the company in a position like this? Or maybe it wasn't carelessness, maybe it was deliberate. He pulled out the phone he used when he called Byron.

"Joe, I'm glad you called. I was going to try calling you tonight."

"Hopefully one of us has some good news."

"That doesn't sound good. What's happened?"

Joe quickly explained the situation to Byron. "I need to start correcting those contracts, but I don't want to tip our hand."

"Linda found all this?"

"Yes, and I can tell you she's pissed that I'm not doing anything about it."

"You need to tell her Joe. But in any case I think you can go ahead and start correcting things. Linda was checking things and found problems. I don't think it will tip our hand if you don't blame Gwen."

"Okay, I'll give Linda the go-ahead when I get back tonight. But I'm not telling her anything until I know the company and all of us are safe, especially her and the kids."

"Well, maybe that won't be too long. We just got some good stuff, and as soon as we can nail it down better for the police and courts we'll be set to move."

"Do you know who's behind it?"

"We're pretty sure. But we need to tie it to him before I accuse anyone. I'm working on that now."

Joe ground his teeth. "All right, Byron, but let me know the second I can fire Gwen."

"I will. Don't get discouraged, Joe. We're close, very close."

* * *

CHAPTER TWENTY-ONE

Linda tiredly put away the payroll records. They were finished and ready for the checks to be issued Monday morning. It had been a week since Linda had talked to Joe about the contracts. He had come back and admitted that they couldn't be ignored and then had cajoled Gwen into going with him to the customers to have them sign the corrected contract. Gwen had thrown herself into the role of playing the oh-so-contrite little girl that had made a mistake. It was all a show for Joe's benefit, but it would probably work well on the customer.

She surveyed her office, wishing there was something else she could stay and work on, but she had so completely organized things that there was nothing left to dig into. Her earlier routine was to have dinner with Joe and the kids when he was home and with the kids when he wasn't. Whatever happened between them, the kids shouldn't be living 24-7 with just the housekeeper, no matter how good she was with them. But lately things had been strained and he hadn't seemed to want her around. So she wasn't sure if she should show up for dinner tonight or not. Joe would be home all weekend if all went according to his plan. The way things were between them, maybe she should give him a chance to be with the kids without her. She had been almost a surrogate mother to them for a long time now, but if things didn't work out Joe would be all they had.

She had forgotten to breathe and her body took over with a ragged gulp of air that shook her back to reality. But the subject of her thoughts wouldn't go away. If she had it to do over again she wouldn't let herself come to love kids that weren't hers, or let them get so attached to her. She was filling a mother's role, and she had known this for quite some time now. She had thought she was going to be their mother though. Joe had even talked about it. Then they came here and it all went away. He met Gwen.

Lela appeared at her door. "A delivery man is here with a special delivery envelope for you. He says it's marked private, and he has to have you sign it." She waited for Linda's okay.

"Send him in." Linda was almost relieved that something else was turning up that would keep her here just a while longer.

The young man handed her a clipboard. She signed the receipt, and he handed over the brown manila envelope. He was out of the office and on his way before she noticed that the delivery had no return address.

Curious now, Linda applied a sharp edged letter opener to the security tape on the envelope and looked inside. It appeared to hold pictures. She tipped it up and three glossy prints slid onto her desk pad.

"What in the world?" Linda didn't grasp at first glance what she was looking at. *"Why would someone send her pictures of naked...* Her arms and legs turned to concrete, legs trapping her in her chair so she couldn't get up, arms too heavy to lift. She wanted to push them apart, look closer, but she couldn't move. There was an enormous drum in her head that was beating rapidly in time with her heart. She swayed slightly and subconsciously realized she was close to passing out. She leaned forward and let her head drop onto the desk and closed her eyes. It felt like the room was a tilt-a-whirl at a carnival, and her stomach threatened to reject its contents. Eventually her heart slowed, and she began to breathe. She opened her eyes and the room settled down. She didn't think she passed out, but she was never sure afterwards.

Head still on the desk she continued to concentrate on breathing. She realized what she had seen in her first brief look. She needed to look again. She had to sit up, but it seemed such an enormous job. She had to though. Lela and Seth would stop by to say goodnight and check if she needed anything more. She had to look normal. The concrete in her arms seemed to be going away so she sat up. Without focusing on the pictures she picked up the envelope and dropped it over them, then leaned back in her chair and waited.

It wasn't long until Seth stopped by and bid her goodnight. Lela followed a few minutes later. Linda had asked her once why she never left until Seth, Gwen, and Joe were gone, and she said Wallace told her not to. Once Linda heard Lela close the front door she laid the pictures out side by side and studied them, carefully this time. Her stomach roiled a bit as she looked but she was getting over the shock now and would have to deal with this knowledge, not just collapse and ignore it.

Both Joe and Gwen were naked. All three pictures showed Gwen on top. In one she was on her hands and knees leaning over him, her breast in his mouth. Another she had her head buried between his legs. The third one she sat astride him, riding him, her hands holding her breasts up to titillate.

This was it, Linda realized. The thing she had been fearing. The end of her life as she had been expecting it to be. What had she done wrong? She had gone to bed with Joe, but they had been discrete because of the children. Was Gwen that much better in bed than she was? Was that why he hadn't seemed to want to spend time with her since she'd come to Alaska? Did Joe just like Gwen's type better than Linda's?

Whatever the reason it was over now, and she had to move on. She had experienced her moment of pain and now she would bury it and continue to do her duty to the company until the moment came for her to leave.

She slipped the pictures back in the envelope and placed them in the safe at the back, behind the journals and current work she was doing. The heavy door swung slowly shut. She made sure it was locked. Picking up her handbag she switched off the light, locked the door to her office, and headed for her apartment.

Glad that she didn't run into Mrs. Ramsey and the kids in the elevator or the hallway, she entered her silent apartment and locked the door behind her. A thoughtful look around showed her an apartment that really hadn't been lived in. She'd spent more time in Joe's apartment across the hall than she had here. She'd rarely eaten anything here, and if she did it was more fast food or snacks while she was on the run with a busy schedule. There were a few personal items but no decorations. The focus of her life had been across the hall in Joe's apartment and at the office, helping to run his company.

She checked the kitchen cabinets and found a can of soup and some stale crackers. She wasn't hungry but she had once been athletic and she knew that sooner or later she needed to eat or her body would let her down. Now, of all times, she needed to be strong. She managed to choke down some tomato soup with the stale crackers soaked in it. As she ate, she planned. She would make a list of things to be done and their priority. She would do them one at a time and not think about the future. Once back home, she would go to her parent's house for a short time while she decided which direction to go with her life. Now she just wanted to get away from here with as little notice as possible.

Going to the spare bedroom that she had never bothered to do anything with but use for storage, she pulled out a couple of boxes from the stack she had never disposed of when they came here.

I wonder if that was a premonition. She sighed and began taping the boxes. First were the things she wanted to take back with her. Other things she set aside in boxes for donating to charity. It was pathetic really, how little she had. A medium size wardrobe of quality clothing, a couple of sets of sheets and bath towels. Even her kitchen only sported a setting of dishes and silverware for four. Her furniture was nice and had been moved here when she came, but she had no desire to take it back with her. It would be a reminder of her life before today, and she wanted a clean slate when she left—had to have it that way or she couldn't stand it.

Her phone buzzed, and she checked it. It was Joe, probably wanting to know why she wasn't there for dinner. Sure enough, when she opened it the text asked where she was.

"Sorry," she answered. "Have a headache, going to bed early. Have shopping and errands to take care of this weekend, so I'll see you at work."

He answered with, "Can I come over and do something? Get you something?"

She tamped down the urge to respond with, "No, just leave me alone!" and responded instead with, "No, thank you anyway." In a few days he would be free to have Gwen to dinner. The idea of Gwen having dinner with the kids truly did give her a headache so she went to bed.

* * *

Monday morning Joe called for the chopper and headed out to inspect the site of a prospective new customer who had contacted him. Gwen would be mad as a wet hen that he hadn't included her, but he would deal with that when he got back.

The chopper found a big cleared area near the small structure on the water's edge. They were about a hundred miles from Anchorage on the coast. The property was a small cannery about a mile from the nearest town. The owner wanted to build a new facility and tear down the existing one.

A man emerged from the building when the chopper approached. He came forward wearing a large smile and holding out his hand. Joe guessed from his appearance, dark but not as dark as most Native Americans, short but not as short as most, that he was of mixed blood. They shook hands and the man's grip was firm.

"Mr. Black! So happy to have you come here. To be honest, I did not think this job would be big enough for you to bother with."

Joe smiled. "Call me Joe. I like to think no job is too big or too small for us to bother with as long as we can do it." They walked toward the building, talking as they went. "Tell me about this place and what exactly you're wanting to do."

An hour later they sat on wooden folding chairs on a dock. Joe now had the story of the business. The owner, Yancy Washington, had started a small fishing business about a mile out of the nearest village when he was a young man. He had done well and over the years had hired many people. He paid them well, and twice a month the catch was distributed among them. Now he was nearing sixty years old, operating at capacity and needed more space and wanted to buy new modern equipment. He wanted to build a modern facility to leave to his family and employees.

"Do you realize, Yancy, just how expensive this is going to be?" Joe asked gently, trying not to be offensive because he liked the man and admired what he had done.

The older man smiled happily at Joe. "Yes, Joe, I do. I will share something with you because it is necessary to making our deal. No one but my financial manager in Seattle knows, not even my family, especially my family." He laughed. "I am a very wealthy man. I graduated from high school. That was very unusual here when I was young, but my father was white and thought I should go at least that far in school. He hadn't been able to and always felt less of himself because of it. I was a very good student, and the business classes fascinated me. After I graduated I kept reading books and magazines about business and investing. I worked hard and always saved a little money out of what I made. After two years I got married and couldn't save as much, but after five years I was able to buy this property. Then I could fish on the side as well as work. After a while I fished only. Then I found I could sell more than just my own fish, so I started to buy from others, and this business was born. We worked out of our two room house at first and added space as we needed it and because my wife and I needed help with the fish.

He stopped and smiled at Joe again and raised his eyebrows. "But that isn't the whole story. You see, before I married I made a trip to Seattle. I wanted to invest my money. I had read all about it. I didn't want to do it with anyone here in Alaska where they knew me or might talk about me. In Seattle nobody cares. So I went there to find an investment man for my money. I went to all the major companies, and they would look at this half Indian kid in my clothes that looked tacky to them but were the best I had and the little amount of money I had and wouldn't even talk to me."

He laughed and continued. "The joke was on them. I happened to be shuffled off to this young guy just starting out, and no one wanted to put their money with him because he *was* young and had no experience. Well, I was young too, and he was the best I was going to get, so I gave him my money. Every year since then I go to Seattle and give him more. He is now one of the most successful investment brokers in Seattle. In fact, he is an officer and only has a handful of clients now. I'm one of them. He has paid me back thousand's fold for having faith in him. He has made me a wealthy man. So, yes Joe, I can easily afford whatever it takes." He leaned back and waited for a reply.

Joe chuckled. "I admire you, Yancy. You remind me of my father. He started Black Capital with nothing. He ran it out of a cheap apartment off a card table and fed my sister and I peanut butter and jelly, but he made it." Joe was silent for a moment. "So now that I know we don't have financial constraints, let's talk about this project. It's a bit different than the usual because you sit right on the ocean, and we have to do a lot of testing to make sure we have good footings. Part of this will be new docks and a breaker wall. I'll subcontract those things. I'll find someone good to do that as it is so specialized, but we will still be responsible if there is a problem."

"Sounds good. I researched Black Capital, and you are the best and have a great reputation. When can we start?"

"I'll get it started right away. I want to bring in an architect from California, have him come up here for a few days and work with you on what you need. Tell him any and all equipment you'll be buying and how much room it takes and so on. Plan in advance so you don't wish ten years from now that you had added another ten feet. Also I want to see if we have someone who has experience in building things right on the water's edge like this. We'll try to put it where you want it, but a lot may depend on where we can put good footings under it. If we decide to put it in the same location as your current building, you are going to have to shut down during construction."

"I would prefer it to not be right where we are, but if that is best we can go with that."

"Good. I'll get a man up here, and we'll talk after he has something for us."

"We have a deal, Joe." Yancy held his hand out to shake on it.

"We sure do." Joe leaned forward and sideways to reach the older man's hand. Somewhere in the middle of that move a thunderbolt moved across his shoulder. His breath came out in a huge puff as he toppled sideways out of his chair. Before Joe hit the dock, Yancy was in motion, moving like he had never seen a day of his sixty years. Disregarding the fact that Joe had been shot, the old man gave him a massive shove and rolled him off the dock, diving over himself at the same time.

Tide was low and they landed in only a couple of feet of water. Yancy grabbed Joe and helped him sit up. He starting shouting toward the building in a language Joe didn't understand. No one came out, but Joe heard what he thought sounded like windows opening and lever action rifles being readied for action.

"We need to get you inside." The old man spoke to Joe.

"I'm okay," Joe's voice trembled. He looked at the dock above. "He's still out there."

"I think, no. I sent men out with rifles to find him. Either they find and kill him or he will leave quickly because he will know men are tracking him." A yell came from the area of the trees where the shot had come from.

The old man smiled. "All is clear. Whoever he was, he is gone." By the time they waded out of the water and entered the building the sound of a motor could be heard. "That will be the closest we have to a doctor here. My wife will have called him. He was a medic and came here one summer many years ago to fish. He fell in love with us and stayed. He married my cousin."

Joe allowed Yancy to guide him to a straight backed chair at a table. He tried not to show how shaky he felt. "You're taking this pretty calmly. Do people shoot at you often up here?"

Yancy smiled. "We are pretty remote here. There are some bad elements that prowl the woods. We stay alert. But this, I think, was meant for you. I have followed your problems here in Alaska. I think someone doesn't like you, my friend."

A man Joe estimated to be in his early fifties entered carrying a black doctor's bag with him. Joe tried to think if he had ever seen one of those outside of a movie. The doctor had already been told it was a gunshot wound.

"Ah, glad to see you just have a graze. I wasn't looking forward to digging through anyone's interior today. I'm Marty, by the way."

"Glad to meet you, Marty. I'm Joe. Wish we had met under better circumstances."

Marty covered the red swath of flesh with antiseptic. Joe grit his teeth and held onto the chair. "You just lucky or did you piss somebody off?"

"Guess I'm just lucky." Joe answered. "Does this need any other attention? It's not that serious is it?"

The man tending him frowned. "Not really, unless it gets infected. If it doesn't heal and gets red and tender get yourself to a doctor. It's a deep graze and you're going to have a scar whether you see a doctor or not. Want some pain pills?"

"I'll be fine without them."

"I will get you some fish to pay you." Yancy hurried off.

"You're kidding?" Joe asked. "They pay you in fish around here?"

"They pay me in whatever they have," Marty smiled.

"In that case so will I." Joe retrieved a soggy billfold from his pocket. Pulling out five hundred dollars he handed it to Marty. "You may have to dry these out a little."

"You sure about this, man?"

"Oh, yeah. I'm very partial to medical care when I get shot."

Marty smiled, picked up his bag, and went to collect his fish.

When he was gone Joe had an honest discussion with Yancy about the problems Black Capital had been having. He was more than a little surprised to find that Yancy was already aware of them.

"You will find who is doing this. Here it is all about the money. As they say in the mystery books, 'Follow the money.'"

"So you aren't hesitant to have us do your job?"

"Send your man. Let's get started."

Joe sent his pilot to start the chopper up and was soon on his way. He went right home and thanks to his jacket managed to get past Mrs. Ramsey and the kids without them realizing anything was wrong. He changed into a loose sweat suit and joined them for dinner. Mrs. Ramsey cleaned up from dinner and left for home. By the time the kids went to bed, Joe was feeling the effects of a stressful day. He sat on the edge of his bed and called Byron. Once he had related the incident, he went on to explain that he hadn't reported it because there wasn't anyone there to report it to and no evidence to show them if anyone had been there. He could have told his story, and he had lots of people to testify it had happened, but in the end there was nothing they could do.

"Okay. I'm getting concerned about this but I think we almost have all the information we need. I think you can let Gwen go, but don't tip her off about us investigating."

"Thank God. My life may get better after all." Joe hung up and eased himself into bed gratefully, thinking maybe he should have taken a few of those pain pills.

* * *

Joe's shoulder was sore the next morning. It was difficult to bandage, so when he found the wound had dried he decided to try going without a bandage in favor of just being careful. He wore a silk shirt that would slide over it easily. A light jacket would have to do. By the time he had himself ready, the kids had eaten breakfast and were prepared to leave for school. He spent a few minutes with them before Mrs. Ramsey shooed them out the door.

Joe wasn't sure which way to go first this morning. At the top of his list was to terminate Gwen's employment with Black Capital. After he did that he would go talk to Linda. He still didn't want to tell her about the investigation details, but she would be happy to have Gwen gone. They could work on all the mistakes Gwen had made on the contracts. The tension between them would go away, and as soon as Byron gave the go ahead they would go to the law, and these attacks on Black Capital would stop. Then Linda and the kids would be safe and he could concentrate on them. On that note, he smiled. He needed to get to a jewelers and pick up a ring soon.

Joe took out his phone and wandered into the living room. His call was answered immediately. "Gwen, it's Joe. I want to see you this morning. Are you headed for the office?"

"Oh Joe honey, I'm in Juneau. But I can head right back and be there by noon."

"Won't do. I'm headed for White Mountain. I'll see you at the office later this afternoon." Joe ended the call before she had a chance to say anything else. He knew her well by now, and she would just start asking questions. He didn't want her to get suspicious. He wanted this to be quick, clean and final.

Linda answered her phone on the first ring. She had just arrived at the office. No, nothing needed his attention at the office. Yes, she was on top of the office work and had no problems to discuss with him. Did he need to speak with Seth or Gwen? Neither were in yet. Linda sounded clipped and stiff. He asked about her, and yes, she was fine, and yes it was a good day for him to go to White Mountain.

He had some feelings of relief. He did need to go up to the White Mountain site and check on Ashton to see how things were progressing there. He didn't want Linda to notice he had a problem with his shoulder. He thought he was handling the discomfort well, but Linda would notice if anyone did. Going to White Mountain should be a relaxing day. As far as he knew Ashton was having no problems. Although with what had happened yesterday, they could have trouble at any time. He would talk to Ashton, and then this afternoon he would take care of the Gwen problem. He ended the call to Linda and put another call in to the chopper pilot. He was loading to take the morning flight of supplies to White Mountain and assured

Joe they would be loaded and ready to leave by the time he arrived. In less than an hour he was in the air and on his way.

* * *

Gwen was beside herself. Joe asking her to come see him was a big change in his attitude. He was finally coming around to seeing what a catch she was, and now she could move forward quickly with her plans. A big wedding would be nice, maybe a couple of months from now. Of course if Joe was skittish about that she wouldn't be against a weekend elopement. She could come back as Mrs. Black, and wouldn't that show all of those who didn't think she could pull it off. Of course if she became Mrs. Black then she would take over Linda's position, and Linda would have to go.

In the meantime she would surprise Joe and just go to White Mountain and meet him there, show him how eager she was to please him. She called the pilot and arranged to meet him at the heliport as soon as possible. If they got off quickly they shouldn't be much over an hour behind Joe.

She made a quick call to cancel a customer meeting she had later in the morning and began throwing things in her suitcase. She was so pleased with the way things were finally going that she felt she was floating on a cloud of happiness.

* * *

Ashton was glad to see Joe and eager to show him around, bring him up to date on their progress. Joe, having missed breakfast at home, suggested they start with a verbal update while he got some breakfast in the meal tent. Everything he heard was good. He had made a solid decision when he picked Ashton to replace John. They were aware of the small far away thumping of a chopper coming in.

"You have two loads coming in this morning?" Joe asked.

Ashton shook his head. "No. The chopper you came on is all I have this morning."

Setting down their coffee mugs they left the tent and watched until the chopper came in sight and began to descend. Joe could see now that it was a Black Capital chopper and a sour knot formed in his belly. *Surely not! But—that would be just like her.* Sure enough, Gwen bounced out of the chopper and ran towards Joe.

"What in hell are you doing here?" Joe growled.

"Oh, honey, when you called me to come I wasn't going to make you wait until you got back home. I decided to go ahead and come join you." Gwen made a quick move toward Joe and managed to plaster herself against him. Wrapping her arms around his neck brought a sharp exclamation as Joe dropped his shoulder where Gwen's arm lay.

"What's the matter?" Gwen looked startled.

"Nothing." Joe stepped back from her. Frowning, he decided the day had just ceased to be enjoyable. He had planned to be more professional about this at the office and have a final check drawn up and all that. But with Gwen you could never keep anything professional. Just as well do it here and get it over with. The sooner she was out of the company the better.

"Is there someplace we can talk in private?" Joe asked Ashton.

"You can have my little office. Have Wallace and the man monitoring the security equipment take a break. It should be okay for a few minutes."

Gwen pursed her mouth and raised her eyebrows in an unanswered question. Joe nodded for her to follow him and turned toward the little building that served as office and for security monitoring. Once the two men had left the office, Joe turned to Gwen and motioned for her to take a chair sitting near the desk. He seated himself behind the desk.

"What's going on, honey? You look so serious."

"I am serious, Gwen. I'm truly sorry it has come to this, but in spite of everything anyone has tried to tell you nothing has changed." Joe paused and watched Gwen's face begin to settle into a defensive look.

"If this is something---," she began.

"No!" Joe stopped her in mid-sentence. "This has nothing to do with anyone but you, Gwen. You refuse to listen to others and learn how to do things in a professional way. You have been completely resistant to the business practices and ethics of this company. Rather than work with other employees to get the best job done for the customer, you demean them and undermine them. You have made mistakes that could put the company in a position of liability. I'm sorry, Gwen, but I'm letting you go. I'll see you in the morning and give you your final check or I can mail it if you would like. Please give me the keys to the main door and to your office."

Gwen sat immobile. Joe thought she looked like an alabaster statue. He watched in fascination at how her tightly compressed lips turned her normally pretty face into something ugly. Her struggle not to lash out was obvious, and he waited for it. It didn't come.

"Are you sure, Joe? I could help you be successful here. I love you, you know. We'd be so good together. You'll see. No other woman could satisfy you like I would."

"Gwen, you haven't cared so far about helping the company be successful here. As for loving me, you're like a teenager with a crush. I've never encouraged you in any way, and yet you refuse to get the message. I really think you have some growing up to do."

"It's Linda, isn't it? She's complained about me. This is her fault."

"Linda doesn't even know I'm letting you go. But speaking of Linda, you have done everything you could to make her life miserable and circumvent her efforts at the office. That sort of behavior doesn't work in business, Gwen, and I suggest you remember that in your next job. Now, give me your keys, please."

Gwen rose, and reaching into her pocket for her keys, she tossed them onto the desk. Giving him a look so malevolent it sent a chill down his spine, she spun around and walked out. She walked calmly to the chopper and speaking briefly to the pilot, got in and they took off.

Joe watched them leave. *Damn, the woman is toxic.* He could feel the weight lift off his shoulders now that she was gone. He would have to step into her job for a while until he was able to replace her, but eventually he would find someone. Soon they would know who was causing them all this trouble and that would be gone too. In the meantime, he decided, he better go tell Ashton about his being shot yesterday and make sure they were especially vigilant here until Byron was ready. He straightened his shoulders and went to find Ashton. The worst part of his day was over.

* * *

CHAPTER TWENTY-TWO

Linda's arms and legs felt wooden as she pushed the 'send' key down and watched the tab pop up telling her the message was on its way. It was done. She no longer belonged to the company that had been her home and family for the last seven years. That life ended with the resignation she'd just sent. She took inventory of her office and noted the neat stack of paperwork in the out basket, pen in its holder, telephone placed just right and the information binders lined up on the shelf in perfect order. Her desktop was clean of any work. She had been meticulous this morning after she made her decision to leave—leave her job, her life, and the man she had and still did love desperately.

Opening the bottom desk drawer she removed her handbag and stood, rolling her chair back in place out of habit. At the door she turned and took one more look at the room she had entered three months ago with such hope and enthusiasm. The door clicked softly as she pulled it shut behind her.

She paused at Seth's drafting room. She had hoped to say goodbye before she left. He hadn't been in the office all morning, eliminating any opportunity to thank him. He'd been a friendly and helpful presence in the office. Turning away, she nodded to Lela at the reception desk and walked purposefully out of the building for the last time.

At her apartment she poured a plastic cup full of wine. Her four glasses were packed and sealed in the box they would travel back in. Fortifying herself with a large gulp of wine she settled into a chair and took out her phone.

"What do you have leaving tonight for the states, direct to Denver or anything that will get me there?" She waited, absentmindedly taking another sip of the wine. "I see. No, that's all right. Put me on the LA flight and the first connection to Denver." She listened a moment. "Thank you." She moved her thumb across the disconnect button.

She supposed she should be crying, but she'd steeled herself not to cry. That could come later, sometime when she was more removed from here, a long way from here. She would visit her parents while she decided what to do next. She would tell them she was taking a long and well-earned vacation. They wouldn't question it. They quit caring what she did a long time ago. She would take the late flight to LA and change planes for an early flight to Denver. There were shorter more direct flights, but this one would get her out of town sooner, and that was what mattered most to her now.

Linda carefully packed two boxes with items she didn't want to part with. Two suitcases held all the clothes she was taking with her. She would stop at a shipping office on the way to the airport and have the boxes shipped to Denver. Everything else would stay here. She wanted none of it around to bring back memories.

Her cell phone chimed, announcing a text had arrived. She checked the message. It was from Joe. He had arranged a special birthday party for Art and wanted Linda to bring Art and Renee by company helicopter to Gold Post as soon as she got the message. She answered that Mrs. Ramsey could bring them. A couple of minutes later Joe replied that the kids would be more comfortable on a helicopter ride if Linda was with them.

Linda had arranged for a birthday gift to be delivered to Art the next day. She wasn't sure Joe would even remember Art's birthday, but apparently he had. No, that was unkind. Even with his being gone with Gwen a lot he tried to make time for the kids.

She hadn't planned to see the kids. She would cry if she tried to say goodbye, and Linda Sloan didn't cry in front of anyone. Joe was right though. They wouldn't be as at ease with Mrs. Ramsey for an unexpected trip in an aircraft. She could take them to Gold Post and hand them over to Joe and make the return flight with the pilot. She could still make an early Saturday morning flight.

"OK." She sent out the answer.

"Great." The reply immediately came back.

She called and changed her flight. She'd be taking one of those early, more direct, flights after all. Taking a deep breath she crossed the hall to Joe's apartment. She found the kids working on their homework under Mary Ramsey's watchful eye. Both seemed hesitant about this unexpected surprise. *Joe should have prepared them for this.* Linda made sure Art packed what he would need while Mary helped Renee pack an overnight bag.

A few minutes later they were all in the Suburban headed for the airport where a company pilot waited to give the kids their first helicopter ride.

"Do we have to go?" Renee clutched Linda's hand.

"It's my birthday trip. Dad expects us, and it will be fun." Art sounded more determined than excited as he eyed the large helicopter that was not meant for passengers but for transporting building materials.

Linda smiled and putting an arm around each, hugged them tight. "It will be fun. You'll see. It's amazing how much you can see from a helicopter. Remember how much you liked looking out the window when we came here on the plane?"

A smiling pilot came forward. "Hey, here's my passengers. Let's get these put away and we'll be off. Only two bags?" He looked at Linda for confirmation. She nodded.

"I'll be coming back with you tonight."

He picked up both bags and headed to the chopper. A few minutes later they were buckled in with the rotors spinning.

A lump rose in Linda's throat as she watched Art bravely trying to pretend he wasn't the least bit concerned about this new experience. Renee appeared terrified. Linda reached for her hand and assured her as best she could through the intercom in their headsets. Thirty minutes into the flight, Linda was pointing out small lakes and rivers to a considerably less nervous little girl.

"I want to learn to fly one of these." Art declared this with his usual certainty and determination.

"Ask your father," Linda replied with a smile.

She fought back tears at the complete confidence Art had that he could fly a helicopter. Why was it that a woman who held it together and cried over almost nothing could be brought to tears over the simplest thing these children, who were not hers, said or did?

Dropping down into the dense, green mountains, the pilot brought the chopper to rest at a small heliport carved out of the surrounding trees. A beat up old Jeep waited for them.

"Seth! What are you doing here?" Linda stopped in surprise as Seth exited the driver's seat. She had expected Joe to meet them.

"Hi, Ms. Sloan. Everyone is up at the camp sight, and they sent me to get you."

A burning anger rose in Linda's chest. He didn't even come to meet his own kids. The kids barely knew Seth. Linda pulled out her phone and started pounding Joe's number only to find she had no bars—the phone was useless.

"There's no cell service here?" She glared at Seth.

"I'm sorry, Miss Sloan. This area is awful for communications. Have to get right on top of a mountain to get any bars at all. There's a spot up at the campsite where you can usually get a couple bars."

"How far is the campsite?"

"Bout a thirty minute drive on these roads. It won't take us long."

Linda turned to the pilot. "How soon will you be going back?"

"Right away. I have instructions to have the chopper back by dark unless Mr. Black tells me otherwise. But I can be back first thing in the morning if he sends for me."

Linda took a deep breath and thanked the pilot, anger coming through the words. Seth had already loaded the kid's bags and had them buckled in their seats. Climbing into the passenger seat next to him, she couldn't wait to get started. Wait until she saw Joe. Her fists clenched as she pictured braining him with the nearest lethal object within reach.

* * *

Seth was less than forthcoming about the camping party. Absorbed in navigating the rutted primitive road, he gave her only grunts and vague answers to her questions. As the jeep bounced them along Linda observed the forest that looked to be reaching out at them. The air in the high altitude made her feel sluggish, like she needed to breath deeper. The tangy forest smell she might have enjoyed under other circumstances felt only cloying. She thought about her situation. She would have Joe call the pilot back in the morning and would take the first available flight out when she got to Anchorage. There was nothing she wanted less than to be around a party with Joe.

Seth hit a bad rut in the narrowing tracks that bounced all of them hard on their seats. More than likely Gwen would be there making it more humiliating for her. Joe couldn't have planned something like this without Gwen. He had become so enamored and dependent on her that she practically ran his life. *Like you used to do?* The thought intruded on her anger, and she felt the hurt, not only of a woman scorned but of one displaced and left behind. Demoted, that's what had happened to her, demoted from lover to secretary. She didn't even get to pretend she still held a valuable position in the company.

She had never planned to see Joe again, but she would get her emotions in check and get through tonight, take care of the kids, if needed, and get out of this place in the morning.

Emerging from the trees at the edge of a bare area that had once, obviously, been a parking area Seth parked the jeep. A late model Ford pickup sat a few yards from them.

"Where is everybody?" Art beat Linda to the question. They both looked to Seth for an answer.

"Over there a few yards up that hill, where you see the big boulders. There's a cave up there where the party will be. You can go on up."

The kids clambered out of the jeep and attached themselves to Linda as she studied the silent, wilderness around them. The hair on her arms and the back of her neck seemed to rise and she wished she could have come up with a reason to not have come here.

"Where's Dad?" Art sounded as puzzled as Linda felt.

"I don't want to go to a party here. I want to go home," Renee almost whispered as she took Linda's hand.

"Where is Joe?" Linda turned to Seth.

"Up at the cave."

Surveying the surroundings again, Linda saw no sign of people having been here other than the other truck. What on earth was Joe doing? She took the children's hands and headed for the area up the hill where the cave and party were supposed to be. This just seemed all wrong. What had gotten into Joe? When they reached the numerous rocks and boulders they could see the entrance to the cave. It was approximately twelve feet wide, six feet high and it was dark and quiet. Linda stopped and looked back. Seth had disappeared.

"Joe?" she called. "Joe?" she called louder, the sound disappearing into the trees.

"Seth?" Linda turned to retrace their steps to the jeep.

"What's the matter, Linda? Hunting for Joe?"

Linda whirled around to see Gwen step from behind a ten foot tall boulder. She was carrying a rifle.

"Gwen! What's going on? Joe texted that there was a birthday party for Art."

Gwen's laughter rolled maniacally across the silence.

"That was me, and you fell for it."

"It was Joe. It came from his phone."

"We were in bed. I told him I was texting my cousin. I texted you instead. Then I texted my cousin." Gwen nodded over Linda's shoulder.

Linda glanced back and froze in shock. Seth stood behind her thirty feet away. He also carried a rifle.

"Seth? I don't understand. Cousin?" Seth shrugged.

"I would never have guessed. I know why Gwen dislikes me, but what do you have against me?"

"Nothing." Gwen answered for him "He works for me and does what I tell him. Today he's going to help me bury you three."

"What?" Linda blanched, suddenly realizing they were in serious trouble.

"If you had just stepped back and let me have Joe there would have been no problem. I could even have coped with the brats, but you never stopped trying to block everything I did. So now you go, and the brats go with you. Joe will come crawling to me for consolation."

"You don't have to worry about me now. I'm going back home. Joe's all yours. Just let me call the helicopter to take us back, and you're free of us."

Gwen snorted a laugh. "Too late even if I wanted to. You and the brats would talk. I never wanted them anyway."

Gwen began lifting the rifle. Linda whirled and found Seth's rifle trained on them also.

"Run for the cave, Art. Take Renee." Linda spoke softly, hoping Gwen couldn't hear.

Art grabbed Renee's hand, and they sped as only children can for the cave's mouth only a few feet away. Linda watched helplessly as Gwen brought the rifle up. Dashing between the kids and Gwen, she followed them. She felt the bullet hit her leg a few seconds before the pain but somehow she could still walk. The next one slammed into her side. That one hurt. Then they were in the cave. Bullets followed them, ricocheting off the cave walls.

"We have to move back. One of those bullets might hit us or they may come in." She tried to speak calmly, hoping the kids didn't go to pieces on her. Her side was hurting badly.

The darkness closed around them more with every foot they retreated. Linda called a halt and attempted to inspect their surroundings. The cave had narrowed to not more than three feet wide and what she could see was merely varying shades of black and grey. The dim light at the front barely penetrated the sixty or so feet they had come.

"Stay close and be quiet." She cautioned them.

"Will they come after us?" Art asked.

"I'm afraid so." Linda wouldn't lie to the kids. They needed to be strong now. "If there is another opening we can find and get out of here, we might have a chance to get away from them."

"I'm scared." Renee clung to Linda.

"Yes, honey, so am I, but we can't think about being scared. We have to figure out a way to get away from them or hide. Okay?"

"Okay." Renee's voice quavered.

"Now, I want you to both be very quiet and only whisper if we need to talk. We need to listen for them in case they follow us. Okay?"

"Okay," they both whispered.

Linda fought to stay focused through the pain of two bullet wounds. Pain in her leg was excruciating when she tried to walk, but it supported her so she thought maybe it hadn't hit the bone. The wound in her side was less painful if she stayed still and kept her breathing shallow. She could feel the wetness of her clothes and knew she was bleeding.

She felt in her pocket for her phone. Thank God she hadn't left it in her hand bag. It was useless to contact anyone from here, but it would give a tiny amount of light. An instant after it produced a tiny amount of light a shot rang out, and a bullet slapped the wall close to her, ricocheting back and forth, like a ping pong ball. They couldn't go back. They had to go on. She put the phone back in her pocket.

"Hold on to me. I'm going to move very slowly." Linda whispered as she slid one foot in front of the other. It was slow working through the pain and total darkness. She grit her teeth.

"You're going to die in this cave." Gwen's voice echoed around them. "It's dangerous in there. It had signs and was closed off but we opened it up just for you." Her wild laugh followed and another shot bounced off the walls.

Linda continued feeling her way along the wall with one hand, the other pressing against the hole in her side. Art gripped Linda's belt and Renee held fast to her pant leg. More shots rang out.

Dear God, please don't let a bullet hit one of the kids.

She had just advanced another couple of feet when the earth let go with snapping and rumbling, and they were sliding into nothingness.

* * *

CHAPTER TWENTY-THREE

L inda held onto the screaming kids with a death grip as dirt and rock buffeted them. Then her feet hit something, and they were slammed to a stop so fast and hard that she couldn't react or breathe. Fear drove the pain to the back of her consciousness, and she remained motionless, never relaxing her grip on the kids. Renee continued to scream.

"Shush, shush, quiet." Linda whispered because that was all she had enough breath for.

"Renee, Renee," Art yelled. "Shut up." The screams became sobs.

"Renee." Linda tried again. "Renee can you hear me?"

An "Uh-huh," came between sobs.

"You need to be quiet now. I know you're scared. So am I, and so is Art, but you have to stop crying now. They'll hear you."

Renee's sobs chocked off after a minute. Linda was somewhere in the midst of a black void. Dust made her want to choke. The kids were coughing.

"Okay, we have to be very careful now. I want you both to stay very still and only move when I tell you. Okay?"

"Okay." Art responded. Renee only whimpered.

"Art, can you feel anything solid under your feet? Are you touching anything?"

"I'm standing on something. I don't know what. I think we are next to a rock or something."

"Renee are you standing on something solid?"

"Yes." Her answer was whispered.

Linda closed her eyes against the blackness and the pain. Art was on her left. Renee had her arms wrapped around Linda's injured right leg. The leg screamed its pain as the little girl clung to it desperately.

"Art, is your back to the rock or your face?"

"My back."

"My back seems to be against rock also. Now here is what we are going to do—very slowly. Renee, are you listening to me?"

"Yes."

"You are hugging my leg. Without letting go I want you to move your foot up against mine and then over between my legs. Can you do that? And remember—very slowly."

A minute passed. Linda felt no movement.

"Renee?"

"Yes."

"Did you understand? I want you to start now."

A few seconds later the small body hugging her leg shifted slightly, and Renee straddled her leg.

"Good, Renee. Now very slowly move your other foot between mine." This time Renee responded promptly.

"All right, sweetheart. You're doing great. Now I want you to take your right arm and move it to my other leg. Hold on to it tight. Keep leaning against me."

Once Renee had managed that, Linda had her move the other arm. She took a few seconds rest as the now unburdened leg throbbed.

"Art, it's your turn. I don't know what our situation is yet so I need to get my phone out. I want you to let go of me with one hand and take hold of Renee. You'll have to turn around first and face the rock. Then I can let go of her and get my phone out. Okay?"

"Sure, I can do that." His voice shook.

"Go slow. Don't get off balance. Renee, you stay very still."

Linda held firmly to Art's jacket as he rotated to face the rock.

"I'm turned." Art's voice sounded calmer than before.

"Now I have a hold on you, and I want you to reach over and take a tight hold on Renee's jacket. We all stay very still, and I will let go of her and get my phone out of my pocket."

"Don't let me go, please," Renee begged.

"Sweetheart? Sweetheart?" Linda tried to sound soothing. "You have your arms around my leg, and I want you to hold on tight. Art will hold on to you. I just need a minute to try to see around us. I need you to be a big girl now."

Linda eased her free hand into her pants pocket and felt for the phone. Her heart froze when she heard sounds from above. A beam of light appeared above them.

"Be quiet, don't talk," she whispered. Her heart thudded as she struggled to hear.

"Don't get too close. This whole damn thing may go down."

It was Seth. Linda watched the light play above them. They were too far back to aim it down.

"I wish I could get to the edge and see them," Gwen's voice complained.

"They probably went too far down to see. There's a reason this thing was boarded up."

Gwen's shrill laugh echoed. "We were going to dump them in here after we shot them anyway. The dumb bitch just dumped herself."

"Come on Gwen. Let's get the hell out of here before this thing caves in on us too. We can sleep in the vehicles and get out of here first thing in the morning."

Linda waited. She was losing her perception and wasn't sure if it was seconds or minutes. She heard nothing else. Easing the phone out of her pocket, she touched the screen, and it came to life. She aimed the light at their feet, and a wave of nausea hit her in the belly. They appeared to be on a ledge less than two feet deep. It was maybe three feet wide, a miracle they had come to a stop on it. She aimed the phone outward, but the feeble light had no chance of penetrating the darkness. Turning the phone to the side, she tried to see what was behind them without moving. It appeared to be solid rock, too steep and smooth to climb out. Two feet above her head a rock jutted out a little over a foot. It aimed upward.

She aimed the light at Art and Renee. They were dirty and bruised with some bloody scrapes. Renee had blood all over her arms, and panic claimed Linda until she realized Renee had been hugging her leg where the bullet wound had bled. Her face was pale and terrified. Art's face showed fear but also determination.

Linda turned the phone off and slipped it back into her pocket. She slipped her hand back onto Renee to comfort her.

"What are we going to do?" Art was already thinking ahead.

"I think we don't have anything we can do but wait. Your father will come but it may be a while."

"If she tricked us into coming here, how will he know where to find us?"

"Mrs. Ramsey knows. When he doesn't find you at home, he'll find out from her. It just may take time."

A wave of dizziness sent a lightning bolt of fear through Linda. She had to remain still. If she lost her balance in a dizzy spell they would all plunge to certain death. If she could hold on to the rock jutting out above her, it would help, but she couldn't hold on forever. She was still losing blood, and while she didn't know much about these things, she knew at the least she would get weaker and at worst lose consciousness.

My belt! She was wearing a webbed belt. If she could get it loose and loop it over the rock above and around her hand, it would keep her from falling if she was unsteady.

"Art, do you have a belt on?"

"Yes."

"I'm going to let go of both of you for just a minute and take off my belt. Then I'll have you take yours off. If we can loop it over the rock above, it will help us a little.

"Okay."

The small amount of movement involved sent a numbing shock wave across Linda's mid-section. She clamped her jaw tight at the pain and tried to breathe shallowly as she waited for it to pass. *Keep going, you don't have time to stop.* Gently running her fingers over the belt, she began to maneuver it out of the loops. Once free, she passed the end through the buckle and put her hand through the loop, pulling it tight. Working in the dark, trying to remember how big around the rock formation looked, she attempted to fashion a self-tightening tie she had learned as a child.

Damn, I need to see. Slipping her phone out again, she paused as the movement set off a new wave of pain. She aimed the light at Art.

"Art, take off your belt and hand it to me, very slow."

She buckled his belt to the end of hers and then slowly reached up to put the big loop over the rock projection above her. She was getting weak, and it took an epic effort before, on her fourth try, she hooked the belt securely over it. Sweat beaded her forehead, and pain wracked her body. She pulled the loop tight and realized she had just secured herself to the rock outcropping, probably for the rest of her life. It would take more strength than she had and more movement than she had room to make, to get it loose. If she lost consciousness, as she was certain she was going to, and one of the belts broke, she would go down into that black endless chasm in front of them, taking the kids with her. But if the belts didn't break, and they held her weight she would not be endangering the kids. They would be on their own, but she wouldn't be dragging them down with her.

"Renee, I want you to move around my leg so you are behind me. Can you do that?"

There was no answer but the arms around Linda's leg tightened.

"All right. Start now, Renee." Linda tried to sound as firm as possible in her weakening condition. Renee slowly began to move. Linda felt a ray of pride at the little girl's courage.

"Now I want you to turn with your back to Art and keep your shoulder against the rock. Then I want you to sit down. Then you have to stay still and most of all keep against the wall."

Once Renee was in place, Linda instructed Art to do the same.

"Can you reach the end of the belt, Art?"

"I think so." He took a hold of the last six inches of the belt dangling above him.

"You know how to turn my phone on and off don't you?"

"Yes."

"Good. Here's what you do now. It's very important. I'm going to give you my phone. I want you to turn it off now and put it in your jacket pocket. You need to leave it off unless you really need it so the battery doesn't run down. If it does, you'll have no light at all."

"Why don't you keep it?" Art's voice was wary.

"I've been shot and lost a lot of blood. I'm feeling weak and dizzy, and I may faint eventually and not be able to talk to you or help you. You understand?"

"Yeah."

"I fixed the belt so that if I pass out, it may keep me from falling. You have to be the adult now. I want you to promise me that if I do fall or slip, you will not try to do anything. The belt may not hold so you and Renee must hug that rock wall no matter what. Your life and hers is going to be up to you if I pass out. Can you do it?"

"Are we all going to die?"

"Of course not, Art. Your father will find out where we are, but it may take time. You and Renee can sit still and wait. You'll be all right for a long time. I will probably pass out before help comes. *I do not* want you to try to help me no matter what happens. What I want more than anything is for you and Renee to be all right."

Linda paused and swallowed. "I love you both."

"I'll try." Art's voice was close to breaking.

Renee started to cry. "I don't want you to fall. I want to go home."

"I know sweetheart. I want to go home too. For now why don't you hold Art's hand and be brave so you can help him." Linda took a shallow breath. "Art, put your arms around Renee and let her lean against you and she'll feel better. Now, Art, turn off the phone and put it away and we'll start waiting."

* * *

Linda existed in a black void. There had been no pain, no sensation, no sound, no awareness for hours. She could have left this world gently, without struggle, but that was not to be.

First came a sound, a noise, unintelligible and far away. She fought against it, wanting to stay in her blessed black void. But it kept coming back, like a mosquito coming back to buzz her brain again and again. Then there was light, annoying light that came through her eyelids. Her body was jostled and her comfortable void was jerked away. She heard a long high pitched sound that she realized was her own scream.

The sound and the light went away leaving her in a vacuum as she fought to understand where she was and what was happening. She began to focus on the sound next to her. Someone was talking.

"It's okay, Linda. Dad's here. He took Renee up, and he's coming back for us. He saved us, Linda. He came like you said he would. You have to be all right. Promise me you'll be all right, Linda."

Was she really in a cave with the children or was she dreaming? Then the light was back, and there was more talk.

"Hang in there, Linda. I'll be right back for you. Don't move now. I'll be right back."

The light went away again, but this time Art didn't talk. Could Joe be rescuing them in this dream?

The light came back, and her body was moved. She screamed, then felt something tight around her, and the pain came again. Then she felt her feet leave the ledge and panic overtook her. She tried to find something to hold on to, but her slightest movements were feeble. Her weight came off the belt and pain seared her shoulder as her arm was lowered. She screamed again. Then she was floating out in space, and she knew that Joe had come for them because his arm was around her, making the trip up with her. Her eyes adjusted to the dim light, and men's arms reached out to her. A few seconds later Joe was beside her, scooping her up in his arms and carrying her out of the cave.

An old battered green cargo van sat nearby with its two side doors open. He took her directly to it and settled her on a blanket on the floor where seats had been removed.

"The kids?" She half whispered the words.

"They're all right. One of the men is a medic of sorts. He's checking them out." Joe held a water bottle to her lips. "Try to drink. You're dehydrated."

Linda managed a sip.

"What the hell happened?" Joe was searching for the wounds that resulted in her blood encrusted clothes.

"Kids," she whispered. "Need you."

"You've been shot!" Joe looked at the bullet wound in horror.

"The kids need you." Her head dropped back on the blanket, and her eyes closed. "Go, please," she whispered.

"I'll get them and the men, and we'll get you all to the chopper. We'll get you to a doctor, sweetheart."

Joe left, yelling for the three men. One was with the children, the other two gathering up the ropes and equipment they had used to get them all out of the cave.

"Joe!" His name rang across the clearing. "Did you come here to find me? Did you want to apologize?"

Joe spun around to see a figure emerge from the dense foliage at the edge of the forest. "Gwen? What are you doing here?"

"This is my uncle's property. That witch, Linda, brought the kids up here to trespass in his mine."

"What the hell's going on? Linda's been shot."

"Dad! Dad!" Art called from where he stood next to Renee and one of the men. "She shot Linda, Dad!" Renee began to sob.

Linda heard the hated voice from where she lay in the van. There was no escape from the woman from hell. Linda looked around the empty van. There were only two seats, driver and passenger. Almost everyone here carried a gun, and between the seats lay a rifle.

Putting her tongue between her teeth she bit down, making a supreme effort not to scream at the pain that movement triggered. She reached as far as she could, until the tips of her fingers touched it. She couldn't get a hold on it. Bending her good leg up, she pushed as hard as she could. The pain was blinding, and she closed her eyes and focused only on getting a grip on the gun. She pulled it toward her. Her left arm wasn't working right and still felt numb so she pulled the rifle across her body, using her right hand to release the safety. She knew it would be loaded. In this wild country guns were always loaded.

"Too bad you had to find them, Joe. Now you have to go too." Gwen raised her rifle. The men with Joe began to back away. "You three stay put. I'll decide what to do about you later."

Joe started to move and the rifle jerked up pointing not at Joe but at Art, standing next to Renee.

"You move again, Joe, and the brat goes first. You should have been nicer to me and got rid of that bitch, Linda. Guess she's still alive huh? I'll take care of that right after you and your brats." She laughed hysterically.

Gwen was still laughing when her face disappeared. She hung in the air a second before another bullet slammed into her heart, sending her lifeless body backward. Another bullet bit into it as it lay on the ground.

Everyone whirled around and saw Linda leaning against the open van door. The rifle was propped on her bad arm as it gripped the door.

"Linda!" Joe started toward her as the rifle slipped to the ground, followed by Linda.

Her last thought before she hit the ground and darkness enveloped her was, *"He loved her."*

* * *

CHAPTER TWENTY-
FOUR

Five minutes later, Linda was again in the van with Art and Renee huddled next to her, both crying, although Art was trying hard not to.

One of the men who flew back with them had some experience with emergency care, but there was little he could do for Linda with his rudimentary knowledge. He did tell Joe that she had lost more blood than anyone should, and she needed surgery—soon.

The pilot radioed ahead to get permission to land at the heliport at the hospital. By the time the chopper settled to the ground, there were gurneys there. Linda was whisked away. Art and Renee each got a gurney ride, and Joe followed them off to emergency where they would be examined. Both were dehydrated and had bruises, cuts and scrapes. Renee kept crying off and on, refused to talk, and screamed at any attempt to separate her from Art. They were admitted to the hospital for the night, and the doctor gave them a sedative that would allow them to sleep. Joe hoped they didn't dream of Gwen's face disintegrating in front of them.

Joe called Mrs. Ramsey, and by the time she arrived, the kids were asleep. Leaving her to watch over them, he went in search of Linda.

He was told she was still in surgery. He was asked to fill out her admitting forms and sign permission forms and various other requirements. As they preferred a relative, he identified himself as her fiancé, which he would be as soon as she woke up.

She would wake up. She had to make it, and when she did he would do nothing but hold her close and never let her go.

They showed him to a waiting room and promised the doctor would come when the surgery was over. While he waited, Joe called his father and related the situation.

"Well," Billy said. "If the damn woman was going to kill Linda and the kids, she belongs dead. I'm sorry Linda had to be the one to do it." He paused. "Does this have anything to do with her resignation?"

"Her resignation? What are you talking about?"

"Martha came to see me first thing this morning. She had an email from Linda, sent at closing yesterday. She resigned as of this morning. Didn't you know?"

"No. No, I didn't. I was coming home from up north, and when I couldn't find them, I didn't check the office messages."

"What's happening, Joe? We had the impression you two were a couple. Were we wrong? Is that why she's resigning?"

Joe rubbed his eyes with one hand.

"It was Gwen, Dad. They squared off from day one. Gwen did a number on me and made me think we needed her. I have Byron working on the problems we've been having. He thought Gwen was involved and asked me to keep her happy so he could use her to take us to whoever is doing this. He gave me the go ahead to fire her day before yesterday. She kept throwing the fact that I took her side on things in Linda's face. I fired Gwen yesterday morning, but Linda didn't know yet. I had no idea she was leaving. I was going to propose when I got home. I should have told Linda about everything. I thought I was protecting her and the kids."

"You need help up there?"

"I have one inexperienced receptionist to answer phones. Linda's back-up and our draftsman turned out to be Gwen's cousin and helped her ambush them. There was just me and Gwen in the field. I don't know what I can do now. Kids are traumatized, and Linda is going to need care. I just don't know yet."

"You'll figure it out. I'll send you a temp from here who knows the office end to keep it running until you get help. You call as soon as she's out of surgery and let us know how she is. And Joe, if you need help don't be too proud to ask."

"I'll keep you up to date, and I'll call if I need anything." Joe was silent a moment. "Dad?"

"Yeah?"

"How did you get Kate to forgive you?"

There was silence for several seconds. Then Joe heard a low chuckle.

"I groveled a lot."

"Got it. I can do that."

* * *

Linda fought to withdraw back into the blackness, but she was again being pushed up into a world of pain. A voice was saying something and wouldn't go away. Somewhere in the little awareness she had, it made her mad. A nurse kept telling her she was doing fine. She wasn't fine. She was in pain! God, she was so sick. Turning her head, she groaned and began dry heaving. The nurse seemed more interested in getting a tiny plastic pan under her head and protecting the bedding than she was about Linda being sick enough to die.

Finally, her body quit its spasms. She lay still, head resting on the pan still under her head. She grunted angrily when the nurse made a move to remove it. She didn't want any tiny movement, just to be let alone and lay there. The nurse left it there and busied herself with other patients nearby. Linda's foggy mind processed the fact that this must be the recovery room. She dozed off back into blissful sleep. The next time she woke, the doctor was there looking at her chart and talking to the nurse about how she had been in recovery.

"She's doing good, doctor." She smiled at Linda. "Won't be long, and we can move you to a room, and you can see your fiancé."

"No!" Linda croaked in a hoarse voice. Her body jerked, and she cried out in pain. She reached out feebly for the doctor. He moved closer and took her hand.

"You're doing fine. We'll give you something for the pain." He nodded to the nurse, and she twisted a knob to increase the painkiller in the IV feeding into Linda's arm.

"No one visit. Don't want to see anyone."

"Not even your fiancé?"

"Don't have fiancé. Don't want to see anyone."

"There's a couple of policeman waiting also. They need to speak to you."

"Just them. No one else, please." She was begging now, visibly upset.

"All right. We'll talk about it more when you're out from under the anaesthesia."

"Thank you," she whispered, closing her eyes. The increased dose of painkiller began to take effect, and she drifted back into sleep.

The doctor moved away from the bed and spoke softly to the nurse.

"Interesting that she doesn't want any visitors at all. If she does well and her vitals are still good, you can move her tonight after visiting hours. That should reduce the likelihood of those who want to see her interfering with the move. I'll tell the nurses and hospital security just in case someone doesn't abide by the sign. The police can see her in the morning, and maybe that will change the situation."

* * *

With the kids sedated and asleep in the children's ward, Joe had spent the night sitting in the waiting room while Linda went through surgery and into recovery. The doctor reported to him after the surgery that she would be fine. The bullet hadn't hit anything vital, but she had lost a lot of blood and it would take a little time for her to recuperate. She had hung on her arm for hours, and it was pulled and strained.

Therapy would be required for a good recovery. Joe breathed a sigh of relief for the first time since he'd found the three of them missing.

He was still trying to piece together what exactly had happened, other than Gwen had gone crazy and tried to kill them. Art told him Linda said they were to go to Gold Post for a birthday party that Joe was supposed to be giving for Art. He told a story of Gwen shooting Linda, and Linda telling them to run to the cave and of the cave floor giving way. He told Joe in detail how they had moved slowly around on the tiny ledge as Linda told them to and how she had tied herself to the rock so she, hopefully, wouldn't fall. He told Joe how she put him in charge if she were to fall or not be able to talk to him. Art cried when he told Joe that she told him not to try to catch her if she fell, but to hold tight to Renee. Joe cried with him.

Once Linda was in recovery, he returned to the kids room and sent Mrs. Ramsey home. Tired as he was, there was no question of sleep. Questions kept going round and round in his head, wondering how Linda could have believed he was giving a party up there. He thought of her phone. She had given it to Art, and it was in a bag with his clothes in the cabinet. Joe quietly retrieved it and proceeded to check her calls and texts. Finding the texts from Gwen, he realized she must have taken his extra phone from the office. So Linda would have seen that the calls did come from his phone. He read them and came to the one where he was supposed to have answered Linda's comment that Mrs. Ramsey could take them. It was clipped and cold. An order expected to be followed. Did she really think that was him? Did he talk to her like that? He spent the next two hours thinking about that as he shifted in the so-called 'sleep chair,' listening to the occasional stirring of the kids.

The hospital began to stir quietly at about five in the morning. There was the quiet padding of feet down the hall followed by a quiet murmur of voices at the nurse's desk. Joe thought about the morning and wondered how he could be with the kids and Linda and check on the company at the same time. He had help arriving on this morning's plane. Billy and Kate had decided they were coming up and bringing someone who supposedly could keep the office running. He hoped to be able to check in at the office tomorrow or the next day. He'd talked to Byron last night while Linda was in surgery, and Byron also would be arriving today.

At six there was considerable activity in the hospital, and to Joe's delight an angel in the form of Mrs. Ramsey showed up to relieve him.

"Mrs. Ramsey. I didn't expect you at this hour." Joe struggled to his feet from the uncomfortable clutches of the chair.

The matronly woman smiled. "I thought you might need a little help with all that's going on."

"You were right." Joe stretched his back. "I need to go see Linda. The kids are still asleep. If you could be here with them, and as soon as I see her I'll come back. Hopefully, we'll know by then what the plan will be for the rest of the day."

Mrs. Ramsey nodded, and slipping out of her coat, took a peek at each of the children and then took Joe's place in the chair.

Slipping into the tiny bathroom, Joe studied himself in the mirror. His full head of black hair was a mess. His eyes were red and had bags under them, and he had a dark stubble of beard. He washed his face and ran his fingers through his hair. That was about all he could do for now.

In the surgical waiting room he studied the screen that showed the status of all the patients having surgery. They were either scheduled, in surgery, in recovery, or assigned a room. Seeing that Linda had been assigned a room he hurried on to the nurse's desk for a room number.

"I'm sorry, Mr. Black, Ms. Sloan is not allowed visitors."

"What? Why not? The doctor told me after her surgery that she was doing fine."

"I have no information on that, Mr. Black. Doctor will be making rounds between 9:00 and 11:00 this morning if you wish to see him."

"But I'm her fiancé."

"I'm sorry sir, our orders are *no one*." The nurse was becoming colder by the minute.

Joe turned and started to walk down the hallway.

"Mr. Black!" the nurse stood and called firmly. "If you don't leave immediately, I will call security and the police."

Joe turned and they engaged in a standing stare-off. The nurse won, and with a feeling of complete defeat, Joe left the area. Back in the main lobby he tried making calls. No one answered. All were in the air in route to Anchorage. The doctor would be in this morning, and he could get answers then, but in the meantime he needed to be with the kids when they woke up. He returned to the children's ward.

The pediatrician apparently had no reason to be there early any more than the surgeon, and Joe had no choice but to wait with Mrs. Ramsey until he showed up. At 9:00 A.M. Joe returned to the nurse's desk. The same nurse scowled at him, and before he had a chance to ask, waved a finger in the air and pointed to a chair at the end of the hallway.

"Doctor is making his rounds, and he knows you want to see him. I'll let him know you're here, and he'll come by when he's done."

Joe took the chair and waited. Thirty minutes later the doctor came walking down the hall. Joe rose and waited for him.

"What is this that Linda can't have visitors? I thought she came through the surgery without big problems."

"She did. I was hoping you could tell me why she doesn't want any visitors."

"Me?" Joe looked at the doctor in astonishment. "Wait a minute. This is because she doesn't *want* any visitors?"

"That's right. She'll talk to the police about what happened, but doesn't want anyone else at all. Very adamant about it. You have no idea?"

"No." Joe's voice expressed his bewilderment. "Could you tell her I said I love her, and would she please see me? And if she won't see me how about the kids? They want to see her and know she's all right."

"All right." The doctor didn't look hopeful. "I'll go ask her. Wait here."

Joe knew when he saw the doctor come out of Linda's room what the answer was. He returned to the children's ward to find the police there waiting for his permission to talk to the kids. They were friendly, a man and a woman, and assured Joe they only had to get the story in the kids own words. It was necessary, and they felt the sooner they did it the more accurate it would be. Joe let Mrs. Ramsey go on to the apartment, assuring her he would be along soon with the kids. He sat in the uncomfortable chair while the kids answered the detective's questions—rather while Art answered their questions. Joe tried to hold Renee to put her more at ease, but no matter what the coaxing she would only nod her head. She struggled out of Joe's arms to climb up in the bed next to Art where she held on to him firmly.

"She hasn't spoken since we found them," Joe explained worriedly.

They nodded in sympathy and said they thought they had all they needed, but if not would be back in contact. Once they left Joe sat and held his children tight until the doctor finally arrived. He proclaimed them in good shape physically. After a few efforts to get a response out of Renee, he drew Joe to the side of the room and gave him a business card.

"If she doesn't began to speak and communicate in a week or so, give this doctor a call. She's one of the best, and if you allow this to go on, it will just be more difficult. Even if she does talk you may want her to have a few sessions with the doctor about it."

Joe's heart was one big ache that threatened to engulf him as he helped the kids into their jackets and prepared to leave. The nurse's showed up with wheelchairs to take them out of the hospital. Joe realized how badly the kids were traumatized when Renee was afraid of it and had to be assured it wasn't dangerous before she would get in it. Art, who would normally have considered a wheelchair great fun, was completely indifferent. Outside the hospital Renee broke from the wheelchair and ran back to the doors of the hospital. Joe caught her by the hand and she turned screaming.

"Linda! Linda come! I want Linda!" she howled.

Joe gathered her stiff little body tightly against him, and stroking her hair, he whispered in her ear. "It's okay, Renee. It's okay. Linda has to stay in the hospital a little bit longer to get better. She can't come home with us right now." Other cars waited to take his place in the pick-up line, and he had to go. He made sure she was buckled into her seat belt and that Art had his fastened before jumping into the Suburban and heading for home.

"Dad?" Art asked solemnly. "Is she going to die?"

"Linda!" Joe was shocked at the question. "No, she's going to be fine. But she was shot and lost a lot of blood, and it's going to take time for her to get better. I thought you knew she was okay."

Art settled back in his seat, apparently satisfied but still solemn.

* * *

At noon, Joe was beside himself as to what to do with his children when the doorbell rang. He opened it to Billy and Kate, and to his astonishment Martha was with them. Martha had been his father's first office employee when the office had been a ratty two bedroom apartment in a walk up and her desk a card table. She had been part baby sitter and part disciplinarian when Joe wasn't following his father around a construction site. She headed all office departments now and was a powerhouse in Black Capital. She was a square, solidly built, practical woman who oozed the confidence of her success and position. Linda had been her prodigy, and Martha had hand selected her for the personal assistant's job in California years ago.

"I'm so glad to see you all." Joe hugged his Dad and Kate.

"Martha? What are you doing here?" Joe hugged her affectionately.

"You need someone to run the office don't you? Well, you got it. Now I want the office keys and directions to get there. One inexperienced receptionist won't cut it, Joseph."

Billy grinned at Joe. "You're going to run the office?" Joe asked. "Don't you have more important things to do?"

"I'll take care of them when your office is running well, and someone is in charge that knows how to stay on top of it. By the way, I want to go see Linda tonight."

"That's a problem." They all turned to look at Joe. "She's refusing any visitors. She saw the policemen that came to question her about the shooting, but she won't agree to anyone else, even the kids. Renee hasn't talked since we found them except to scream that she wanted Linda when we left the hospital. The kids are holed up back in their rooms. I have to admit, I'm about at the end of my rope."

"Well, give me the keys and I'll go get one problem taken care of." Martha reached out and Joe handed her his keys with instructions on what key was to what. He gave her the street address to the office and called her a cab, telling her to pick up the extra vehicle parked there.

"I'll call Lela and tell her you're coming. She's a good kid, and Linda likes her, but she hasn't been around long and doesn't know a lot yet."

They went down the hall to Art's bedroom where the kids sat, Art on his computer with Renee next to him humming to her doll. It had been a while since she had played much with her dolls. Both kids were happy to see grandma and grandpa but in spite of smiles and hugs, Renee didn't speak. She only shook her head yes or no. The adults went back to the living room, and the kids chose to remain where they were. The adults exchanged concerned looks as they took their seats.

An hour of conversation brought Billy and Kate up to date on the problems with sabotage and the attacks. While Billy was aware of most of it, Joe brought him up to date on Byron's progress and that Byron was arriving in Anchorage. He explained the problem he had encountered with Gwen, his early naivete about her importance and how she had been highly recommended by Donald Larson when he retired. How when he finally realized what a problem she was, Byron had asked him to keep her happy so he could use her to lead them to the source of their problems. He told them how he fired her, and when he arrived home, discovered Linda and the kids missing. Joe explained how no one had known about his draftsman being Gwen's cousin and how he had helped her when they lured Linda to the fake party. Now that things might be coming to a close, Linda had resigned a few hours before he had planned to propose to her and wouldn't talk to anyone.

Mrs. Ramsey served up a late meal of a tasty stew and put what was left aside for Martha when she returned. After cleaning up, she left for home, assuring Joe she would be in at the usual time unless he needed her sooner. She had seen to it the kids had their bath and were ready for bed. Joe tucked them in and returned to the living room.

"I don't know what I'm going to do with them. I don't think they're ready to go back to school, especially Renee. She can talk, but she won't. She won't let Art out of her sight." Joe told them step by step what Art had told them of the ordeal, how Linda had told them exactly what to do and secured herself to the rock, and gave Art her cell phone with instructions not to try to stop her if she fell. Art sat for hours in the dark holding Renee and talking to her after Linda lost consciousness. Now she only felt safe with Art and Linda, and Linda was gone.

"And you feel guilty that you can't provide that feeling for her." Kate sat back observing Joe with a knowing look.

"I feel guilty about everything. Seems like I haven't done a damn thing right since I got here, and I almost got Linda and my kids killed."

"You talk to her, and you'll work it out." Billy smiled and looked at Kate who smiled back.

The doorbell rang and Joe went to admit Martha. She looked unhappy.

"What's wrong?" Joe asked.

"The good news is that Linda is a jewel. It didn't take me an hour to take a look at everything, and it's all up to date and perfect. That little girl she has out front will be very good when she has a chance to learn. Linda is almost as good at picking out people as I am."

"So why the serious face?" Joe knew there was another shoe to drop, and he had a feeling it wasn't good.

"I know why Linda resigned." Martha was as grim as Joe had ever seen her. "Lela didn't have the combination to your safe, so she couldn't put away the last two days mail safely. I opened it up, and right there in front addressed to you in Linda's handwriting was this." She reached in her handbag and pulled out a manila envelope that she tossed at Joe as if it was something she didn't want to touch. "Any liquor around here?" She surveyed the room, and finding no liquor cabinet, sat down with a huff.

Joe studied the writing on the sticky note that was obviously Linda's. It read, *This must have been misaddressed. I believe these belong to you.* The original envelope was addressed to Linda in block letters. Joe slowly opened the flap, knowing he wasn't going to like whatever this was judging from Martha's reaction. He knew the moment he touched the contents that it was photographs. Pulling them out he felt his stew rising and thought he might deposit the contents of his stomach right there on his living room floor. He swallowed and took a deep breath, holding still until he was reasonably sure his stomach was settling down. The bitch. The damned bitch. He was glad she was dead. He wished he had killed her himself. He knew exactly when these had been taken. Why hadn't he suspected then that this might happen?

He handed the photos across to Billy and Kate. Martha had seen them, and he didn't think he could feel any lower than he did now. He wasn't going to try to keep anything secret any longer. He hadn't known about these, but who would believe he had been unconscious when they were taken. He took a deep breath and began to explain.

"Byron said to keep her happy and not let her go yet." He finished and sat silently.

"I'm sure there's a specific term for it, but crazy seems to cover her," Kate murmured.

"Never would have pictured Linda taking someone out, but maybe this is what did it." Billy mused.

"Why not?" Martha asked. "Don't any of you know about her background?" Met with blank looks, she shook her head. "I hired her and know her history. In college she was on the rifle team and only missed by a point or two of making the Olympic team."

After several seconds of silence, Kate commented quietly. "I guess we all neglected getting to know the real Linda."

"How can I ever get her to talk to me after this?" Joe groaned.

"Don't worry about it." Martha spoke up. "I'll take care of getting her to talk to you. You better start giving some thought to what you're going to say when you do talk to her. Now show me where I'm going to sleep."

* * *

CHAPTER TWENTY-FIVE

Byron was at the office by 6:00 A.M. Joe and Billy met him there, along with Martha who began on the last two day's work. Byron had all the evidence they had collected, and he laid out who and where it had come from. He had an appointment with the sheriff's department and the FBI that morning. Joe was to go with him. Billy announced that this was Joe's problem, and he should be given room to solve it. He would be there if all else failed, and he was needed. He looked pointedly at Byron, and Byron got the message, sending back an almost imperceptible nod. He was to look after the heir apparent and help make him worthy to be that. Billy returned to the apartment and what he considered more important— spending time with his traumatized grandchildren.

They were shown directly to the sheriff's office the minute they arrived. Sheriff Britone was a big, no nonsense type of man that was cordial and polite but gave the impression he could be hard as nails if needed. FBI agent, Carl Filbert was there because of the interstate smuggling that had come to light.

Byron started by explaining the problems they had at first getting supplies to the sites and accidents that couldn't be explained. He told the sheriff why they suspected Gwen blew up her own car. He detailed what Joe had done to stop some of it by hiring extra security men and other procedures. It had gotten worse. Mickey Paxton had seen someone before he was almost killed in the accident at Fairbanks. There had been the fire and the man murdered at White Mountain. Then there was the attack on Josie and Joe related his experience of being shot and why he had not reported it. He drew his shirt back off his shoulder as evidence of his story.

"I've been aware of rumors about you folks having problems. I even reviewed some of the reports on the occasions you reported things to the police."

"And what was your conclusion?" Byron asked.

"That you were having problems. Also that there was no evidence we could take action on. You see gentlemen." He leaned back in his chair. "We have crime here just like all the states do. One of the things we have is theft of shipments coming into the ports. It can be cargo from the other states or from twenty miles down the coast. It's all fair game, and unless we have a man there on every boat or ship, we can't keep a handle on it. Too many people involved to get anyone to rat them out. Everyone's afraid for themselves or their family. I don't doubt someone is behind this, but whoever is doing this to you didn't leave anything for us to work with."

"And if I can give you that?" Byron asked, lifting a heavy file out of his briefcase.

The sheriff gave a broad smile. "Then I will bend over backwards to get these guys for you."

Byron smiled back. "Then let's get to work." He began at the beginning, laying one document after the other out for the sheriff to observe. When he got to the transcript of the recordings from Mit's hidden equipment the sheriff stopped him.

"So Rodney's back! We thought he'd drowned in an accident. No wonder you had problems. He's as crazy as they come, nothing he wouldn't do. Also that information is coming from Bull Smith's cabin. He's Gwen Smith's father. Bull is the biggest criminal on the docks. Has been for years. I'd love to take him down too." He glanced over at Joe. "Sorry to hear about the trouble Gwen gave you and your office manager. She's always been crazy as her old man. Went off to Juneau for a couple of years and then came back." He shifted his gaze to Byron. "You still have equipment up at that cabin?"

"I sent men up yesterday to pull it out if they could. They promised the girl nobody would know it was her."

The sheriff nodded, and Byron finished giving him all the information he had. The sheriff called in two officers and gave them a list of men and places with orders to plan raids and arrests.

"Okay." The sheriff turned his attention to Byron. "We'll get Rodney for that murder at White Mountain. Bull will give him up to protect his interests. Bull will also give us the information we need to get the senator. All these connections to Gwen and the others will add to the net we put out."

"I'll be checking in with you often. I expect to be kept up to date." Byron was polite but left no doubt that he was not to be discounted.

The sheriff looked over at Byron and smiled. "No problem."

* * *

By the time Joe and Byron returned to the office, Martha had things humming along smoothly and had a stack of phone calls for Joe to return.

"I can't return those until I know what to tell them." Joe stared at the stack of notes Martha had presented him with.

"Oh, for goodness sakes, Joseph!" Martha planted her feet apart and jammed her fists on her hips. "Do you or do you not run this company? And after you return those calls, there are several things the site managers are waiting on from the draftsman."

"Yeah, well, the draftsman guy is nowhere to be found, and if he is, he will be in jail." He looked up to find Martha hadn't moved and was still glaring at him. Meeting her glare he shifted his feet, and a tiny tick that might have been the start of a smile appeared at the corner of his mouth. "You want me to go in and do the draftsman's work, don't you?"

"Either that or your father needs to demand a refund on that expensive education he paid for. Not to mention that you've been hanging over Billy's shoulder reading blueprints ever since he started this company."

"All right, Martha. I'm going home to check on the kids for a little while, and then I'll come back and start on those. Byron is going to work out of one of the empty offices while he's here."

"Good. I'll feel safer with him here." Martha turned and marched back to Linda's office.

Byron watched her go. "I think maybe I'm the one will feel safer. I should hire her away from you."

"Good luck with that. She's the family angel, guardian, and dragon all in one." Joe showed Byron to an empty office next to his and left for home.

A few minutes after Joe left, Martha appeared at Byron's door and announced that she would be gone, possibly for the afternoon, and that if he needed anything Lela could possibly help him.

An hour later the hospital was in a full state of activity. Nurses were trying to finish up with the lunch trays. Patients were trying to get checked out after finally being released by doctors running late. Rooms had to be cleaned and readied for new patients, and the first flood of anxious people crowded the halls as visiting hours started. Winding her way through all this was a stout woman in a white doctor's coat, carrying a clipboard. No one had challenged her when she stepped behind the nurse's desk and retrieved Linda's file, and no one challenged her now as she pushed open the door with the no visitors sign. She was just another doctor in the middle of a very busy shift.

She let the door swing slowly closed behind her and watched the astonished expression spread across Linda's face. "Hello, honey. You look better than I expected."

"Martha? What are you doing here?"

"I'm doing your job. Now, aren't you glad to see me?" She sat on the edge of the bed and carefully gathered Linda up in a hug.

"Of course I'm glad to see you." Linda's voice began to break and tears escaped down her cheeks. "Damn! I haven't cried until now."

"Maybe it's about time you did." Martha continued to hold her and rock back and forth as Linda dissolved into quiet sobs.

When she was able to stop the tears, Linda leaned back against the pillows and smiled weakly at Martha. "I can't believe he called you up here."

"Joe? He didn't. He said he only had one inexperienced receptionist in the entire office, and I decided you needed someone to keep the office in hand until you can get back to it."

"Didn't you get my email?"

"I did, and we'll talk about that later. Right now we have more important things to talk about. I hear you won't see anyone."

Linda gave Martha a small smile. "Is that the reason for the doctor costume?"

Martha chuckled. "Worked great. Not a single question about who I was, but we need to discuss this not talking to anyone. I know why you won't talk to Joe. I opened the safe." Martha waited for Linda to say something.

Linda wiped at her eyes with a tissue from the bedtable. "Those were just the last in a long line of things that finally made me realize that whatever was between Joe and I was over. I couldn't stay here. Gwen sabotaged the office and hated me. I hated her too, actually." She faced Martha. "I was just a few hours from getting on a plane when all this happened. As soon as the doctor says I can go, I'll be on the next plane out and let Joe rebuild his life."

"Things weren't quite like you saw them, Linda, and that's Joe's fault. But you need to talk to him. There's a lot he hasn't shared with you that he should have."

A small bitter sob escaped from Linda. "Obviously, he was sharing more with Gwen than he was with me. Don't you understand, Martha? He was in love with her. It's not just the pictures. It's so many other things. He defended her and humiliated me. I killed her." Linda paused and took a deep breath, and a hard look settled on her face. "Don't misunderstand, Martha. I'm glad I did. She could have killed just me, but she didn't like the kids, and she was going to kill them too. I wasn't going to let that happen, but he still loved her, and I'm the one that killed her. That can never be changed."

"Okay, let's put the subject of Joe aside for now. I'm most concerned about the kids, especially Renee. She hasn't talked since she was rescued. She can because when she left the hospital she was screaming for you. Hasn't said a word since, clings to Art like glue, like he is the only one to keep her safe. Art's so quiet it hurts. They spend all their time in Art's room with him playing video games and Renee sitting right beside him, leaning against him or holding on to him. There's no question of sending Renee back to school. She may need professional help. Art could go I think, but I also think he needs help too. He asked Joe if you had died." Martha looked sternly at Linda. "They need to see you, Linda."

"Oh, God, the kids. All that time in the dark and afraid. If I could have just stayed awake to talk to them, it might have been better. Then they had to see me kill Gwen." Linda again had tears flooding down her face. "Oh, Martha, I'm so sorry. I love them so much."

"I know you do, honey, but you need to see them now. I think you, better than anyone, can help them get through this."

Linda cried and wiped her eyes and cried some more. Martha waited. Then Linda sniffed and faced the older woman. "All right. I'll see the kids as much as I can while I'm here. I don't know how much longer the doctor will keep me here, but as soon as I'm able I'm going home to Colorado."

"Even if the kids need you?"

"I hope after they see me they will be okay, but I can't stay. The longer I stay the harder it will be, not just for me but for them. They aren't my kids. I killed the woman that would have been their stepmother."

"There is more to that than meets the eye, Linda. You have to let Joe talk to you."

"No. Not Joe. But I'll see the kids if you bring them."

Martha was smiling at dinner in spite of Joe's foul mood. Billy and Kate had spent the day with the kids without much success. Their faces showed concern. The quiet children weren't even interested in the fried chicken Mrs. Ramsey had made for dinner. In the end Martha was the one that broke the quiet up.

"I want you kids to clean those plates. Then go wash your hands and get your jackets. You and I are going somewhere." The kids looked up, half curious and half resentful. The adults looked surprised.

"Where?" Art asked in a flat voice.

"It just so happens," Martha drew the story out, "that I went by the hospital today and saw Linda. And," she held up a finger to silence all the voices that started up around the table, "you two kids and I are the only ones on the list allowed to visit her for now." She looked pointedly at Joe. "So," she continued, "are you going to eat that fried chicken or are you going to stay home?"

Five minutes later the kids had gone to wash up and get their jackets, and the adults had a moment of privacy.

"How is she, Martha?" Joe asked. "Will she see me?"

"I don't know, Joe. Physically she's going to be fine. I don't know what the hell was going on up here before this mess, but she thinks that you were in love with Gwen. Told me those pictures were just the last little thing that made her realize she didn't belong here anymore. Says she killed the woman you loved. I could have told her the truth, but that's not my place to do. It's yours. So now excuse me, and I'll go see if she can help those kids get over this."

* * *

Mit had been watching Bull constantly ever since he showed up earlier that morning. He was upset and in one of his foul moods. She knew this had to be something serious because he wasn't interested in food, and more than that had only had one beer over the morning. His phone rang, and he barked into it and disconnected the call. Thirty minutes later the noise of a horse being rode hard through the trees could be heard, and in a few moments Rodney emerged. He rode to the edge of the porch and dismounted, tossing the reins to Mit without a word. She took them and led the lathered animal away, her lips coming together in a thin line of hatred.

"What the hell is the emergency? That message you sent made it sound like a war had started." Rodney was belligerent.

"It damn well has, you bastard. First I get a call from the senator looking for you. Seems he knows you botched some job he gave you, and he's pissed. Then I get a tip from one of my contacts in the sheriff's department that they're going to make a sweep of raids. They have a stack of warrants, and you and I are on top of the damn list. What the hell did you do to pull me into this?"

"I didn't do nothing. That gal of yours got you into this."

Bull's face flushed red, and his voice dropped a notch. "You be careful what you say. She had her faults, but she was my kid and you aren't going to bad-mouth her. I talked to the cops after she was killed, and they know I wasn't involved in that."

"So, it has to be something in your business that they're onto." Rodney pushed past Bull and into the cabin. He looked around. "Mit!" he yelled. "Where the hell is that good for nothing bitch?"

Mit slipped quietly in the door behind them, keeping her eyes down.

"Get me some damn food and a beer!" Rodney yelled at her.

Mit hurried to the stove to comply. She had just dipped a ladle into the stew when an explosion went off behind her, causing her to drop both the tin plate and the ladle. Backing away as far as she could get, she stared at the scene before her. Bull stood with his rifle looking at Rodney's dead body sprawled across the floor. He turned and looked at Mit with steely eyes.

"No son-of-a-bitch is gonna cause me this much trouble and live." He grabbed his pack and began loading it. Mit stood where she was, and he glanced at her. "Don't just stand there. Go get his horse ready. I'll take it for a ways. Then pack me some grub."

Mit watched him pry out a stone at the foot of the fireplace. He kept money there, she knew, but she had never been brave enough to count it when he was gone. Moving toward the door, she had to pass Rodney's body. She studied the handgun still clipped to his belt. He'd had no idea what was coming or he would have had it out.

"When you be back?" she asked Bull.

"Never. They know about this place, so I'll have to get another hidey hole." He continued working packages out from behind the stone.

"Where I go?"

"You can stay here or go back to your people. I can't be responsible for you anymore, you understand?" Bull's phone pinged, and he listened for a moment and disconnected. "What are you waiting for? Hurry the hell up. Cops just passed the bend. I got maybe thirty minutes until they get here." Bull was stuffing packages of bills into his pack.

Mit bent over Rodney and slid the pistol out of its clip. "No hurry." She spoke calmly, and Bull spun around ready to yell at her. Instead he found her pointing a handgun at him. He opened his mouth to say something, but Mit never knew what it would have been. She shot him three times in the heart. Then she put the gun in Rodney's hand, pointing it towards Bull, laying just a few feet away.

Bull had loaded his pack with a lot more money than Mit had ever seen. She stuffed it in a bag as fast as she could and ran to the last dog kennel in the row. The box she had kept the phone in was still buried there. She stuffed the money bag in it and covered it back up, adding some old dog stools to the top to camouflage it even more. Running now, she returned to the cabin, replaced the rock at the foot of the fireplace and scattered some ashes over any telltale signs it had been tampered with. The space the money had taken in Bull's pack she hurriedly replaced with clothes and food before placing it back next to him. Then she went outside and huddled down on the porch to wait for the sheriff's men to come.

* * *

Linda had to go home. She was physically ready to leave, could get around well enough to care for herself, and needed no help other than someone to drive for her as that wasn't allowed yet. She had stalled the hospital as long as she could, and they were now insisting she was well enough to go home, which indeed she was.

The last few days she had seen Martha and the kids on a daily basis. The first time they came there had been a lot of tears, both hers and the kids. At the second visit she took a firm and practical tack.

"You both understand you have to get back to school don't you?" Art nodded his head, his expression sober.

"I don't want to go back to school. I want to stay home with Art and you." Renee was adamant.

"But Renee, honey, you can't stay home forever. Bad things happened, but we are all here and we are fine, and Gwen is gone. We can't let this ruin our lives because of one bad person and one bad experience. Life is full of hard things we have to go through. Besides, I won't be at home after the doctor says I'm healed, and both of you have to get back to school so you don't have to repeat a year. And Art needs to get back to his soccer team so he doesn't lose his place."

"I don't want to leave Art." Renee's eyes teared up.

"You'll be right there in the same school with him in case you really need him. You can see him at lunch for a minute or two, and maybe Martha or Mrs. Ramsey will stay with you and watch his soccer practice if it's okay with the coach for a day or so. You were very brave in the mine. You're strong on your own you know." The little girl buried her head against Linda's neck and sniffled.

"Tell you what," Linda continued. "How about you go back to school. You know you are going to have a lot of work to make up. You have Martha bring you over to see me, and Martha and I will oversee you two doing your homework until you catch up. Does that sound okay?" There was a hesitant nod from Renee. They had gone back to school, and the familiar routine had started helping put the terror of their experience behind them.

Linda sat in the visitor's chair, waiting for Martha to come take her home. Without realizing it she had both her jaw and her fists clenched. She didn't want to go back to her apartment right across from Joe's, and run the risk of seeing him in the hall or having him come knocking on her door. She didn't think she could bear seeing him again. She just wanted to go get on a plane and fly back to Denver and start over. It had been so hard seeing the kids every day, and now she had to create a distance between them again for their sakes as well as her own.

By the time they reached the apartment house, Linda was leaning on Martha's arm. She had been up and dressed waiting in a chair or working with the office personnel who came by with discharge papers, for the entire morning. Once in the apartment, she declined Martha's offer of fixing her something to eat in favor of a nap. Exhausted, she went straight to bed and lay down fully clothed.

* * *

CHAPTER TWENTY-SIX

Linda woke feeling sluggish, regretting that she had refused the doctor's offer of pain medication. Back in the privacy of her own place and in her own bed, she had slept more soundly than in the hospital. Groaning in pain, she attempted to sit up, only to freeze in horror as strong hands reached out to lift her to a sitting position.

"Take your time. I've got you." Joe spoke softly, holding her in a firm grip as she struggled to get her bearings and throw off the stupor of sleep.

"I'm all right." She pushed frantically at his hand holding her arm. "You shouldn't be here, go away!"

Joe sat back, elbows on his knees, hands clasped together, and leaned toward her. "This is where I want to be. If I had been here when I should have been, you wouldn't have had to go through this." His voice lowered. "I love you, Linda." She lowered her head, and he paused, waiting for a response that didn't come. "Martha told me you think I loved Gwen. I never did. I was dumbfounded when she told me that."

Linda looked up, tears tracing a path down her cheeks. "How can you say that?" Her shoulders slumped, and she hugged her arms across her chest. "I realized you were falling for her and that I couldn't stay. I lived with that. I had *already* decided to leave when I got those pictures. That hurt, Joe. That really hurt."

"Oh, sweetheart, I'm so sorry. I didn't know about the pictures. She drugged me, and all I knew for sure was that I passed out before she left my room. We had been going over client information. She implied the next morning that we had sex, but I knew that was impossible. I told Byron, and he said there was a possibility of pictures, but we didn't know for sure until we found the ones she sent to you."

"Oh, stop. Get out! Just Go!"

Joe reached for her, and she pulled back, hands out, fending him off. "Get out or I'll call the police!" Her voice rose in panic, and she started to cry.

He sighed and dropped his hands. "All right. You're upset now, and there's so much we need to talk about—more than I ever dreamed. I've been an idiot. Rest today, sweetheart. I'm coming back tomorrow, and we'll talk more. It can't be left like this, Linda. We love each other."

Catching her off guard, he quickly cradled her face in his hands and placed a gentle but brief kiss on her lips. "I love you," he whispered, then turned and left the bedroom.

Linda put her hands over her face and swallowed a painful lump in her throat. A tiny whine emerged that she tried to smother. She didn't want anyone to hear, to check on her. She wanted to hide. Her effort to thwart her emotions failed, and she fell back on the bed, uncontrolled sobs wracking her.

*　*　*

Linda had cried until she could cry no more and then fallen into a deep exhausted sleep. She awoke tired and listless but determined to take her life in hand. After the limited opportunity to maintain personal hygiene at the hospital, due to her wounds among other things, she stood under the heavy stream of hot water and let it help loosen the knots in her muscles. It didn't help her heart feel less broken.

Martha had unpacked some of her clothes from where her bags had been sitting near the front door when she received the fateful call from Gwen. Her brow furrowed as she realized her wardrobe contained nothing casual. She had running shorts for those times she had imagined she would go for runs. *Well, that hadn't happened.* One pair of sweat pants and shirt was her only option for the comfort she needed while she finished healing.

"I need to make more room in my life for casual," she mused.

Now, she stood taking in the view from her apartment window. She hadn't had time to enjoy this view or even be very aware of it since she had been here. Too much work, too many problems to be taken care of, no one to share the load, work or emotional.

The muted chime of the doorbell sounded through the apartment and Linda took a deep breath. Her shoulders slumped. Martha had checked in on her earlier so this could be no one but Joe. She moved to the door and checking the peep hole saw Joe standing there as she had known he would be. Nothing for it but to get it over with. There would be no avoiding Joe.

*　*　*

Joe left Linda's apartment thinking his heart was going to quit beating any second. Tears were beginning to escape down his cheeks. Mrs. Ramsey would be arriving soon after picking the kids up from school. He couldn't deal with their questions in his current condition. In a matter of minutes he was pulling out of the parking garage and wondering where he could find privacy. It came in the form of the lookout over the bay where he had once sat with Linda. There, with only the sound of the waves rolling in, he cried.

The next afternoon Joe stood in front of Linda's apartment door, stealing himself for whatever came next. He had to make this up to her but he wasn't sure how. Squaring his shoulders, he pressed the doorbell, and waited. Just when he thought she wasn't going to answer, the latch clicked and the door swung open. Linda stood there in a sweat suit looking wan, pale, and defeated. Nothing of the strong and confident woman that had run his offices was apparent. His heart broke for her and for himself.

"I don't suppose if I asked you to leave you would go away, would you?" Her voice was flat and emotionless.

"No, Linda. We have to talk this out."

She opened the door fully and stepped back. He walked in and turned to face her. His instinct was to gather her up and rock her like a child.

"Can we sit down?" He knew this would take some time, and she didn't look like she had the strength to stand up long. She shrugged and motioned to the living area, settling in a chair, denying him the opportunity of being close to her on the couch.

"I don't know how to go about this, Linda, but I have to explain that I did not, ever, for even a second, have any feelings for Gwen." Her eyes flashed and the Linda he knew was behind them.

"You broke every company rule in the book for her and let her cram it down my throat." Anger was coming out in every word she spit at him. "I had to fight to run the office anywhere near professionally, and when I showed you things that could make problems and should never be allowed, you sided with her. And then!" Linda's eyes began to flood with tears. "You were sleeping with her!" She blinked several times, but when that didn't clear the tears away, resorted to wiping her eyes with the back of her hand. "How could you do that to me, Joe?"

He pulled his handkerchief out of his pocket and handed it to her. She clutched it and wiped at her eyes. He took that as a good sign.

"I didn't realize at the time. I want to tell you everything that happened so you can maybe, if not forgive me, at least understand."

For a couple of hours, Joe related in detail what had happened that he hadn't shared with her. Sometimes he stopped while she asked questions or wiped tears away. When he finished, they sat in silence, giving her a chance to compose herself.

"You shut me out. You didn't trust me to be able to help you."

"I took you so much for granted, and I was so wrapped up in doing a good job and solving the problems up here. The more I found out, the worse it was. I deliberately made the decision not to tell you everything that was going on because I thought if you knew it would put you, and maybe even the kids, in danger. When you pressed me on things I couldn't explain without telling you everything, I didn't handle it very well. At first I thought Gwen was of some value as she had contacts and was our only sales person, and all this other stuff was happening. By the time I realized I needed to get rid of her, I had brought in Byron, and he found out enough to suspect she was a part of it. He wanted me to keep her around and see if she led us to anyone, and she did. But I put you and the kids in danger anyway. I was wrong, and I will regret that for the rest of my life."

"Byron was in on everything?"

"Yes. He'd just told me he didn't need Gwen anymore, and I could let her go. I did that the morning she pulled this off. I should have called and told you, but I wanted to tell you in person over dinner." Joe paused, swallowed, then cleared his throat and continued. "I was planning to ask you to marry me."

"Then I got home, and you were all gone. Once I talked to Mrs. Ramsey I knew where to look but still didn't know what was going on except that you thought I had told you to go there. I've never been so scared in my life. I knew then that I had been overlooking what was really important in my life, I was terrified because of everything that has happened, but it never occurred to me that it was Gwen. She was a mental case of some sort, tormented by her own demons. I guess we'll never know, and frankly I don't want to. I just want to get on with my life without all these problems and come home every night to you and the kids."

Joe reached into his pocket and came out with a small velvet black box. He pressed it gently into her hand. "Do you think that could happen, Linda? Would you be my wife?"

Linda clutched the box, not opening it. "I don't know, Joe. I need to think about all of this. I don't think either of us is terribly good in the communications department. It almost wrecked us this time. If we are going to make this work, we have to both make an effort to correct that. We need to get to know each other all over, regain some trust maybe. Then we'll see."

"I'm good with that. Whatever it takes. Do you feel well enough for me to take you to dinner?"

"Not today. I'm very tired, and I need to think about all this. We could try tomorrow night."

He knelt by her chair, taking her hands in his. "I love you, Linda. I'll do absolutely anything for you." A tiny quirk at the corner of her mouth might have indicated a smile, but it didn't develop.

"Then go now. I'll see you tomorrow night."

* * *

For Linda, the next week was full of resting and thinking over what Joe had told her. Martha popped in every day and fussed over her and brought food items she thought might tempt the now too thin Linda. Joe took her out for a while each day; a short walk in the park, a drive for a change of scenery, lunch at a fish and chowder stand on the waterfront, or to dinner, always making sure she was home to get in bed early.

By the end of the week Linda was stronger and looking more like her old self. At an upscale restaurant where Joe had made reservations, they sat sipping after dinner drinks. Joe once again reached into his pocket and brought out the little black velvet box and placed it in her hand.

Linda held the velvet box a few seconds before nudging it open. Gleaming up at her was the most beautiful diamond she had ever seen. It sat in the middle of a nest of tiny diamonds where each twinkled in its own right. She smiled. "If I put this on, we will have to work as a team from now on."

"Is that a yes?"

"Yes, I think it is."

* * *

Exactly six weeks after Linda was admitted to the hospital, she received a clean bill of health from her doctor. The next day was her wedding day.

Joe was smiling from ear to ear and as close to floating on air as a human could manage. Linda wore a form fitting white gown with heavy gold threads running through it. The tight sophisticated roll that usually adorned her head had been discarded for this special day. Her hair had been brushed until it gleamed, and fell in golden waves over her shoulders, matching the gold in her dress. She had foregone a train, claiming that would be overdoing it. Joe had pretty much been ready since daylight, and if it hadn't been for Billy and Byron he would have forgotten everything. All he could think about was Linda. It was finally going to happen, and he could hardly stand or sit still for more than a few seconds. Byron threatened to handcuff him to something to keep track of him until time for the ceremony.

A large yacht had been volunteered for the occasion by one of Billy's wealthy friends and a past client of several large projects. It would whisk the couple away for a two week honeymoon after the guests departed.

Joe stood in the bow with Art and Renee and watched his bride-to-be walk the length of the deck to him. The minister asked Linda if she took this man and these children, and she opened her arms to them. The children jumped forward to hug her. She answered, "Yes, I do." Joe stepped forward and wrapped all of them in his arms, and they were pronounced man, wife, and family.

There was an extravagant reception aboard ship, and about twenty couples who had flown in from various states expressed their good wishes for Joe and Linda and began to drift away to sample the sites to see and things to do in Alaska before heading back home. The family hugged and left to pick up their part in filling in for Joe and Linda for the next two weeks. As evening closed in, the yacht moved out and carried the happy couple south.

What they had come to think of as their Alaska family returned to work. Kate and Mrs. Ramsey stepped in to care for Art and Renee and see that all went well on the home front.

After much discussion, it had been decided to offer Wallace the job Seth had filled. Wallace had the education to do the job, and he had done well with any other duties he had been given with no complaint. He deserved the opportunity. He did lack some knowledge of the way Black Capital's building engineers worked and the company standards they were expected to uphold, so Wallace was taken from the wedding reception and promptly dispatched on a plane to California for an intense month of training.

Josie sent Seyma home with Kate and Mrs. Ramsey, and went for dinner with Ashton. Morning saw him on the chopper headed back to the White Mountain site and Josie and Seyma on a plane back to California.

With Joe away on his honeymoon, the office once again had no draftsman to check plans and see that everything was correct. Billy rolled up his sleeves and declared he needed something to do while he and Kate waited for Joe and Linda to return. He enjoyed the work, and Kate noticed he came home to dinner in a good mood.

Martha, having had six weeks to run the office, declared that Linda had trained Lela wonderfully. That didn't stop her from working every day to mold Lela into an even more perfect employee. Martha managed to train her in several of the functions Linda normally did. Linda would be returning after the honeymoon, but there would come a time Martha thought, that children would come, and Linda needed someone who could run the office.

Byron flew in and out several times over the length of Linda's recovery and during the honeymoon. He reported to Billy that Seth had been located working on a fishing boat in a little town far to the south. He would go to jail. The senator's brother, Byron continued, had a construction company that the senator had invested heavily in. They stood to lose a fortune if Black Capital remained in business. The problem was that while everyone knew he was behind it, and many other nefarious activities, there was no paper trail to him, and those they had thought would be witnesses against him had ended up dead. So the senator would remain untouched by all but a lot of unsavory talk. Time would show him reelected. His cousin's construction company folded.

A few months later, the poor ignorant little widow of Bull Smith was declared the sole heir of his estate of property on the waterfront. Unfortunately, Bull had been a wanted man when he died, so the state moved in and claimed all his money and property, leaving Mit penniless. Nobody cared what happened to her, and she faded into the background until the next running of the Iditarod. A tiny, native woman that nobody seemed to know much about entered her team and literally left the other entries in the snowflakes behind her. She collected her winnings and promptly booked passage to Seattle on a tourist boat. She reportedly left with only one suitcase and a backpack and was never seen again.

About the time Mit was running the Iditarod, there was another wedding. This time Wallace and Lela were married in a small ceremony in Anchorage. A very pregnant Linda was the maid of honor.

* * *

ABOUT THE AUTHOR

Elsa is a country girl at heart and lives with her husband on a small acreage in the central valley of California. They are hosts to a continuous parade of various animals that find their way to them.

When not writing romance Elsa can be found working with an extensive collection of house plants or pruning over thirty rose bushes. Raised in her parents' mom and pop restaurant, she can't bear to see a holiday or weekend pass without tables heaped with food for her children, grandchildren, and friends to gather around and partake of.

She loves to read, her favorites being suspense, mystery, spies or historic tales set in the early days of the west and most of all loves romance in her stories.

Life has taken her through huge cultural changes beginning with a prairie childhood in Kansas to the metropolitan east coast to the high plains of Colorado and beautiful picturesque New Mexico before landing her in California.

OTHER BOOKS BY ELSA BAYLY

Dangerous to Love
Objection to Love